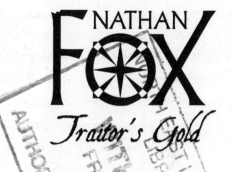

NATHAN FOX

Traitor's Gold

*J*hey stood there, sodden and shivering, as the rain and wind whipped themselves up into a fury; then, as quickly as it had started, it died, and there was a silence.

Nathan stepped forward to comfort his horse but, as his hand touched the horse's neck, he felt the point of a knife press into the side of his own neck.

'Make no move, or you will die,' said a quiet voice in Dutch. Nathan held his breath. Then he heard a small squeal from Marie and the sounds of a brief struggle in the darkness.

The knife point in his neck was pressed a little harder and Nathan realized that they had been successfully ambushed and resistance was not an option.

L. Brittney lives in Axminster, Devon, and is a full-time
writer. The Nathan Fox titles are her first books for
children.

Also by L. Brittney

Nathan Fox: Dangerous Times

To find out more about the world of Nathan Fox, visit

www.nathanfox-traitorsgold.co.uk

NATHAN FOX

Traitor's Gold

L. BRITTNEY

MACMILLAN CHILDREN'S BOOKS

First published 2008 by Macmillan Children's Books
a division of Macmillan Publishers Limited
20 New Wharf Road, London N1 9RR
Basingstoke and Oxford
www.panmacmillan.com

Associated companies throughout the world

ISBN 978-0-330-45421-6

1 3 5 7 9 8 6 4 2

A CIP catalogue record for this book is available from
the British Library.

Typeset by Intype Libra Limited
Printed and bound in Great Britain by Mackays of Chatham plc, Kent

To the historian Geoffrey Parker, whose fascinating
published work on the Spanish army in the Netherlands
gave me the foundation for the plot of Traitor's Gold.

North East Lincolnshire Council	
Askews	
	£5.99

Introduction

*J*hirteen-year-old Nathan Fox, an exceptionally gifted boy actor in the same theatre company as Will Shakespeare, has been recruited into Sir Francis Walsingham's fledgling Secret Service as a partner to England's most skilled agent, John Pearce. After arduous training at Robey's School of Defence in London, Nathan and John undertook their first mission together in spring 1587 when they were sent to seek an English alliance with the State of Venice against the threat of invasion by the Spanish Empire. Tragic circumstances led to the ultimate failure of Nathan's first mission but Sir Francis Drake's raid on the Spanish Armada at Cadiz, where he sank or disabled most of the Spanish fleet, gave England a temporary reprieve. However, the Spanish Empire continues to advance and, as Nathan undergoes training for his second mission, events elsewhere in Europe mean that speed is of the essence.

In the autumn of 1587 the Spanish Empire covers most

of the Western world. Philip II of Spain had inherited half of the Empire ruled over by his father, the Emperor Charles. The other half of the Holy Roman Empire was inherited by Philip of Spain's uncle, Ferdinand. This comprises Austria and a large part of Central Europe and is, of course, firmly allied with Spain.

There is also an uneasy alliance with France, but that country is torn by religious wars. Philip of Spain is financing the Catholic League of France in an effort to stop France becoming a Protestant country, but the Protestant faction remains strong and it is only a matter of time before they succeed in taking over the country.

All Philip of Spain's vast possessions are administered by the largest (and possibly the slowest) bureaucracy in history. Armies and navies have to be maintained in some of the farthest-flung corners of the known world. Wars are being fought, sometimes on several fronts at once, and this adds to the pressure on money and administration.

Two thorns are stuck firmly in Philip of Spain's side. One is England, now committed to the Protestant religion by its queen, Elizabeth, and the other is the Protestant revolt in the Netherlands, which Philip has been trying to crush for nearly thirty years. The Dutch rebels in the northern region have organized themselves into the United Provinces and, with financial and military help from Elizabeth of England, are proving impossible to overcome.

At times ill-equipped and starving, the Dutch nevertheless use all their knowledge of the land and surrounding sea to fight off everything that the Spanish Empire can throw at them. Even though Philip swamps the Netherlands with over 60,000 troops – sometimes outnumbering the Dutch and English forces by three to one – he cannot defeat what he calls 'those stubborn heretic rebels'.

Prologue

'REVENGE IS A DISH BEST SERVED COLD' – SICILIAN PROVERB

Bernardino de Mendoza, Spain's Ambassador to the Court of France, turned to the man standing in front of him.

'You understand now what you have to do?'

The man nodded and picked up the bag of gold Mendoza had placed on the table in front of him.

Mendoza looked steadily at him. 'I want no mistakes. I have promised His Most Catholic Majesty, King Philip, that we will deliver everything safely. It is important that you understand that.'

The man nodded again.

'You need have no fear,' he replied. 'I understand everything perfectly.'

Mendoza looked satisfied.

'Then God go with you,'

After the man left, Mendoza knelt in prayer before the shrine to St Odilia, the patron saint of the blind. He could barely see her statue in the niche, his eyes were now so clouded.

It had not been a good week for the Spanish Ambassador. His monetary support of the Catholic League in France had suffered a severe blow when they had lost a major battle at Coutras against the Protestants. There had been a moment of panic when it was thought that the Protestants might press on, take Paris and claim the throne, but it had not happened and Mendoza had thanked God for that. But it would only be a matter of time before France fell to the rising tide of Protestantism in Northern Europe, and the Spanish could not afford to fight a war on yet another front.

He sighed and tried to turn his thoughts to his prayers but he failed. All that was in his mind was the task ahead. Ever since Sir Francis Walsingham, England's Spymaster, had persuaded Queen Elizabeth to banish Mendoza from the English court, he had waited for an opportunity to exact his revenge. Three weeks ago, the King of Spain had unwittingly presented him with such an opportunity. There were important tasks to be undertaken in the war-stricken Netherlands and Mendoza knew that Walsingham's spies would have already informed their master of what was about to happen.

But Mendoza, whose own abilities to plot and deceive more than matched those of Walsingham, had already made his own plans. He smiled with grim satisfaction. Spanish agents would be briefed and this time he would undermine the English Spymaster. He had waited three long years for this and he would savour every moment of humiliation suffered by his enemy.

A knock on the door interrupted his thoughts and he struggled up from his knees. These would be the men he had been waiting for – who would put the next part of his plan into operation. He surveyed them calmly as they bowed low. Although his sight was failing he was still able to appreciate the unusual white-blond hair of the younger of the two men who stood before him.

'I have your orders here, my friends,' he said quietly, handing the older man a parchment from his desk. 'Make sure that you instruct our friend in London as to the part he must play.'

'We shall not fail you, Signor Ambassador,' the younger man said with confidence.

'This time, the task is more complex,' Mendoza murmured. 'There are two separate missions outlined in this document. The English must be stopped from succeeding at all costs. Once you have read the document, burn it. It must not go with you to England. May God guide you and keep you.'

The two men bowed and left swiftly. Mendoza turned back to his devotions. All his agents were now in place and he could do no more.

It was extraordinary, he reflected, that the deep game of espionage throughout the whole of Europe was controlled by two sickly old men – a half-blind Spaniard and a crippled Englishman. His next prayer, Mendoza decided, would be that both of them live long enough to see this next adventure brought to its just conclusion.

MASTER OF THE HORSE

*S*word clashed against sword with such speed that, at one point, Nathan's hand was stung by one of the sparks that flew from the blades. Nathan watched in astonishment as the Silver brothers fought each other with a ferocity that was excessive, even for them. They were oblivious to everyone – even their tutor, who was standing on the sidelines, fruitlessly screaming instructions in Dutch.

'George, *breng omhoog uw linkerwapen!*'

'Toby, *u zich verdedigt, de heer niet!*'

'*BEGRIPT U MIJ?!*'

The last instruction was shouted with such force that it finally penetrated the deaf ears of the brothers and they ceased their battle to stare at the hardened soldier in front of them. The man repeated himself, in English this time.

'Do you understand me?' he said testily, glaring at the vacant faces of the Silver brothers, 'and did you hear any of my instructions?' George and Toby Silver shook their heads and grinned.

Jan Groesbeck let out a sigh of defeat. Trying to teach the Dutch language to this pair of wooden-heads was testing his patience to its limits. He turned to Nathan. 'Tell them what I said,' he asked.

Nathan replied, 'You told George to bring his arm up, and then you told Toby that he was not defending himself. Then you asked them if they understood you.' George pulled a face at Nathan's ready answer.

Groesbeck turned back to the hapless brothers. 'Listen to me, you *domoors*,' – Nathan sniggered at Groesbeck's use of the Dutch word for 'nitwits' – 'Meister Robey tells me that in a very short time, you will all be going over to the Netherlands to aid the Dutch rebels. How in God's name – please tell me – can you expect to stay alive if you don't understand the simplest instruction that may be shouted out to you by a Dutchman who is fighting alongside you?'

George and Toby shuffled their feet, at a loss for an answer. Groesbeck made a dismissive sign at them and they gratefully stampeded out of the weapons hall without a backward glance.

'They are very good fighters,' Nathan offered by way of an apology.

Groesbeck smiled at him. 'You and I both know that that is not enough. The war in the Netherlands is not a normal situation. There is no clearly defined enemy.

9

There are Protestant Dutchmen who are fighting with the Spanish Army and Catholic Dutchmen fighting with the British. Most of the Spanish army is made up of Italians, French and Germans. Units desert and defect to the opposite side – the fighting is made up of ambushes, sorties, sieges. There are very few pitched battles where you know exactly who you are fighting against and that is why . . .' he pounded his fist into his hand in exasperation, 'it is important to know the language!'

Nathan sympathized with him. Jan Groesbeck was a veteran soldier of the Netherlands conflict. A man to be respected. The ugly scar that slashed across the side of his neck showed he had faced death and survived. This was precisely the reason why Robey had recently taken Groesbeck into his School of Defence – to teach the Dutch method of warfare, as well as the language. Groesbeck was a man who fitted right into the experienced team of soldiers that Robey had built up. His other men, Bardolph, Pistol and Nym, had embraced Groesbeck into the fold as one of their own.

Groesbeck cut into Nathan's thoughts. 'Still, Meister Nathan Fox, you, at least, are an apt pupil. By the time you have finished your lessons with me, you will know enough Dutch to be able to listen in on people's conversations with confidence – and that, I understand, is what your work is all about.'

Nathan nodded, and thanked Groesbeck for the compliments. Secretly, he had struggled with the language because of its strangeness. While Italian, French and Spanish flowed from his mouth with ease, speaking Dutch was like hawking and spitting, so much of it was produced in the back of the throat. He also knew that learning another language was really a matter of having a good memory and, in his days as a boy actor, he had been able to memorize a different play every week. Toby and George Silver did not have that facility.

'Come now.' Groesbeck began to put away the swords in their places on the wall racks. 'Today you have other work to do and, from what I hear about you, it is work that you will love.'

Nathan was curious as he followed the Dutchman into the kitchen. What could his next task possibly be? He loved most of his work at Robey's School.

'Ah, there you are, lad,' Nym said gruffly as Nathan appeared. 'Today we're all going to Kent. You and me – the Silver brothers and . . .'

'. . . Me!' said a familiar voice, and Nathan spun round joyously.

'John Pearce!' Nathan flung himself at his friend, hugging him so fiercely that he almost knocked the wind out of him.

'Steady! Steady! I've only been away a month!' Pearce laughed.

'I was beginning to think that you would never come back!' The edge of genuine concern in Nathan's voice made Pearce look into his eyes.

'Did you really think that I would abandon the best newly recruited spy in England to fend for himself?' Pearce asked with a twinkle in his eye.

Nathan shook his head and smiled. He felt that all was well with the world, now that John was back. The wounds he had sustained on their first mission together had been so severe that Nathan had feared his partner would be disabled forever. The thought of continuing his espionage work without the guiding hand of John Pearce had been almost too much for him to contemplate. Only now did he realize the degree of relief he felt that John was back in harness and able to be his mentor once again.

'When did you get back to London? And what do you know about our next mission?' Nathan was a fever of questions.

'I got back this morning and all I know is that we are going to the Netherlands. Jan Groesbeck here is going with us . . . oh, and we have to take the Silver brothers with us, God save our souls.'

'What are we going to do in Kent?' asked Nathan, his mouth full of the first crisp bite of the apple that Nym had just tossed to him.

'Well, first, we're going to Pointz's farm!' exclaimed Nym with a beam of delight. 'You're going to put Santa Cruz through his paces and then I'm going to see how you do with the bow.'

'Santa Cruz?' Nathan asked, wondering what the great Spanish admiral would be doing on a farm in Kent.

Nym chuckled. 'Finest horse that ever lived, and the cussedest. John here says that you are good on horseback. We'll see if you are. I warn you, boy . . .' he carried on saying something about the horse's personality but Nathan wasn't listening. The sheer joy at the thought of spending a day on horseback had welled up inside him and his smile was so broad that it threatened to split his cheeks. Pearce, Nym and Groesbeck shook their heads in amusement at the transformation in Nathan's face.

'Well, you've amazed me a-plenty in your time here, lad, and no doubt I shall see another wonder today,' confessed Nym. 'Come, young sirs, let's be on our way.'

George and Toby Silver were already in the back of the cart – looking relieved at the thought of a day without learning Dutch. They waved cheekily at Jan Groesbeck, who disappeared inside the house, shaking his head in dismay. Pearce and Nym climbed up behind the horses and Nathan clambered into the back. There was plenty of hay to sit on and he sat peacefully munching his apple as Nym slowly negotiated the passage out to the street and turned the horses eastwards. It was an hour after dawn and the inhabitants of Southwark, night creatures all, were still sound asleep, except for the merchants and delivery carts that were making their way towards London Bridge.

From behind Robey's School came the fearsome sound of wild animals – bears groaning in their cages in the bear-baiting pits, dogs beginning to bark, bulls shuddering at their tethers. The animals were hungry but Nathan knew that they would not be fed until they had provided sport for the masses who, tanked up with ale and blood-lust, would shout themselves hoarse and wager their last coin on the outcome of the bestial fights.

As the cart passed the ominous entrance to the Clink Prison, Nathan held his hand to his face to mask the stench wafting out from the grilles in the walls.

Southwark looked innocent in the half-light of the dawn but Nathan supposed it was a godless place. Filled with taverns, gaming dens and prisons, it was a strange area for Master Robey to have chosen to set up shop. Even St Saviour's Church seemed to bow with shame. Once the pride of the Bishop of Winchester, it had fallen into disrepair and now, according to Pistol, was lived in by a baker and a herd of pigs.

Nathan finished his apple, except for the core, which he tucked into the top of his jerkin for later. The cart passed the massive gates of London Bridge. They were locked now and would remain so until the bell of Bow Church in the City announced the start of the day, but already merchants, beggars, travellers and assorted other people were queuing silently, waiting to be allowed to pass into the City to conduct their business.

The cart trundled on, and gradually there were no more signs of habitation, with only green fields to be seen. In the distance, on the riverside, Nathan could see men and women cutting rushes with their scythes –

rushes that would be sent to London to dress the floors of houses. Turning back to the other side he could see fields of sheep grazing on the dewy grass, as the sun slowly climbed in the sky.

'Why are we going riding today?' Nathan asked Pearce, as the cart swayed gently along the Old Kent Road.

'Because we will spend most of our time on horseback in the Netherlands,' answered Pearce. 'The war is being fought by small groups that move swiftly between engagements. Although,' he added, 'the Spanish army relies very heavily on its foot soldiers and has only a few thousand light horse cavalry. But the Dutch rebels use their horses well, to give them an advantage against the sheer numbers of the enemy.'

'The Dutch sound very brave,' Nathan commented, thinking how exciting it must be to be part of a small band of rebels, attacking the might of the Spanish army and then riding off again.

'They are,' Pearce agreed.

Leaning over the edge of the cart, Nathan could see a small house in the distance and two fields of horses a short way from the house. He counted twenty horses in all and he wondered which one was the fabled Santa Cruz.

'Have you been here before?' he asked the brothers, who were busy eating a late breakfast, and they nodded.

'Best food in England,' said Toby, spraying a mouthful

15

of mutton and bread over Nathan, who flicked it off his jerkin with a grimace. George laughed and squeezed some wet bread through his teeth, and Nathan sniggered despite himself.

When they reached the house, a man and a woman were waiting for them. The man was short, wiry and dark and looked like another veteran soldier to Nathan. The woman was equally small, with a jolly smiling face.

'Bless us if it ain't old Nym . . . and John Pearce!' she exclaimed with pleasure. 'Well, we ain't seen you, Master Pearce, since afore harvest last year! And look if it ain't them two young rascals, George and Toby Silver!'

The cart stopped, everyone leaped down and there was a flurry of embracing, back-slapping and hand-shaking.

'Nathan!' Pearce motioned to him. 'Come and meet Abel Pointz and his wife Bess. Don't be shy, lad.'

'Master Robey said you're a good horseman,' said Pointz, looking at Nathan intently. 'So are you ready to ride, lad?'

Nathan's eyes glittered. 'Yes, sir. I should like to see Santa Cruz, please.'

Everyone grinned and the Silver brothers nudged each other. Pointz sucked his breath in through his teeth.

'So it's to be the old devil, is it? Are you sure you're up to him, boy?'

Nathan nodded firmly. Pointz winked at Pearce, then led them to the first field.

Without being told, Nathan knew which horse he was to ride. In the centre of the field, several hands taller than the other horses, was a fabulous black stallion. From the fence, Nathan could see no imperfections in the horse at all. He was about seventeen hands high, black as jet, and his muscles moved fluidly under his skin like black oil. Nathan felt his heartbeat quicken with excitement. The horse stopped grazing and raised his head, fixing the group with a baleful glare. Nathan marvelled at the arched curve of his neck, his large strong hocks and his well-developed quarters. Every part of Nathan ached to just touch the magnificent animal.

'Arab?' he asked Pointz softly.

Pointz raised an eyebrow and nodded. 'Partly,' he replied. 'He's a Neapolitan with an Arab sire. The breed is much prized by those who need a horse with power and speed. Most are docile and make good war horses – but not this one. He has the arrogance of a king, and he's choosy who he'll let sit astride him.'

'Can I try?' asked Nathan.

Pointz laughed and slapped Nathan's back. 'You've got nerve, I'll give you that! Most take one look at the beast and turn away! I'll bridle him up and take him to the training field.'

With that, he took a bridle off the fence post and entered the field. The other horses scattered but Santa Cruz stood his ground, waiting for Pointz, defiantly sizing him up. Nathan could hear Pointz muttering softly to the animal, words of reassurance and gentle command. Santa Cruz's nostrils flared as he caught his master's scent and Nathan heard the horse whinny, as if giving permission to be approached. Slowly and carefully, Pointz stroked the horse's cheek. Then he slipped the bit into the animal's mouth and expertly slid the headpiece on. Santa Cruz tossed his head and snorted with irritation but allowed his master to continue. Pointz adjusted the throatlatch and clipped on a lead rope, and then led the horse into another field.

Nathan watched the way Santa Cruz walked perfectly straight. He had never seen such a beautiful horse and his desire to ride him grew more and more powerful.

Finally, Pointz motioned to Nathan to enter the field. Breathing slowly and calmly, he approached the stallion. The horse made a sound of warning but did not move. Nathan moved closer until he stood within an arm's length of the powerful head. The nostrils flared to seek a scent and Nathan slowly slid his hand into the top of his jerkin and retrieved the apple core. Santa Cruz gave a soft whinny but his big, shining eyes held a look of devilment still. Gingerly, Nathan held out the apple core on his open hand. The horse hesitated for a moment then brought his big muzzle down and took the gift. Nathan kept his hand up and moved it towards Santa Cruz's cheek. The first contact of his fingers brought a sudden rearing of the horse's head and a baring of teeth but Nathan persisted. He was used to horses – most gypsies

18

spent their lives rearing them, and Nathan had inherited that instinctive skill. He kept his hand close to the horse's face and began to talk to the animal. At first he spoke in English but the horse's lips kept curling above his teeth in a menacing way until Nathan had a flash of inspiration and switched to murmuring in Italian.

'Good horse. How are you? What's the matter? Good horse . . .'

Santa Cruz shuddered in recognition and turned his head into Nathan's hand, allowing himself to be stroked. Nathan closed in and turned the horse's muzzle until the nostrils were in front of his mouth, then he gently blew into them. It was an old gypsy trick which made horses calmer. The great beast nuzzled Nathan's face in response and a faint expression of amazement came from the group watching by the fence.

Having won Santa Cruz's confidence, Nathan gently placed both hands on his back and vaulted nimbly up. It was a great height but he landed gently, with the expert control of a natural acrobat, and Santa Cruz made no movement of protest. Nathan grasped the horse's mane and, laying his head alongside the horse's ear, he murmured, 'Let's go.' Santa Cruz whinnied an agreement, before breaking into a disciplined canter. Nathan passed his friends with a boastful grin as they shook their heads in disbelief.

'That boy is a wonder,' said John Pearce ruefully.

'When I first mounted that beast, it threw me clear across the field.'

'You wouldn't get me up on it,' muttered George Silver, with a touch of envy in his voice.

'You wouldn't be *allowed* up on it,' said Pointz acidly. He had had a bitter experience of trying to coach the Silver brothers in horsemanship.

Pointz allowed Nathan a good fifteen minutes on the stallion's back before making him come down. To ride him was like riding on the shoulders of a giant. He was so high, and each measure of his powerful legs seemed to cover twice the ground of a normal horse. When he was told to stop, he felt cheated. Pointz had already called out to him to stop him from trying to gallop on Santa Cruz. To urge such a horse into full speed would have been like riding the wind.

'You can't run him fast without a saddle, boy, so don't even try!'

Nathan knew that the warning was right. He could have galloped a pony bareback but the sheer bulk of the stallion meant that Nathan's legs were not long enough for him to grip with his thighs and raise himself up. He slipped down off the horse with ease and Santa Cruz tossed his head sideways in acknowledgement. Nathan sadly patted the horse's great head and took his leave but was cheered by Master Pointz promising that he could take another turn on Santa Cruz in the afternoon. For now, it was time to eat.

The noonday meal was the greatest repast that Nathan had ever seen. Bess had braised six rabbits and there were peas, carrots, turnips and cabbage. This was followed by a fruit tart, washed down with warm spiced milk.

He felt happy and comfortable, seated with his friends around the large table in the farmhouse. Bess Pointz looked flushed and proud to have so many men-folk eating at her table. She was animatedly discussing with Nym the provisions they would be loading on to the cart.

'I told Master Robey that I could let you have some capons. Oh, and we've got some salted pork, some mutton pies and plenty of sausages. We're down to the last couple of crocks of salted beans but I can let you have one . . . ooh . . . and we've got a bag of lentils . . .' On and on she twittered, bustling about her kitchen, putting things to one side to be added to the cart.

John Pearce interrupted. 'Bess, you'll have to leave Nym be, now. He's got to take Nathan and the brothers down to the butts for a bit of archery practice.' So she turned back to her kitchen work, happy and satisfied that she had done her job of feeding the men.

Outside, Pointz took Nym into the barn and showed him where he kept the bows. Then he took his leave and went to tend to his stock. Nym carefully unwrapped each bow from its oiled cloth.

21

'Ah, good,' he said to himself. 'He's kept them dry and well.'

Handing John, Nathan, George and Toby a bow, a quiver of arrows and a leather shooting glove each, Nym pointed to the far field, where four target butts were set up. The straw butts had canvas targets stretched over them and they were all painted with pictures of animals. Nym put all of them in position, about a hundred yards from the targets.

Nathan didn't see why he had to prove himself with the bow. After all, Nym had schooled him well before his first mission to Venice. But he pulled the leather glove on to his right hand, placed the end of the yew bow under his foot, pulled up the grip of the bow and braced the string. Nathan nocked the arrow and, raising the bow with his left arm, pulled back on the string with the first two fingers of his right hand until the index finger rested on his right cheekbone. He took aim and loosed. His first arrow hit the painted boar on its tusk and he cursed because he had rushed the shot. His next arrow was true and hit the boar in the eye.

George and Toby were surprisingly good with a bow, even though their preferred method of combat was the sword. Toby looked relieved that, at last, they had managed to earn praise instead of criticism.

Nym nodded to Pearce to take his turn. John took aim and hit the boar squarely between the eyes and, before Nathan could comment, loosed another arrow, which spliced the first arrow in two. Nathan laughed his loud approval. *John is always the best at everything,* he thought with amusement.

'You see, Nathan, it ain't enough to be accurate,' said Nym. 'You have to be fast as well. Still, lad, I've no doubt that you will improve in the next hour or so.'

Over the next hour, Nathan shot quiver after quiver of arrows, until he almost matched the speed of John Pearce and the accuracy of the Silver brothers. Then Pointz appeared leading three ponies and one horse, all saddled up and ready to ride. Nathan broke into a smile.

'More riding?' he asked eagerly, putting down his bow and patting the nearest pony.

'Ride and shoot,' said Nym firmly, 'so pick up your bow, lad, and climb aboard.'

Nathan slung his bow over his back and mounted the pony. Nym looked enquiringly at the Silver brothers, who had made no move towards their own steeds.

'Let Nathan go first,' said George obligingly. Toby nodded in agreement. Neither was anxious to make a fool of himself. Nathan struggled to hold back a grin.

'Very well,' said Nym. 'Give her a good ride first, Nathan.' Needing no further encouragement, Nathan sped away at a fast gallop.

The pony was easy to manoeuvre and she obediently went in whichever direction Nathan guided her. He took several turns around the field and wheeled back to where the others were standing.

'What now?' he asked Nym breathlessly.

'I want you to ride at full gallop, crossways to the target, leave go of the reins, stand up in the saddle and try to loose your arrow at one of the targets.'

'Right,' said Nathan. He trotted the pony over to the far left of the field, and reached for his bow. Then, taking the reins in his right hand, he kicked the pony into a gallop. He stood up in the stirrups almost immediately and, as he neared the target, he dropped the reins, grabbed an arrow out of his quiver and nocked it but, as he pulled the string back he realized that he had already passed the target and it was too late.

Not to be defeated, he grabbed the reins again and brought the pony to a stop. Then he replaced the arrow in the quiver and trotted back to start again. Nym came over.

'Judge the distance, lad, judge the distance. You did the right thing by standing up straight away, but you need to nock your arrow at the same time as you stand. You left it too late.'

Nathan nodded and steadied the pony. This time he did as Nym told him. As he stood in the stirrups, the arrow was out of the quiver and on to the string. He pulled the string back and took aim. This time he was ahead of the target but, whilst the arrow hit the butt, it did not hit the boar's head. *Well, I shall just have to try again,* thought Nathan defiantly, and wheeled round for another turn.

The others sat down on the grass to watch and Nathan was determined to give them his best performance.

Time after time, he thundered past the targets, shooting his arrows until by the eleventh attempt, he had perfected the technique of hitting the boar's head from about thirty yards – at full gallop.

Toby Silver groped to find the right words to express his admiration.

'He's like one of those mythical creatures. You know, John – the top half is a man that shoots a bow and the bottom half is a horse. What are they called?'

'A Centaur,' replied Pearce.

Toby took a deep breath. 'That's what he's like. A bloody Centaur.'

Nym looked at Pointz. 'I ain't never seen a Centaur,' he said.

'Nor me,' replied Pointz, 'but I know a determined bugger when I see one!'

Nathan trotted the pony back to the men, satisfied that he had done his best. Everyone stood up and congratulated him as he dismounted.

Then it was the turn of George Silver, who managed, Nathan thought, passably well. He certainly showed an aptitude for hitting the target but, being bigger and heavier than Nathan, he was less skilled at manoeuvring his pony. Still, it was obvious from his flushed grin that he felt he had not disgraced himself.

Toby had less luck. He was good at riding and good

with the bow. He was just less good at putting them both together. Twice he fell off as he raised himself up to shoot and was about to fall a third time when Nym shouted at him to stop.

'Hold up! Hold up!' he shouted, flinging himself at the pony's bridle and dragging it to a halt. 'You'll fall on an arrow and either kill yourself or the horse! We have to find another method for you, lad, because this way you are more of a danger to yourself than any enemy.'

Toby slid out of the saddle in a lather of sweat and Nathan could see that his face was grim with humiliation. Nym patiently walked Toby and the pony across the field and stopped on the far side. He seemed to be giving fresh instructions to Toby, who was nodding.

'Let's see if this works any better,' Nym said once he'd trudged back to the group.

This time, Toby spurred the pony on to a gallop, holding the reins with one hand and a loaded bow in the other. Then, as he approached the target, he pulled the horse up sharply to a halt, raised himself up and loosed his arrow, hitting the centre of the target with a smack, before urging the pony into a full gallop again.

'It makes the rider more vulnerable when they have to stop to shoot but, in Toby's case, I think it is the lesser of two evils,' Nym said sagely. Nathan nodded in agreement.

Toby cantered back to his companions with a happy smile on his face.

'Trust you to do it differently to everyone else,' George joked, cuffing his brother round the ear.

'That's because I am unique, brother,' Toby replied good-naturedly.

When it was John Pearce's turn he mounted up, arrow ready-nocked, and set his horse to a gallop. He shot an arrow straight into the boar's eye then, still raised in the stirrups, he swiftly nocked another arrow and managed another amazingly accurate shot. Before Nathan and the Silver brothers could break into appreciative applause, Pearce wheeled the horse around, set it to gallop again and performed the same double-shot sequence using his other hand. Nathan brought his fingers to his mouth and began whistling loudly, George started clapping and cheering, while Toby just slumped to the ground and muttered, 'He's such a show-off.'

When the spectacle was over, Pointz tapped Nathan on the shoulder.

'Nathan, have you done with riding for today?' he enquired. For a moment Nathan was stricken until he realized that Pointz was jesting with him.

'Just one more turn with Santa Cruz?' he pleaded.

As the others loaded up the cart with the provisions, they watched Nathan and the magnificent stallion canter around the training field. As he rode, Nathan kept stroking and talking to the horse.

'D'you know . . .' Pearce observed, 'there is nothing

more powerful than a man's love for his horse? Not even the love for a woman.'

Nym pulled a scornful face. 'Never knowed a horse that could make a decent apple tart,' he said, giving a bashful smile and a wink at Bess Pointz as she pressed a large slice into his hands. Pearce laughed heartily and agreed.

On the way home, Nathan dozed fitfully in the back of the swaying cart and dreamed of riding Santa Cruz at full pelt across a great plain, the wind coursing through his hair and laughter bubbling up inside him as the great animal thudded across the ground. He awoke with a start when they reached Southwark, and realized that they were back in the midst of the swarming city. Taverns were open and lit from within and noisy drunks spilled out on to the streets. On one corner two men were brawling, and a crowd had gathered to shout encouragement and derision. All the smells of London came flooding back into Nathan's consciousness but as they pulled into the yard of Robey's school, the only smell in his nostrils was of a warm, powerful horse, sweating gently beneath its rider.

'TO BECOME A MASTER REQUIRES MORE THAN SKILL WITH A SWORD'

*O*ver the next few days, Nathan excelled in his Dutch lessons while the Silver brothers made little progress. Robey was adamant, however, that the lessons should continue.

'The Silver brothers must go to the Netherlands with John Pearce,' he said on one occasion when Groesbeck had called him into class to protest at their lack of improvement. 'I am afraid, Jan, that you must persist.'

No further explanation was given about the mission and Nathan became more and more curious.

'We will know everything in due course,' Pearce had said, when Nathan asked him. 'Walsingham is still finalizing the details. We will be summoned soon,' he added reassuringly, and Nathan had to be satisfied with that.

They all had a few days' leave coming up and Nathan noticed that the Silver brothers seemed to be almost conspiratorial in the week before the break. *What mischief are they up to?* he wondered. But his mind was too full of the happy prospect of seeing his sister Marie again.

As much as he loved the atmosphere of Robey's school, Nathan had missed his sister fussing around him like a mother hen. *Not that I would admit it to her*, he thought. It had taken him the best part of six months to assert his independence and he was not going to give Marie an excuse to take it away from him again. Even though they had made contact with their father once more, Marie's habit of taking full responsibility for her younger brother was so ingrained that she could not help herself. *But I suppose I love her – despite her bossiness*, Nathan acknowledged fondly. She was after all the only family he had known, for most of his life.

He was glad to be back in Shoreditch for a few days. He visited the theatre where he had once performed and met with his friend Will Shakespeare once more. To Shakespeare, Nathan was proving to be an important source of stories and adventures. Nothing was too insignificant to be scribbled down in Will's battered notebook.

'Where are you off to next?' Will dropped his voice to a confidential tone when they sat by the fire, at home, after eating a substantial breakfast.

'The Netherlands,' Nathan replied quietly, 'but don't ask me anything else because I can't tell you.'

'Oh, I understand,' said Will eagerly. 'Now you work

for Sir Francis Walsingham, you must keep your plans secret.'

'No . . .' was Nathan's faltering reply 'Well, yes . . . I mean that is true. But actually, I can't tell you because I don't know anything yet.'

Will nodded. 'Well, it's a shame it's to be the Netherlands. Such a boring place. So flat. I prefer Italy. There is romance in Italy. The Dutch are too practical. They have no passions. I would never set a play in the Netherlands. The audience would be asleep in half an hour.'

Nathan laughed and Marie, who had been sitting by the fire quietly darning Nathan's hose, pushed back her dark curls and raised an eyebrow.

'I doubt whether the thousands of Dutchmen who are fighting for their beliefs at this very moment would regard themselves as having no passion, or regard their existence as being boring,' she said sarcastically.

Will rolled his eyes but she persisted.

'I hear they had a *very* boring time during the reign of The Council of Blood.' Marie's comment bordered on the withering and Will cleared his throat in embarrassment.

'What's the Council of Blood?' Nathan asked Marie, seizing upon what sounded like a spine-chilling piece of information.

'The Dutch version of the Spanish Inquisition,' Marie answered, biting off a woollen thread. 'Twenty years ago, the Duke of Alva set up the Council to punish the Dutch heretics. Over nine thousand people were condemned and thrown into prison, hundreds were executed in various horrible ways and thousands more fled the country. I expect they found it very *dull*.' Marie glared at Shakespeare, her blue eyes darkening to violet as they always did when she was angry. He wisely decided that he had outstayed his welcome.

'We are rehearsing a new play, Nathan,' he said, rising to his feet and trying to avoid looking in Marie's direction. 'Will you come to the theatre with me tomorrow?'

Nathan was about to happily agree when all three of them were startled by an urgent knocking on the door. Brother and sister looked anxiously at each other and Marie drew a knife from her bodice. Since they had entered the shadowy world of espionage they had learned to be suspicious of any unexpected visitor. Marie nodded towards Nathan and before approaching the door he also drew a knife from the hidden compartment in his boots. He opened it a crack and, to his surprise, found himself looking into the face of his dearest friend.

'John!' he exclaimed, as he flung open the door.

Pearce strode into the room, with a strange look of half-anger and half-amusement on his face. Marie flushed, as she always did when the handsome agent was present. Pearce, as usual, smiled but always made it a point to be professional and detached although Nathan suspected that he really rather liked Marie.

'I apologize for the intrusion,' he said, bowing low to Marie. 'But I thought you should see this.' He brandished a piece of paper towards Nathan. 'It was pressed into my hand by a complete stranger this morning as I was riding through the City. Those idiots have excelled themselves this time!'

Nathan grabbed the paper and read it out aloud.

'The brothers George and Toby Silver,
insomuch as they desire to prove themselves
as Masters of Defence, challenge all
Italian Fencing Masters abroad in London
to a duello at the Black Friar's Inn at noon on
30th October 1587. The Silver brothers seek
to prove that the Italian method is inferior and
will take all comers.'

Nathan's eyebrows rose but he could not resist a small smile of excitement. *Today! The duel is going to take place today!* His half-smile faded, however, when Pearce spoke.

'Robey will kill them for this! By all the saints, they must have a death wish! I have said before that they have not a cupful of wit between them!'

'I think I know why they are doing this,' said Nathan seriously. 'They have both been struggling to learn Dutch and then Toby could not manage the horseback shooting and has not been himself ever since. I think they have decided that they must prove themselves.'

Pearce shook his head. 'They have yet to undertake

their first mission for Walsingham, yet they seek to be dismissed from his service, for I can see no other outcome . . .'

'We must try to stop them,' Nathan said quickly. He liked the Silver brothers and also felt in some part responsible. It embarrassed him when he found tasks easy and the brothers struggled.

'I should like to come as well!' Shakespeare seemed gleeful at the thought of some excitement.

'Then I shall come too!' Marie was never happy to be left out. 'Quick, we'll borrow Mistress Fast's cart.' There was no stopping her once she was determined, and she swept past them to find their landlady.

'You must follow after us as best you can!' Pearce called to her as he and Nathan ran down the stairs to their waiting horses. 'We can make faster time on horseback,' he added, as he and Nathan spurred their mounts on.

When the two of them arrived at the Black Friar's Inn, a crowd had gathered. In the courtyard of the inn was a wooden stage. *Recently used as a theatre*, thought Nathan, with a heart-leap of recognition. He had acted on many a makeshift stage such as this, when Burbage's players went touring.

Pearce and Nathan hitched their horses and pushed through the crowd. As they neared the front, they saw George and Toby, laughing and joking, standing to one side. They were kitted out for business – leather fencing gloves with chain mail on the backs of the hands, thick skirted leather jerkins to act as breastplates and protective leather neck collars.

Pearce was trying to struggle through the last two rows of spectators, when a mixture of cheers and catcalls went up from the crowd. The Italians had arrived. Nathan realized that they were too late to stop the proceedings now.

There was silence as three very elegant and very menacing men pushed through the crowd, which parted silently to let them through. One, who seemed to be the leader, wore a black doublet with a high-standing collar and his black hose was slashed with gold.

'Hardly dressed for a fight, are they?' said Pearce as he made his way back to Nathan's side.

The crowd murmured its appreciation as the three Italians began to strip off their finery and their servants handed them leather gear similar to that worn by the Silver brothers. Three of the finest Italian rapiers were produced, which gleamed in the morning light.

George Silver bounded up on to the stage and the lead Italian made a more leisurely ascent on to the platform. They bowed to each other, raised their swords and began to engage, cautiously at first, each getting the measure of the other.

Nathan shouted to Pearce above the noise of the crowd. 'Apart from trying to prove themselves to everyone, why do you think they have chosen to challenge the Italians?'

'Every fencing pupil has to give a public display of his skill in order to achieve the title of Master,' shouted Pearce in reply. 'Robey is always saying that the Italians are the best street fighters in the world and so I suppose the Silver brothers decided to pit themselves against the toughest opponents. But if they think to impress Robey, they are sadly mistaken. He will be furious when he finds out what they have done.'

The duel was gaining momentum. The Italian was fast and he had already cut the side of George's jerkin with his razor-sharp sword. George was still grinning though, and he was beating the Italian back towards his side of the stage. Just then, the Italian stumbled and, as he went down on to one knee, he raised his hand and caught a dagger, thrown by his servant. The crowd roared its approval at this turn of events. Quick as a flash, Pearce pulled out his own dagger and threw it so that it stuck in the wall above George's head. George grinned even wider and yanked it free. Now they were equal and both crouched into a dagger and rapier fight. The Italian slashed with his dagger and George leaped to one side, bringing his rapier down with lightning speed to cut the Italian's dagger arm just below the elbow. The Italian brought his sword round to cut George's exposed sword arm but he was thwarted by a well-aimed kick from his opponent, which struck him in the jaw and knocked him senseless.

The crowd screamed with delight, and a servant

dragged the Italian off the stage. A second Italian, who looked meaner and younger than his countryman, took his place.

There was a shout from Toby and he leaped on stage to take over from his brother. This time the fight started at top speed. All rules had been abandoned. The Italian lunged and grazed Toby's shoulder but Toby retaliated with a swift kick to his opponent's groin and, when he doubled over in pain, another hard kick to the shoulder sent him flying off the stage. The third Italian came on the stage slowly, with two rapiers, indicating with a sadistic smile that he would take on both Silvers at once. The crowd made a collective sound of warning. Toby and George threw down their daggers and circled their opponent. They made a concerted attack on the Italian, but he was good.

Robey always says that you should be able to fight with both hands, thought Nathan. *I would be able to do that now, probably better than the Silvers.* He marvelled at how the Italian was able to fight in this manner with such ease. He seemed not to tire, whereas the Silver brothers were showing signs of flagging. With a flick of the wrist, the Italian sent George's rapier flying into the crowd, where some fool tried to catch it and cut his hands badly. George was forced to come down off the stage and leave his brother to face the Italian alone, while he recovered his sword from the press of people. The man who had cut his hands beat the hapless George about the ears for his trouble and the man's wife kicked George in the back-side and sent him sprawling.

The fight on stage had stopped. The Italian threw away his left-hand sword, looked hard at Toby Silver and spoke to him menacingly in Italian.

'What did he say, Nathan?' asked Shakespeare, who had suddenly appeared with Marie at Nathan's elbow.

Nathan translated solemnly, 'May whatever gods you worship have pity on your immortal soul.'

'Sounds like he is going in for the kill,' muttered Pearce.

The Italian saluted Toby with his sword and took his position.

Toby's response was a single Italian word accompanied by a crude gesture with his right hand.

Shakespeare looked at Nathan enquiringly. Nathan blushed. 'I think what he said was fairly obvious, Will.'

Suddenly, both swordsmen lunged into a furious and frightening clash of steel – blades flying in all directions as they fought at top speed with murderous intent. The Italian seemed to be getting the upper hand, forcing Toby back towards the edge of the stage, when Toby leaped into the air, both feet landing in the Italian's stomach. The Italian flew backwards into the small group of his fellow countrymen, scattering bodies everywhere. Toby picked himself up off the stage, but the Italian seemed unable to rise. Nathan craned to hear the babble of Italian coming from the knot of servants.

'It seems that Toby has broken several of the Italian's ribs,' he reported to his friends. 'The Italian cannot raise his arms.'

John Pearce looked relieved. 'Then it is over. Thank God.'

'I think not, Master Pearce,' said Will Shakespeare drily and he indicated with his head to where the crowd was parting to let another opponent through.

'My God! It's Felipe Casado!' Pearce's words filtered through the crowd, and the mood turned ugly. Casado was well known – he was one of the few Spanish merchants to have remained in England after the queen had banished Mendoza, the Spanish Ambassador. Since England was not technically at war with Spain – yet – those Spaniards who had business in the country could not be forced to leave. But they led a difficult life amongst the English, who showed their dislike at every opportunity. People began to hiss and boo and several spat on the ground in front of Casado as he made his way through. He seemed unperturbed and a sardonic smile played around his lips. Following closely behind him was a tall young man with white-blond hair, carrying a rapier made of the finest Castilian steel.

'How unusual for a Spaniard to have such blond hair,' murmured Marie, echoing Nathan's very thoughts.

'Who is he?' Nathan asked Pearce, with a certain amount of awe in his voice.

'That is Felipe's son, Carlos. Reputedly the greatest

swordfighter in Spain.' Pearce had a look of despair on his face. 'I suppose I shall have to fight him, for the Silver brothers, good as they are, cannot take him on.'

'That you will *not* do, Master Pearce,' said a quiet, firm voice behind them. Nathan turned to see Robey, his face thunderous. 'You have important work ahead of you, which should not be put in jeopardy by a foolish tavern brawl.' And, with that, he pushed his way through the crowd, which easily parted once they saw the look of intent in his eyes.

The Casados stood by the stage and waited. Nathan saw Felipe Casado nod and bestow a faint half-smile on someone in the crowd, so he craned his head to see who was the recipient of the Spaniard's gesture. He saw the back of a man's head and when that head turned, his blood froze. It was Lord Harcourt – the suspected Spanish spy at Queen Elizabeth's Court. Nathan stared at his feet, not wanting to be recognized by the man whose servant had been sent to assassinate him on his first mission for Walsingham. He nudged Pearce and inclined his head towards Harcourt. Pearce looked and frowned.

'Is your father in London?' he asked Nathan quietly, knowing that Samuel Fox's life was constantly in danger from Harcourt.

'Not that I am aware,' Nathan replied, feeling a surge of hatred for the man who had robbed him of a child-hood in his father's company. Samuel Fox, an apothecary at the time, had disappeared into obscurity after realizing that Harcourt had murdered his first wife using a potion that Samuel had innocently given him. Only recently had Nathan met his father for the first time in eight years.

Nathan's thoughts were interrupted as Robey leaped up on the platform to address the roaring crowd.

'You have all been witness to these two young men . . .' he indicated the Silver brothers '. . . defeating the Italian Masters. Is it your wish that they have earned their Master's titles?' The crowd yelled its agreement and Robey held up a hand to silence them.

'We now have a new opponent. Don Carlos Casado.' He talked over the crowd's boos and catcalls. 'But he was not invited here, for he is Spanish and not Italian . . .'

'That's the Spanish for you! Always going where they're not wanted!' shouted someone in the crowd and the audience broke into raucous laughter.

The Casados looked angry, and Carlos flushed and held his head even higher. Robey silenced the crowd once more.

'This man comes to fight in honour. His skill is renowned the world over. He deserves a fair duel but not, I think, with these young men. Don Carlos, would you do me the honour of accepting me as your opponent?'

Carlos looked at his father, who nodded his approval, and the son stepped up on to the stage. 'Gracias, Señor,'

41

he said by way of acceptance, and the two swordsmen prepared to fight.

Robey was wearing his usual sombre black leather from top to toe, but the Spaniard seemed confident enough, arrogant even, to fight merely in his shirt, with no protection at all.

'What a handsome young man,' Marie murmured, with obvious admiration. Pearce, Nathan and Will all curled their lips in disbelief but Marie kept her eyes fixed on the young Spaniard.

Felipe Casado walked up on to the stage and spoke to Robey. 'You are able to fight in the Spanish fashion?'

Robey smiled sardonically and replied, 'I am able to fight in any style you propose, Señor.' Casado nodded and withdrew.

Carlos Casado dropped on one knee, said a quick prayer and made the sign of the cross. Then he stood and raised his sword as a signal to start.

The crowd fell completely silent. The two men on the stage began to dance around, lightly and nimbly, while their rapiers clashed backwards and forwards continuously. The Spaniard seemed to be able to come from any angle and yet Robey, with speed and intelligence, was always there to break the blow or thrust. They both held their bodies very straight, as opposed to the crouching style of the Italians, and used the full length of their sword arms. The elegance of the swordplay was indisputable and both men were so skilled that they made it look as though it was a demonstration, but Nathan could see the murderous intent in the Spaniard's eyes. Robey fought impassively – there was no emotion on his face at all, merely pure concentration. *There is no one like Robey*, thought Nathan with unwavering admiration. *He truly is the Master.*

The crowd began to get a little restive because there was no blood, no spectacle but then, suddenly, the Spaniard became frustrated by Robey's skill and his body began to lose some of its rigid perfection as he made his attack wider. Robey sensed he had the upper hand and switched his emphasis from parrying the Spaniard's moves to a more concerted attack. The fighting became faster, the Spaniard was breathing more heavily and Nathan caught a gleam of triumph in Robey's eyes. Then, with one almighty slash of Robey's sword, which sounded like a great whip being cracked through the air, Carlos' sword spun out of his hand and pierced the wooden stage, quivering on its point. The young man dropped to his knees, clutching the wrist of his sword hand.

There was a moment's silence, and then a great cheer went up. Caps were thrown into the air and people were hugging each other at this small victory of England over Spain. Robey, meanwhile, had dropped his sword and was tending to the young Spaniard, whose father had hurried to his side.

Robey felt the wrist with his nimble and experienced

fingers. 'Have no fear, it is not broken,' Robey explained to Felipe Casado, 'it is merely dislocated. Hold him still.' Casado obeyed and Robey, with a quick and powerful yank, pulled the wrist bones back into place. The young man slumped down in a dead faint.

Nathan looked over to see Harcourt's reaction, but the man was gone – melted away into the crowd. *No doubt I will see him again*, thought Nathan. *But wherever that man goes, danger follows.*

But, for now, he and Pearce went to congratulate Robey, only to find that he had turned his attention to the unfortunate Silver brothers. He had an ear of each gripped between his thumbs and fingers.

'You beggarly poltroons!' he roared at them. 'Think yourselves lucky that you have got away with a few scratches and bruises! Have you learned nothing from me? *You* do not arrange your own fights, *I* arrange them and you certainly do not enrage the whole Italian population of London with your arrogance and foolishness! You shall come back with me to Southwark to lick your wounds, and then I shall devise some fitting punishment for you.'

Robey turned to John Pearce and spoke firmly.

'Master Pearce, you have dallied too long at this piece of street entertainment. Sir Francis has sent a request that you escort Nathan and Mistress Marie to Whitehall Palace at once. He also requests that Mistress Fox bring

44

medicines.' He whispered into Pearce's ear. 'It is for the queen. She wants a woman to tend her.'

Then Robey pushed the Silver brothers ahead of him and they were gone.

When Pearce relayed this information to Marie, her face went grey.

'The queen . . . wants me to . . . !' Her hoarse whisper faded. *It is not often my sister is lost for words*, thought Nathan wryly.

'We must return to Shoreditch first and collect your medicines.' Pearce's brisk manner seem to snap Marie out of her panic.

'But what shall I take?' she asked as he propelled her and the others through the crowd towards the street. 'Do we know what ails the queen?'

'No. We do not. Take it all, mistress. Take everything you can lay your hands on.'

THE VANITY OF WOMAN

*J*he journey back to Shoreditch had been made in haste and silence. Everyone, especially Nathan, was concerned for the great responsibility that now faced Marie.

'Supposing . . .' she whispered, half to herself and half to Nathan, as she flung every herbal potion she could find into a bag, '. . . supposing the queen is dying and there is nothing I can do? I will be blamed. Everyone in England will lay her death at my door.' Marie's hands were trembling as she filled glass vials with yet more concoctions and pressed corks into them.

While Pearce tried to reassure her, Nathan was set to tearing up pieces of linen into strips, and Shakespeare was despatched to the field beyond the house to strip bark from the nearest willow tree.

'Marie,' urged Pearce, 'we must leave now.'

'I am ready,' she said, grabbing the handfuls of bark from Shakespeare, who had just returned.

Nathan heaved Marie's bag on to the cart and she clambered up beside it, clutching it to her body protectively. Shakespeare grabbed Nathan as he mounted his horse. 'Remember every detail! If I do not see you again before you go to the Netherlands, keep everything in your mind to tell me when you return.'

Nathan reassured him he would and Shakespeare waved them goodbye as Pearce urged the cart towards the City.

He was able to make good speed on the road into the centre of London but once they reached the busy streets of the City they made slow progress. Eventually they eased out into the wide thoroughfare that led to Westminster, but Nathan could see from the sun's position in the sky that it was now approaching mid-afternoon. He looked at Marie anxiously. Her lips were moving in a silent prayer, presumably begging God that they should not be too late to save the queen.

Once they arrived at Whitehall Palace, Pearce held the medicine bag in his arms, as though cradling a child, and strode out for the queen's apartments, Nathan and Marie following in his wake. They found Sir Francis Walsingham sitting on a chair outside the queen's bedchamber, looking old and worn. *He is so devoted to the queen,* thought Nathan. Walsingham rose painfully to his feet as they approached, leaning heavily on his stick.

'Thank God Robey found you!' he said with heartfelt

relief. 'Thank you, Mistress Fox, for coming to Her Majesty's aid.' He bowed to Marie with great difficulty.

'What is it that ails Her Majesty?' Marie spoke in a hushed whisper, overwhelmed by the grandeur of the surroundings and with nervousness at the task ahead.

'No one knows!' Walsingham's voice had an edge of desperation. 'She will not allow anyone except her ladies-in-waiting to enter her bedchamber. She will not let her usual doctor tend her and she will not tell anyone what is keeping her in her bed. She has even forbidden her ladies to open her bedcurtains. All we know is that she is in great pain. She has agreed to see a female physician. Or rather she says that she will only see someone who is skilled – no midwives, bawdy baskets, doxies, trulls, wise women or witches. Whatever is Her Majesty's ailment, it seems that it has not affected her sharp tongue.'

Marie took a deep breath and spoke firmly. 'Would you please tell Her Majesty that I must have my brother in attendance to help me.'

Walsingham looked startled but agreed to relay her request. He knocked on the door and spoke to the lady-in-waiting who appeared. She nodded and the door was closed again. Nathan knew that Marie did not need his assistance and never had. She merely wanted someone to go into the lioness's den with her. Now he was beginning to feel anxious. He half-expected the request to provoke shouts of rage from within, or a chamber pot thrown at the door, such were the stories he had heard of the queen's temper. But, after a moment or two, the attendant opened the door looking sheepish and holding a silk scarf.

'Her Majesty said that the boy may enter only if he is blindfolded.'

'God's teeth!' muttered Walsingham in frustration but he motioned Nathan to step forward and have his eyes covered.

Marie took his hand and Pearce put the heavy medicine bag into his other hand. Together, brother and sister stepped into the room. It was hot and stuffy. Nathan wrinkled his nose in distaste. There was an overwhelming smell of decaying roses, and something else underneath the perfume – a faint putrid smell.

Nathan heard the door close and a woman's voice announced, 'Your Majesty, Mistress Fox is here – with her brother.'

'I want everyone else to leave,' was the command from the queen, but it sounded strange and muffled. *What kind of vile deformity has afflicted the queen that she will not allow even her ladies to see her?* Nathan's heart began to pump with a fresh surge of anxiety.

There was much rustling of skirts and then Nathan heard the door open and close. Marie led him forward, gripping his hand tightly. She stopped and spoke, her voice cracking a little with bravado.

'Your Majesty, I am here to help you, if I can, but I

49

need to examine you. Please will you let me draw the curtains?'

There was a silence and Nathan held his breath while they waited for a reply. Finally it came.

'Is the boy blindfolded?' the queen asked.

'Yes, Your Majesty.' Marie's voice was firm.

'Then you may draw the curtains.'

Marie gently pulled Nathan to one side and placed his hand on the gnarled bedpost. He felt her step around him and heard the clanking of wooden rings as the heavy bedcurtains were pulled apart. He heard Marie take a deep breath in through her nose. *Was the Queen lying in a pool of blood? Oh, if only I could see!*

'Your Majesty,' Marie's voice sounded relaxed now, 'it looks as though you have a bad tooth.'

Nathan suppressed a smile. *That was it? That was what all the fuss was about? A bad tooth!*

Marie sounded matter-of-fact. 'If Your Majesty will permit me, I must climb on to the bed and look in your mouth.'

'You may.' The queen sounded as though she had a mouth full of cotton. Now Nathan understood. Her face must be very swollen and *this* was why she would not allow anyone to see her. Elizabeth was known to be extremely vain. Her white face was always expertly painted, her long elegant hands were always bejewelled and her gowns always decorated to dazzle. She would never allow her courtiers to see her with a *misshapen* face.

50

The queen uttered a groan of pain as, presumably, Marie began to prod in the royal mouth.

'Your Majesty, you have two very bad teeth at the back and they must be removed to allow the pus to drain from your jaw. It will hurt. May I give you some poppy juice to dull the pain?'

'No.' the queen was emphatic. 'No poppy juice. It dulls the senses too.'

'But Your Majesty . . .'

'I said no, Mistress Fox. That is my wish and my command.'

'Very well, Your Majesty, but there is no other way to give you relief.'

'I can bear it. It cannot be much worse than the pain I am in now. Let the boy hold my hand while you do your worst.'

Nathan felt his stomach flip over at this command and then he heard Marie climb off the bed. She took the bag from his hand and gave him a gentle push forwards. Unable to see anything at all, he groped his way along the bed. At one point his hand rested on a projection under the bedclothes.

'Have a care, Master Fox. That is the royal foot you are caressing.' The queen's muffled voice sounded sharp and Nathan moved his hand hastily off the bed.

'A th-thousand apologies, Y-Your Majesty,' he stammered awkwardly.

The queen gurgled a strange laugh.

'How now, lad! I am not averse to having my foot fondled by a handsome pup but I think you will be of more use to your queen if you take her hand.' Nathan felt her long bony fingers grasp his hand and pull him further along the bed.

'There now.' Her hand grasped his more firmly and he felt the cool metal of her many rings. The faint putrid smell he had detected upon entering the room was now much stronger and he realized that it was coming from her mouth. How brave his sister was to suffer the full blast of such putrefaction at close quarters! It was not a job that he would care to undertake. Marie, irritating though she was at times, never ceased to amaze him with her courage.

'Your Majesty, I must send for some salt and warm water. We shall need it to rinse the poison from your mouth.' Marie was fully in command now. Nathan could imagine his sister gazing into the queen's eyes without wavering. He wondered how the queen was feeling about another woman taking charge.

'As you will. I am in your hands, Mistress Fox.' The reply was amiable enough.

Nathan heard the swish of Marie's skirts, then he heard her open the door and demand the salt and water. He also heard Walsingham's voice tremulously enquire if Her Majesty would survive. The queen snorted at this and muttered, 'The Old Moor is more worried about his pension than my health!' but Nathan suspected that she was really quite pleased that Sir Francis was trembling with anxiety outside her door. *She knows how much he loves her*, he thought.

The door closed after Marie had assured all outside that the queen would be in full health very soon, and Nathan heard her return to the bedside.

'Your Majesty,' Marie spoke gently, 'I shall wait for the salt and water before cutting your gum.' The queen stirred but said nothing.

'While we wait, I shall put oil of cloves on some cloth and you must hold it between your teeth. It will give at least some measure of pain relief. I would give you some willow bark to chew upon but it would cause you too much pain to bite down upon it.'

'You seem to know your business well, Mistress Fox.' The queen's voice held a tinge of admiration.

'I had a good teacher, Your Majesty,' Marie replied. 'My father was a renowned apothecary.'

'Ah yes. That old fox Walsingham told me you are an Egyptian. Is that true?'

Nathan was surprised to hear the queen use the old term for gypsy. He knew that it had once been thought that gypsies were 'children of Egypt', and 'gypsy' was a shortened version of that name.

'I am a gypsy, yes, Your Majesty.' Marie sounded guarded, unsure of what the admission would mean.

'Are you a witch?' the queen asked bluntly.

'No, Your Majesty!' Marie sounded shocked at such a suggestion.

The queen's reply astounded Nathan. 'Pity,' she said. 'I should like to meet a real witch.'

'I don't believe that there is such a thing, Your Majesty,' Marie said dismissively.

'No. Nor do I, Mistress Fox. But then you and I are intelligent women.'

There was a strong smell of cloves which passed by Nathan's nostrils and then the Queen was silenced by Marie putting the cloth in the royal mouth. He heard the patient groan slightly as the pungent oil stung her diseased gum. There was a knock at the door and Marie swiftly took delivery of the items she had requested.

'Everything is ready now, Your Majesty. I shall cut the gum and extract the teeth. Your mouth will fill with pus and blood and you must not swallow it but spit it into this bowl. Once the wound has finished voiding pus, you must then rinse several times with the salted water and spit it out, before I pack the wound with linen to stop the bleeding.'

Nathan smelt the cloves as the cloth was extracted and passed by his head, then he heard his sister climb up on to the bed. 'Open your mouth as wide as you can, Your Majesty.' Nathan was not prepared for the blinding agony of his hand being crushed in the queen's vice-like grip. He bowed his head and opened his mouth in a silent scream as her rings bit deep into his skin. He was not sure who was in greater pain – he or the queen – but the shared agony seemed to last for an eternity as Marie panted and puffed through her difficult job. The queen's entire body had gone rigid and she pushed her arm down to the floor, forcing Nathan to his knees. Finally he heard a choking, gasping sound as she spat and retched into the bowl. Suddenly, her hand left his and he rolled gratefully on to his side, cradling his injured fingers to his stomach. They were wet with blood and were beginning to sting furiously as the circulation returned.

'Now the salt rinse, Your Majesty. Force it hard around your mouth to get every last ounce of pus out.'

The queen obligingly gurgled and swooshed, spat and filled her mouth again. Nathan's hand had settled into a quiet throbbing and he attempted to flex his fingers.

'Now, Your Majesty,' said Marie, 'I shall pack the wound and stop the bleeding. Be patient a little longer.' There were more sounds of puffing and grunting and then the job was done.

'Your Majesty, I am going to break off a small piece of willow bark and place it between your gum and your cheek. It will lessen the pain and the swelling which, hopefully, will be gone by tomorrow. But you must sleep sitting up and whenever you feel that your mouth is filled with blood you must spit it out. And you must rinse with more salt water every few hours to keep infection away.'

'I thank you, Mistress Fox. But I shall not be able to sleep unless you stay by my side.' The queen's voice sounded even more muffled now. 'It is my wish that you sleep in my room until I have no further need of your skills. You may take your brother away now and tend to his hand, for I fear that I may have damaged it somewhat. But mind that you return swiftly. I wish no one to wait on me but you.'

'Yes, Your Majesty.' Marie sounded flustered and she helped Nathan up from the floor and guided him towards the door.

'Master Fox,' the muffled voice came from the bed behind him.

'Yes, Your Majesty?' Nathan felt strange talking to the queen while facing the door.

'You and your sister have done me a great service today and I shall not forget it. I particularly shall not forget your bravery in the face of what must have been extreme pain.'

'It was nothing, Your Majesty,' Nathan lied, and Marie led him outside.

Suddenly, he was blinking in the sunlight of the corridor, the blindfold in his good hand whilst Marie fretted over the state of the other.

'John, you must see that he washes this hand thoroughly. When you get Nathan back to Shoreditch, there is some lavender ointment on the table. Put it on his wounds.'

'You are staying here?' Pearce asked, raising his eyebrows.

'Her Majesty has requested that I nurse her until she is well again.' Marie sounded smug.

Walsingham managed a rare smile and he bowed low to Marie.

'My lady, you have saved the queen's life, and for that you have my undying gratitude.'

Marie was scornful, and whispered, 'I doubt whether the queen would have died from a couple of bad teeth, my lord.'

Walsingham looked incredulous. 'That is all it was? But why would she not let her own physician tend to her?'

Marie pursed her lips. 'And let a man see her with a swollen face! I think not, my lord. Now, if you will excuse me, gentlemen, I promised Her Majesty that I would return swiftly.' Then she left the three of them standing by the closed door.

Walsingham shook his head in despair.

'Vanity of vanities: all is vanity,' he said as he stomped away. Pearce, whose experience of women, Nathan knew, was far greater than his employer's, just grinned and winked conspiratorially.

PRISONERS AND PISTOLS

*N*athan was glad to return to Robey's School. It had been too quiet at home, with Marie still detained at the Palace, and Shakespeare busy with rehearsals at the theatre.

The School of Defence was much more entertaining, because the Silver brothers were on punishment duties and rations. Robey had them grooming horses, washing carts, sharpening and polishing weapons and, in a moment of temper at their apparent lack of repentance, on their hands and knees scrubbing the cobbles in the yard. For one whole week they were allowed nothing but bread and milk.

'Infant rations,' Robey called it, 'for infant minds.' But the brothers seemed to take it all with good humour, which only infuriated Robey more.

Nathan watched them as they prepared to scrub the yard – buckets of water and brushes in their hands – and he smiled as Toby said, 'After you, Fencing Master

George Silver,' and George replied, 'No, after *you*, Fencing Master Toby Silver.' That was all that mattered to them – that they had publicly salvaged their reputations as fighting men. He was a little envious, too, of their new status as Masters.

However, Nathan's injured hand had conferred upon him even greater status as he regaled Robey's men with the tale of 'The Hand that the Queen Damaged'.

Nathan unwrapped the bandage and showed Bardolph, Pistol and Nym where each royal ring had bitten deep into his flesh. It could not have caused more interest if it had been a wound caused in battle against the Spanish.

'So you was blindfolded all the time?' asked Bardolph, over an evening meal.

'I was,' Nathan confirmed. 'And I have the queen's silk scarf here.' At this point he drew the long piece of red material from his jerkin. 'It was still warm from her long white neck when they tied it round my eyes,' he said, embroidering the story somewhat.

'Doubtless that will comfort you when you lay down your life for your queen in the Netherlands,' Robey said drily. 'Rather like a knight going in to joust with his lady's favour tied to his lance.'

There were a few chuckles from the men and then they became serious.

'There's little honour and glory to be had amongst the

Dutch,' said Nym quietly. 'Poor beggars. They've been fighting them Spaniards for nearly thirty years now.'

'Aye,' agreed Pistol, 'the country must be bare, stripped to the ground and trampled on.'

'God bless the queen for sending English soldiers out to help them, that's all I can say,' added Bardolph fervently. 'Although she could have sent them a better commander.'

The men then fell to a hard discussion about the shortcomings of Lord Leicester, the Governor General of the Netherlands who had, at one time, been the queen's favourite. There had even been rumours that he had secretly married her.

'I even heard a rumour that she had borne him a child,' whispered Nym with glee. 'And then, of course, Leicester's wife died under mysterious circumstances. They say he got rid of her so he could become the queen's consort . . .'

'Arrant nonsense!' cut in Robey, reminding his men that he did not favour idle gossip. 'Leicester is, for sure, an ineffective Governor of the Netherlands but the queen will replace him soon. Meanwhile, we must send the Dutch the best-trained men we can spare for their struggle.'

Nathan looked at Robey curiously. *I wonder when we shall find out the details of our mission?*

'And speaking of training,' Robey continued, looking at Nathan and the Silver brothers, 'you will need to familiarize yourselves with guns. They are, to my dismay, in constant use in the Netherlands conflict. Hopefully, your hand will stand up to musket training tomorrow.' Robey directed that last brisk comment to Nathan as he pushed back his chair. 'Early to bed now. In the morning, you and our two "Fencing Masters" there,' he spoke with some disdain as his eyes flicked over to the brothers, 'will be setting off to do some gun practice at the Artillery Garden in Spitalfields. Pistol and Bardolph will go with you and you will be collecting Jan Groesbeck from the Tower Armoury on your way.' And with that, he rose from his chair and left the room.

The next morning, everyone was bright and eager to be about their latest challenge. Pistol, however, was not happy.

'It's raining,' he said dolefully. 'We won't get much work done if the matches and powder get wet.'

'Oh, it'll clear up, 'ave some faith, man!' Bardolph slapped his comrade on the back. 'This rain is not set in and I can tell that on account of my feet.'

Nathan, George and Toby all looked down at Bardolph's misshapen but unremarkable feet.

'Curse of a foot soldier, me lads,' he said cheerfully, answering their unspoken questions. 'Bunions. If you spend all your time on your feet, marching, you always get 'em and they are the best indicator of whether we're in for prolonged rain or not. If we are, they ache like priests' knees – and they ain't aching today. So I says it's going to be fine.' And with that confident pronouncement, he ushered everyone into the yard and on to the cart.

Bardolph was right. As they turned off London Bridge and headed towards their destination, the drizzle stopped and a weak sun began to shine behind the clouds. However, the sight of the Tower looming ahead made Nathan shiver in the autumn breeze. Although he had passed its ominous turrets many times, it still filled him with dread. As they passed through Middle Tower and Byward Tower, Nathan's eyes flickered over to Traitor's Gate and then across to Bloody Tower. He wondered what unfortunate prisoners were in residence at the moment, half-expecting to see pitiful outstretched hands through the barred windows. But there were none. In fact the place looked like an industrious army barracks rather than a gloomy prison. Men were loading and unloading goods, a yeoman was walking two large mastiffs on leads, and a small contingent of guards was marching past them towards Middle Tower.

Pistol eased the cart around Bloody Tower and into the centre of the complex. Nathan, George and Toby sat open-mouthed.

'It's like a town all by itself,' said Nathan, as he took in the jumble of houses, towers and fortifications. In the centre loomed the magnificent proportions of White Tower.

'No important executions at the moment then,' Toby muttered. He nudged Nathan and pointed to the left at a scrubby piece of grass. 'That's where they usually build the scaffold.'

'How do you know?' Nathan whispered uneasily.

Toby shrugged. 'Someone told me.'

They all stared hard at the grass as the cart rumbled past, expecting to see a patch of blood, but there was no evidence of a recent beheading. Pistol drew the cart to a halt in front of White Tower and dismounted.

'Here we are, me lads,' he said breezily, completely immune to the effect the surroundings were having on the occupants of the cart. 'Off y'get and warm up yer muscles. We have some heavy lifting to do.'

Inside White Tower, they had to report to the duty officer, a cheerful-looking man who was obviously expecting them.

'This way, this way,' he said, bustling ahead of them. 'Your men are waiting.'

He opened some massive oak doors and there, standing amongst a whole array of weaponry, were Groesbeck and John Pearce. Nathan's spirits lifted at the sight of his partner. He always felt that Pearce's presence spurred him on to do his best at any endeavour, so now he was satisfied that today's artillery lesson would be a good one.

'Ah, good. Now we can load up and be on our way,' said Groesbeck, gathering up an armful of muskets and handing them over to Pistol. 'Come, come. We have much to do.' He turned to a pile of armour – breastplates, backplates, helmets and gorgets – and began to heave them into the waiting arms of everyone assembled.

A steady procession to and from the cart began. Muskets and body armour were followed by a bag of pistols, forked rests for the heavy matchlock muskets to rest upon, two war hammers, two steel maces, three crossbows and several helmets. As they loaded up the cart, Nathan caught sight of a face at one of the windows. *Who is that?* he thought, casting a troubled glance at John Pearce.

'What ails you, lad?' asked Pearce.

'I think I've just seen a prisoner at that window,' Nathan muttered.

Pearce laughed. 'You'd be hard-pressed *not* to see a prisoner in this place!' He slapped Nathan on the back heartily. 'The Tower is packed to overflowing at the moment. Dukes, bishops, priests and all kinds of Spanish sympathizers. Walsingham sniffs out every plot and Her Majesty signs the orders. They shall have to string some of them up soon to make more space.'

Nathan flinched at Pearce's harshness but then he reasoned that to someone like John, who had been working as an agent for several years, the prisoners were the enemy, nothing more and nothing less. *Maybe I will be equally hard when I have done this job for some time,* he thought to himself, but such a thing seemed impossibly remote at the moment.

There was just enough room on the cart for Nathan, George and Toby to climb back in. Groesbeck and Pearce were on horseback. The cart pulled away and the horses plodded on, much slower than before because of the weight.

As they eased the cart towards Bishops Gate, they were all forced to cover their faces with their cloaks to blot out the stench from Houndsditch. This was the place where the City dumped its rotting rubbish and had earned its name owing to the large number of dead dogs that ended up there each week. On a bad day, with the wind blowing eastwards, Nathan could even smell it in far-off Shoreditch. Up close, the stench filled his mouth and nose and made his eyes water. *How could anyone live near here?* Nathan thought incredulously, looking at the workshops and dwellings along the length of the City wall. *Perhaps they get used to it.*

Once they reached the wide road that ran through Spitalfields, the air was sweeter. As Pistol turned the horses down a narrow lane, Nathan could hear the crack of musket fire and smell the burning gunpowder. The Artillery Gardens were straight ahead.

There were a few men shooting muskets at a target in the first field. Bardolph leaped down and opened the gate and they eased through into one corner behind the musketeers.

'Right, me lads, let's start unloading,' Pistol barked while fitting a nosebag on each of the horses. Pearce and Groesbeck dismounted, tied their horses to a nearby fence, and everyone set about the business of unloading the artillery.

Bardolph, meanwhile, rummaged in the bag of hand guns and produced three matchcords made of flax and hemp tow. He went and asked the musketeers for a light and returned with all three matchcords glowing at their ends.

'Providing it stays dry and no fool stands on them, these should keep going for at least two hours.'

'Why does the match stay alight for so long?' Nathan whispered to Bardolph, embarrassed at his lack of knowledge about firearms.

'It's soaked in saltpetre, lad,' Bardolph whispered back.

Nathan nodded. He knew what saltpetre was. His landlady used it as a fertiliser on her garden.

The musketeers, seeing so much weaponry being unloaded, decided to sit down and watch the proceedings.

Pearce had begun to sort out breastplates and was fitting them against Nathan and the Silvers.

'We need to prove them first,' he said.

'What do you mean?' Nathan asked.

'We don't know the strength of this armour,' Pearce explained. 'The lightest weight should be pistol proof, the next weight is caliver or light-musket proof and the heaviest is full-musket proof. It's important to know that your armour will stop a musket ball when you go into a skirmish. It gives you a bit more confidence.' He winked at Nathan, who grinned back.

Having satisfied themselves that the three youngsters had well-fitting breastplates, Pearce and Pistol carried the armour up to the targets and propped them in front. Nathan knew his was the smallest of the three.

Groesbeck picked up one of the large matchlock muskets. Neither Nathan, Toby or George had ever seen one before. Nathan had only ever shot a light caliver musket during training. Groesbeck gave it to each of them in turn to hold.

'How can you fire this gun? It's so heavy!' Nathan was forced to let the four-foot-long barrel fall forward to the ground and Groesbeck caught it just in time.

'Whoa!' he exclaimed as a warning. 'It would not do, Meister Nathan, to let the barrel dig itself into the earth and get blocked now.'

Nathan felt a little foolish and stammered an apology.

'It is not a weapon for holding,' Groesbeck continued. 'It is a weapon for aiming. You rest it on this stand . . .' he pointed at one of the forked rests lying on the grass, '. . . then you prime it and fire. I will show you.'

He rested the stock of the gun on the ground and let Toby hold it while he set up the metal rest some yards away, facing the targets. Then he strapped around his waist a leather bandolier from which hung twelve wooden tubes and a leather pouch.

'In each of these,' the Dutchman said, holding one of the wooden tubes, 'is a charge of powder and in here,' he tapped the leather pouch, 'is the lead shot. Now I shall prime the musket.' He lifted it up, as before, the stock resting on the ground, and the length of the barrel meant that the end was almost up to his chin. Then he took one of the wooden tubes, pulled the cork out with his teeth and poured the powder down the barrel. Next he opened the leather pouch, took out a ball of lead and dropped it in with the powder. Bardolph handed him a ramrod, which Groesbeck expertly slid into the barrel, ramming the bullet firmly down before laying the musket on to its rest. Bardolph then handed him one of the glowing matchcords, which Groesbeck fitted into the serpent, or s-shaped arm, that was fitted on to the side of the stock. Nathan could see that the serpent held the match so that the fire end of it was pointing down towards the priming pan, where Groesbeck was adding more powder.

Pearce and Pistol had returned to the group, and they all stood silently as Groesbeck crouched forward and pressed the trigger. The match dipped down into the priming pan, then there was a crackle and a second's delay before an almighty crack sounded out as the lead bullet shot out of the barrel. There was a loud clang in the distance as the bullet struck the armour.

'It sounds like it's ricocheted,' said Pistol knowingly,

and they all trudged up to the target to see the damage. Sure enough, the first breastplate had just a small dent in the centre and the lead ball, somewhat misshapen, lay on the grass in front.

'We must fire at all of the armour three times, to make sure,' announced Groesbeck, and Pistol volunteered to make the next shot.

Nathan became bored with the 'proving' very quickly. He found the preparation and aiming rather tedious, preferring the fast action of sword and dagger. As he sat down and began to fitfully pull up clumps of grass, Groesbeck sat down beside him and began to tell him about how he had survived the Siege of Antwerp.

'It took the Spanish a whole year to make Antwerp surrender. The Duke of Parma's ships blockaded the harbour so that we could not get food from the sea, and his engineers spent the whole winter building a two and a half thousand foot bridge over the river Scheldt on which they placed 200 siege guns. We had opened the dykes to flood the land but there had not been enough rain. But in the spring of 1585 we sent fire ships packed with explosives down the river and blasted a huge hole in their bridge. Eight hundred Spaniards were killed, but they still maintained the siege. In August of that year, we were forced to surrender because of starvation, but some of us managed to escape and join the rebels in the north.'

Nathan looked at the man with admiration. At his age

he could not imagine going without decent food for a week, let alone a whole year.

Pearce had taken over from Pistol and was showing the Silver brothers, with consummate ease, how to be remarkably accurate with what most people regarded as a very inaccurate weapon.

He called over to Nathan. 'I have put three marks over your heart for luck!'

Nathan smiled but looked puzzled.

'Come and look!' Pearce urged and Nathan trudged behind the others up to the targets. There, on the left-hand breast of his piece of armour, were three small dents.

'Men will think you are blessed because you have survived three shots to the heart.' Pearce laughed and playfully punched Nathan's arm.

George, Toby and Nathan all had their turns with the musket. The Silver brothers eagerly plugged away, achieving some small measure of success. Nathan was reluctant, particularly as he had noticed that one of the musketeers watching from the grass had a leather-bound stump where one of his hands should have been. *Had a gun exploded in his hands?* Nathan shuddered. However, he still managed to give a reasonable account of himself and fired several shots that found their mark.

When Groesbeck produced a German wheel-lock musket, it generated great excitement amongst everyone, as such guns were so expensive to make they were only given to special army units or were owned by very rich men. The advantage of the wheel-lock, explained Groesbeck, was that it required no glowing matchcord. The mechanism struck a piece of pyrites against roughened metal to produce the spark that ignited the gunpowder. This meant that the gun could be loaded and primed, ready for action, and carried around until needed.

'The Dutch rebels have managed to "liberate" a good number of wheel-lock muskets from the German and Italian mercenaries fighting for the Spanish,' Groesbeck said with a grin. 'So accustom yourselves to this weapon. You may very well be able to bring one home as a souvenir!'

So the day continued with more firing of weapons and more explanations of how the mechanisms worked.

The highlight of the day was when George, Toby and Nathan were let loose with the war hammers and maces on some old pieces of armour. Toby, in particular, had reached a restless phase where he needed to exert some physical energy and he battered an old helmet into a flattened gobbet, all the while screaming at the top of his voice. Nathan cursed his over-active imagination as he tried not to picture someone's head inside the helmet and wondered if Toby was demonstrating what Bardolph had described in one of his stories as 'blood lust'.

By the time they trundled up to White Tower it was dark and Nathan thought the buildings seemed even more forbidding in the flickering light of torches. There was an ominous silence about the place. The damp autumn night air made him shiver and he found it difficult to find any excitement within him when Pearce announced, 'You must all get a good night's sleep, for tomorrow we are summoned to Walsingham's office to receive our orders.'

MORE THAN ONE TASK AHEAD

*J*he Silver brothers looked nervous as they entered Walsingham's office in the Palace of Westminster. This was their first mission and their first meeting with the Spymaster General. Robey had given them a stern lecture before they had left his premises that morning.

'You will speak only when you are spoken to,' he had said firmly. 'You will do as you are told. You will venture no opinions and you will accept what tasks you are given without a murmur. Is that understood?'

They had nodded meekly and Nathan had felt slightly smug that Robey had never given *him* such a lecture before *his* first mission.

Then Nathan had been presented with a new pair of boots – without knives this time.

'On this mission you will not be playing the part of a servant,' Robey had explained 'so you may carry a sword.' And he had smiled at Nathan's obvious delight. 'Before you leave, Bardolph will issue you with a suitable weapon and we shall put your special boots away until you need them again.'

Now he and the brothers were standing in the office of the great Walsingham. The room was crowded compared to the last time Nathan had attended a mission briefing. Groesbeck and Pearce were also present, and when Walsingham entered from his inner office, the men parted to let him through.

'Gentlemen.' The Spymaster General acknowledged each of them in turn with his eyes. 'Please be seated.'

Everyone sat down, except for Walsingham, who seemed to prefer to pace a little to ease his aching bones.

He began, 'Philip of Spain is keeping an army of just over sixty thousand men in the Netherlands.' He paused for the effect of this number to be felt by everyone present and then he continued. 'But Philip's greatest problem is that he is not keeping his army well. His men have not been paid for six months and they are perilously close to mutiny on a large scale which, of course, would be to the advantage of the Netherlands – and England. The Spanish have great difficulty in supplying their men with both money and food because the Dutch rebels are restricting access to the sea ports. Most supplies have to come overland from Italy – a route known as the Spanish Road – which takes an average of three months at this time of year.'

He paused once more, stopped pacing and looked directly at all those seated before him. 'My spies in Spain tell me that a vital consignment of one million gold florins, for the army, has recently left Genoa in Italy.'

George Silver made a low whistle but stopped when Pearce glared at him. Walsingham ignored the sound and pressed on.

'Our difficulty is that my spies are unable to tell me whether the consignment is coming by sea or by land. I am told that three ships have been identified as loading "special cargo" and, at the same time, a company of some hundred and fifty soldiers has left Genoa on foot, escorting "special baggage". Your mission is to intercept and take this money, by whatever means possible. Without this gold the Spanish army will certainly stage a mutiny. How this interception is achieved will be up to John Pearce, as he will be your commander in this enterprise. Jan Groesbeck will be your liaison with the Dutch rebels. I am sure that there is no need for me to tell you that this mission must be conducted with the utmost secrecy.'

No one in the room spoke. Acceptance of Walsingham's orders was implicit in their faces. Walsingham finally sat down behind his desk and lowered his voice to a conspiratorial tone. Everyone instinctively leaned forward.

'It is also necessary, gentlemen, to keep your business private from the English army in the Netherlands. As you know, the Earl of Leicester, once Her Majesty's good friend, is not a popular Governor General of the Netherlands . . .' Jan Groesbeck snorted in derisive agreement but Walsingham merely raised one eyebrow and resumed speaking. '. . . Leicester has upset the Dutch on many occasions by his – shall we say – lack of understanding of their needs . . . but he has also spent a great deal of his own money in the service of England. Should he learn of our mission, he might demand that the Spanish gold be diverted into his own pocket. This would not please the queen. Her Majesty wishes that when we are successful the money should be divided between the Dutch cause and our own, to pay for the war against the might of Spain. Have I made myself clear?'

Everyone nodded. Nathan understood that once they reached the Netherlands, the spies would not be able to turn to the English army for help, if it was needed. He suddenly realized how vulnerable they would be – caught between two opposing armies and in the middle of a war.

Jan Groesbeck spoke.

'Sir Francis, we can muster a small independent army of Dutch mercenaries but it will cost us a share of the proceeds. These men do not work for the cause out of loyalty – they work for anyone who pays them.'

'I presume you are referring to Pieter de Ferm's men.' Walsingham smiled at Groesbeck's shocked expression.

'You . . . you know about de Ferm!'

Pearce laughed and slapped Groesbeck on the knee. 'Jan! Have you not learned that Sir Francis knows *everyone* in Europe?'

Walsingham's eyes danced with pleasure. *How he loves the game of espionage!* thought Nathan as he watched the Spymaster's face.

'Pieter de Ferm has worked for me on several occasions,' said Walsingham quietly. 'I find freebooters useful. Like pirates, they respond well to the lure of money. It is much more difficult to get a man of principle and honour to undertake this sort of work. Now . . .' his tone became brisk and businesslike. 'Here is a map of the Spanish Road.' He reached into a drawer in his desk, extracted a rolled parchment and spread it out over the desk. 'It is likely that the company that has just left Genoa is following this route.' He traced his gnarled finger along the road through Lombardy and Franche-Comté up to the Netherlands. 'However, they may reason that we would *expect* them to transport the gold this way and prefer to risk the North Atlantic Sea and bring it in through the port of Antwerp. Therefore we shall enlist the aid of the Sea Beggars to patrol the sea.'

'The Sea Beggars?' The question left Nathan's lips before he had a chance to check it.

'Dutch pirates,' explained Pearce.

'Quite,' said Walsingham, looking askance at Nathan. 'Not always popular in their own country and positively unwelcome in England. Her Majesty banned them from entering English ports some fifteen years ago.'

Nathan was impressed by the assortment of people that Walsingham chose to do business with. Cut-throats, vagabonds, pirates, mercenaries, actors, poets, alchemists – the man chose his agents with care but from the strangest places.

'Now,' Walsingham said, rolling up the map and handing it to Pearce, 'you will ship out from England with Sir Francis Drake . . .' The Silver brothers gave a joint gasp of pleasure but Nathan glanced at Pearce and saw his face set in resignation. He knew that there was no love lost between Pearce and Drake, England's greatest hero. Walsingham continued, '. . . and he will meet up with the Sea Beggars near their base, the Dutch port of Flushing. Drake will stay with the Dutch pirates and wait for any Spanish ships that may attempt to deliver cargo to the Netherlands.'

He continued, 'Meanwhile, you will be landed at Flushing, where you will purchase supplies and proceed north to the city of Dordrecht where, so my agents tell me, Pieter de Ferm has set up camp. Once you have made contact with him and his men, then you can make haste to Amsterdam and await further instructions from Drake. If Drake intercepts the gold he will send you word and you can return home. If he finds that the Spanish ships are empty then John Pearce will give you further instructions on how you will intercept the gold on the land route. Any questions?' he asked in a tone of voice that implied that he was not expecting any. 'Good. Then our business is concluded. But I need to have a further talk with John Pearce and Nathan Fox, so if you other gentlemen would excuse us . . .'

Groesbeck nodded and motioned to the Silver brothers to come with him.

'We shall take a turn about the Palace Gardens, young sirs, and you shall converse a little with me in Dutch.' He smiled grimly as Toby Silver groaned and he ushered the reluctant brothers through the door.

'Her Majesty has requested that we attend upon her,' Walsingham said as he rose from his chair. 'I said that if Drake intercepts the Spanish gold at sea, then you could return home. But that would not be true for both of you – only for your companions. There is another, more private, mission Her Majesty wishes you to undertake. Come with me.'

Elizabeth was seated in her massive chair at the head of the Privy Council table. She was looking magnificent as usual with, Nathan noted, no sign of any swelling about her face. The chair nearest to the queen was already occupied by Marie, who sat there looking quite confident and at ease, in a fine dress that Nathan had never seen before. He could not help feeling jealous that his sister had spent the best part of a week in the queen's company – he should have liked to spend a week at court amongst all the fine ladies and gentlemen. He was also curious as to why Marie was being included in this secret meeting.

Walsingham, Pearce and Nathan bowed very low.

'You may rise, gentlemen – and you may be seated.'

Elizabeth smiled. 'Master Pearce, I am delighted to see you looking so well. I was afraid that the wounds you sustained on your last mission for Sir Francis would exile you forever in the country and that I would not have the pleasure of your company at court any more.'

'Your Majesty, neither age nor infirmity would keep me from your presence.' Pearce knew just the right words to flatter. Nathan could hardly keep himself from smiling.

'And you, brave Master Fox,' Elizabeth turned her full charm on him. 'How is the hand that you damaged in the service of your queen?'

'It was nothing, Your Majesty,' Nathan replied, cursing the fact that his voice chose to break an octave at that moment. He cleared his throat. 'I barely noticed it.'

'Now, Sir Francis,' said Elizabeth, 'I wish you to explain to your two agents the secret service that we require of them.'

Walsingham inclined his head by way of acknowledgement and turned awkwardly in his chair to face Pearce and Nathan.

'I received, some weeks ago, a message through one of my agents in the Netherlands. The message was from the Grand Dame of the Béguinage in Amsterdam. She wrote that she was representing a Dutch patriot who has in his possession a very rare religious relic which he wishes to offer to England. This relic is being hunted by

Philip of Spain's agents and it is only a matter of time before they track it down. It is important that we get to that relic first.'

'Excuse me, Sir Francis – but why? I thought England had done with such things!' Pearce seemed irritated and Nathan was surprised at his vehemence. *What does he mean by 'such things'?*

'Indeed we have!' Elizabeth's voice rang out firmly. 'My first reaction when Sir Francis approached me with this message was not favourable, I can tell you.'

Elizabeth struck her hand forcefully on the arm of her chair.

'My father did not rid this country of Popish nonsense so that I might bring it all back again. God's blood! I will have none of these religious relics, John Pearce! There were enough "fragments of the true cross" in the monasteries of England to populate a small forest – not to mention the untold "vials of Our Lord's blood" which were, in fact, pig's blood, regularly topped up by greedy monks intent on extorting money from the faithful. No, be assured I will have no more religious relics in this country! However . . .' she paused in her anger, her voice became playful and a malicious smile sprang to her lips, '. . . King Philip wants this relic more than anything in the world. Did you know that he is an obsessive collector of relics? Oh yes – he has nearly three thousand of them, I am told, stuffed in his palaces. I am also told that he has a bone from nearly every saint in heaven. And anything that Philip truly desires – like the throne of England or this relic – he shall not have. *I* shall have it. Does that answer your question, John Pearce?'

'Yes, Your Majesty.' Pearce nodded respectfully. 'But what exactly is this relic that Philip so desires?'

Elizabeth inclined her head towards Walsingham, indicating that he should answer. The old man cleared his throat and it seemed to Nathan that he was reluctant to speak.

'It is an ossuary – a burial casket – containing the bones of the Blessed Virgin,' he said in a reverential voice.

Nathan gasped and looked at the shocked faces of Pearce and Marie. The Queen seemed almost amused.

'Indeed the mother of Jesus Christ, herself,' she said softly with a hint of irony in her voice. 'I may be struck down by a bolt of lightning from Heaven for doubting the authenticity of the bones, but no matter. Whoever holds this relic believes it to be what it is and Philip of Spain *undoubtedly* believes it to be so. What matters is that it is important enough for Philip to desire it above all else. Sir Francis, you may continue,' Elizabeth added imperiously.

'Thank you, Your Majesty. I am given to understand that this relic is not in the Béguinage. The Grand Dame is merely acting as a messenger. However, it is necessary for someone to enter the Béguinage in order to be on hand when a further message or messages arrive. Her

Majesty has agreed to allow Mistress Marie Fox to be our agent in this respect.'

Nathan could not contain himself. 'Sir Francis, what is a Béguinage?' In a fit of jealousy he imagined that Marie was to be given a plum job in some Dutch nobleman's court. So when Walsingham replied 'A convent . . . of sorts,' Nathan laughed out loud with a mixture of relief and incredulity. The thought of his hot-tempered sister entering a convent was hilarious. Marie gave him a look of glacial contempt and the laughter died in his throat.

'A Béguinage,' said the Queen, with feeling, 'is a place that I find most appealing. It is a place of refuge for women who seek shelter from the world. They choose to spend their lives in prayer and good works but they do not take vows nor follow the orders of any man – priest or Pope. They are a band of sisters, answerable to no one but themselves.'

Nathan could see why the queen would find such a place attractive. It was well known that she had refused all the potential husbands that the Privy Council had tried to force upon her, saying that she would never defer to any man.

'There is one final matter, Sir Francis, that you must explain.' Elizabeth's voice held a firmness that signalled to everyone that this 'final matter' was not up for negotiation.

Walsingham spoke, again with some reluctance in his

voice. *He does not agree with the queen on this,* thought Nathan, noting the glances that passed between the Spymaster General and his sovereign.

'Once the relic has been found and secured . . . Her Majesty wishes it to be spirited away, back to the Holy Lands – and hidden.'

'I will not have it on English soil. I have made my feelings clear on this matter.' Elizabeth's penetrating eyes fixed firmly on Walsingham. 'Once here, it would become a rallying point for every disaffected Catholic and Spanish sympathizer and it would make King Philip redouble his efforts to invade this country. No. It will be taken away and lost and you will make sure that Philip knows that it is lost forever. If – and I stress *if* – it is the bones of the Virgin Mary, then the blessed lady deserves to be laid to rest somewhere, away from greedy relic collectors.'

Walsingham bowed his head in defeat.

'Forgive me, Your Majesty,' interjected Pearce. 'Does that mean that Nathan and I must then travel to the Holy Lands after our work is finished in the Netherlands?'

Nathan's fleeting hope of travelling to exotic places was dashed when the queen gestured towards Sir Francis to reply.

'No,' he said firmly, 'I have arranged that others will perform that task.'

The queen rose and the audience was over. Everyone else stood and bowed as she turned to leave the room.

'God speed your endeavours. I shall pray for your

safe return . . . Master Pearce . . .' and she extended the royal hand to be kissed. Then she added, with a twinkle in her eye, 'You may escort Mistress Fox home now. She has been of great service to me and I shall miss her company. You may need to borrow a cart from the stables, however, since my ladies in waiting have been extremely generous and have gifted her a whole new wardrobe.' Pearce bowed and, with a swish of many petticoats, the queen left the room.

Walsingham sat down and mopped his brow, then he turned to Pearce and spoke urgently.

'There is a significant problem. I fear that details of this mission have been discovered by the most danger-ous man at court.'

Nathan felt his heart shrink in his chest. He knew that Walsingham was talking about Lord Harcourt.

'How do you know this, Sir Francis?' Pearce asked quietly.

'Because Lord Harcourt has recently been in France and, upon his return, came to my office and requested an urgent passport for him and his daughter, Catherine, so that they may travel to the Netherlands on business. Lord Harcourt has no business interest in the Nether-lands – indeed has never shown *any* interest in the Netherlands until now. I had no reason by which I could refuse him. He and his daughter sailed on this morning's tide. Interestingly, the Spanish merchant Casado and his son left England a few days ago, also bound for the

Netherlands. I understand that you have recently encountered all of them?'

Walsingham was referring to the Silver brothers' tournament. *Is there nothing that escapes Walsingham's eyes and ears?* Nathan wondered, then he volunteered some further information. 'Sir Francis, I saw the Casados acknowledge Harcourt in the crowd at the Black Friar Inn. It was not much – just a nod of the head and a look that passed between them.'

Walsingham nodded. 'I suspect that Harcourt is under instruction from his masters in Spain to go after the relic. We have no reason to suppose that he knows anything about the gold shipment. The fact that the Casados have also left for the same country may be pure coincidence. Felipe Casado *does* have business interests in the Netherlands and makes several visits there each year. However, Nathan, you have observed a connection between the three men and I think it is most likely that they are about to work together against England.'

Pearce grunted as if considering this reasoning, but then he said, 'In some ways it is helpful to know the identity of the enemy.' He grinned. 'Harcourt and the Casados will find it very difficult to follow our movements without being spotted.' *Pearce is always one step ahead of everyone else,* thought Nathan with admiration.

'Will you have enough men to tackle both missions?' Walsingham was concerned.

'We will be enough. As well as Groesbeck and the

Silver brothers, we will possibly have Pieter de Ferm's men and also Samuel Fox and his band of gypsies.'

'My father will be there!' Nathan said in amazement, joy springing up inside at the thought of seeing him again. He flashed a look of happiness at Marie, whose face had lit up at the mention of their father's name.

'Yes. Forgive me, I should have mentioned this earlier.' Walsingham was apologetic. 'It will be their job to take the relic to the Holy Lands. Easy for a band of travelling entertainers. They will meet up with you once you are in the Netherlands. However,' Walsingham's voice took on a note of warning, 'Nathan and Marie, you must be aware that the recovery of the relic must be kept completely separate from the mission to intercept the gold. Speak of the relic to no one except your father and his men. No one,' he emphasized.

Nathan and Marie both nodded.

'But now, Sir Francis, we must make passage for Flushing.' Pearce was anxious to be on his way.

Walsingham rose painfully to his feet. 'I have faith in you, John. If anyone has the intelligence and skill to perform these difficult tasks, it is you. Send me word of your progress by the usual means.'

Once outside, Pearce looked at Nathan and Marie and pulled a rueful face. 'Well, here we are again. The same cast of players but with a different play. Let us hope that this one has a happy ending!'

THE BEGGARS THAT RULE THE SEA

'*I* see that you are expecting to fight,' said Sir Francis Drake acidly, as he watched John Pearce's armour being carried up the gangplank of the *Elizabeth Bonaventure.*

Nathan could see that the great man was not in a good mood. Doubtless it was because, as Pearce had pointed out on the early morning journey from Shoreditch to the docks, the queen would still not give Drake permission to set out and attack the Spanish fleet wherever he found them. Instead he was being forced to twiddle his thumbs in England and perform small tasks for Walsingham, such as ferrying his agents over to the Netherlands. Drake obviously found the work beneath him.

'What! And the boy too?' Drake added in surprise as Nathan's smaller armour was carried on board.

Pearce could not resist goading the Admiral. 'Well, some of us have important work to do,' he said casually, leaving unspoken the taunt that Drake did *not.*

Drake's face darkened but he let the comment pass. Nathan felt embarrassed for the man who had provided the queen, so it was rumoured, with more than £40,000 as her share of the spoils from his raid on Cadiz earlier in the year – yet Drake's reward, apart from the riches he himself had pocketed, was to sit idle while Her Majesty was plagued by indecision.

Pearce had often remarked to Nathan that the queen changed her mind more than she changed her gowns.

'Does this fair lady also have some armour?' asked Drake, brightening noticeably as Marie was helped on board.

'This is my sister, Marie,' announced Nathan, amused at the extravagant bow Drake made.

'Sir Francis,' murmured Marie regally, as Drake straightened up.

'I ask again, young Nathan, does this fair lady also have some armour?' Drake persisted.

'No, Sir Francis,' Marie answered coolly, for herself. 'I go to the Netherlands not to fight, but to minister to the sick and wounded.'

'By the Holy Rood!' Drake broke into a loud, coarse laugh. 'I have many an interesting wound about my body that I should like you to take a look at, my lady!'

Nathan flushed at this vulgarity and Pearce's eyes darkened but Marie merely pursed her lips with displeasure.

'I am sorry, Sir Francis, but your wounds are too *old*

to be of any interest to me,' she said crisply, sweeping past him as though he were a street beggar. Pearce snorted with pleasure and Nathan bit his lip to stop from smirking.

Lost for words, Drake resorted to bawling at his unfortunate seamen.

'Get a move on, you lazy poltroons! We set sail within the hour! God's breath, I'll flog any man who delays departure!'

One of Drake's men showed Marie, Nathan and Pearce down to their cabin.

'Only one?' Marie said in a concerned voice.

Pearce grinned. 'Your honour will be safe, my lady. This cabin is not for sleeping in. The journey will take us no longer than a day. Drake will not take his ship into Flushing, for fear of running aground on the sandbanks around the coast. Anyway, he reckons that we will be stopped by the Sea Beggars in their flyboats before we get anywhere near to port. He knows them and he will negotiate with them on our behalf, with Jan Groesbeck at his side, of course.'

Nathan suddenly remembered that Groesbeck and the Silver brothers were not yet on board.

'Where are George and Toby?' he asked anxiously.

Pearce shook his head.

'I have no idea. It was Groesbeck's job to deliver them.

Drake is insistent that we leave very soon. I hope that they make it, or I shall have to revise all my plans.'

Nathan and Pearce left Marie in the cabin and made their way back on to the main deck. As Pearce stuck his head above the stairwell he said, with a note of deep relief in his voice, 'All is well. They are here.'

Groesbeck looked flustered. *He must have had some problems getting the Silver brothers to the dock on time*, thought Nathan. George and Toby looked as though they had just got out of bed. Their eyes were filled with sleep and they looked more confused than usual. Toby was clutching his sword and belt in his hand, as though he had not yet had time to fix it to his waist, and George had not laced up his doublet. Nathan grinned.

Soon the ship lurched as its moorings were untied, and the seamen scuttled up the rigging in response to Drake's bawled orders. It was barely light and the cold air from the estuary made Nathan draw his cloak around him tightly. The ship groaned and knocked against the quay as it turned into the wind and the sails grew full. A small knot of people, workmen mostly, had gathered on the dockside. Nathan supposed that they were all wondering what great enterprise Drake was embarking upon.

The river looked cold, grey and inhospitable. Rivulets ran backwards, towards the sea, over hidden debris in the water. The tide was fast and strong, pulling them out towards the Channel. John Pearce stood at the ship's rail,

91

breathing deeply in the biting air, trying to stave off sea-sickness. It was his one weakness, and he was beginning to look a little green.

The banks on either side of the Thames grew further and further away and the ship began to roll as it hit the choppy waters of the open sea. Pearce slid down and sat with his back against the rail. Nathan fumbled in the purse on his belt and withdrew a coin.

'Hold this in your hand, John. It will make the sickness less.'

Pearce wrinkled his eyebrows in disbelief but Nathan persisted.

'It's a gypsy remedy, trust me,' Marie had always told him that the belief in the 'remedy' often brought about the cure, rather than the 'remedy' itself.

Pearce nodded and grasped the coin gratefully.

'I was not made to be a sailor,' he shouted to Nathan above the noise of the wind. 'It is a curse to be so feeble on a ship.'

'Never mind,' Nathan reassured his friend. 'There are more than enough mariners to go around but there are not enough men like John Pearce.'

Pearce smiled thinly and they sat side by side as the voyage continued.

Marie appeared, clutching a phial of brown liquid.

'I did not forget that you need medication,' she shouted, uncorking the phial and handing it to Pearce.

'God bless you,' he said and swallowed the liquid.

'It will take effect in, maybe, fifteen minutes,' she advised. 'Come below and lie on the bunk. You will feel better soon.'

Nathan hauled Pearce to his feet and propelled him towards the lower decks. Drake, who was watching from the fo'c'sle, called out in glee, 'We're barely out of the estuary, Master Pearce, and you've lost your sea legs already! By the Rood, man! I've had chickens on board this vessel that sail better than you!'

Pearce raised one finger in insult towards Drake as he tottered down the stairs. Doubtless, Nathan observed, Pearce would have his revenge later, when the world stopped moving under his feet.

The day passed slowly. Nathan, George and Toby periodically went up on deck but there was nothing to see but an unrelenting greyness all around. *It may be exciting to be a pirate*, Nathan thought, *but there must be a lot of boredom in between battles and raids. Nothing but the sea to look at and nothing to do but play cards or dice.* The Silver brothers had joined a huddle of mariners on the poop deck, crouched down over a game of jacks. Nathan wondered if the men would get into trouble if Drake spotted them idling away their time but Drake was standing by the wheel, looking straight ahead, scanning the horizon for any sign of life.

It was almost dark when the mariner in the crow's nest called, 'Ships ahoy!'

Drake immediately instructed his men to break out

the ensigns above the fore and main topgallant sails. He normally kept them hidden, so that he could roam the seas anonymously. This time, however, he knew that the only ships he would encounter in these waters would be Dutch and they needed to know that the *Elizabeth Bonaventure* was English, or they would blow her out of the water. Nathan watched two men shin up the masts and release the green and white striped flags with the cross of St George in each corner.

The flyboats came closer and closer. There were three of them, and they had formed themselves into a crescent. When they were within hailing distance a man who seemed to be their leader bawled across the water.

'Is that you, Drake? You are a bit too far north, my friend!'

Drake roared with laughter.

'Conraadt Visser – as I live and die! Are you the best the scurvy Beggars could find to greet me?'

Nathan smiled as the man called Visser bared his teeth in a mighty grin.

'I *am* the best – and you know that! Permission to come aboard, Sir Francis Drake! I have Spanish wine to share with you!'

'Then welcome, me lad.'

Orders were shouted to drop anchor and break out the boats and ladders. Visser and two of his men were rowed across the choppy sea and Drake's men hauled them over the side when they reached the top of the *Bonaventure's* rope ladders.

Nathan could see that the Sea Beggars were dressed in a variety of curious clothes which they had obviously 'liberated' from Spanish ships. Visser was wearing all black – most notably a pair of loose-fitting breeches called galligaskins, much favoured by the Spanish – with a battered ruff of white and a tall black hat. He looked not unlike a portrait Nathan had seen of Philip of Spain, were it not for the fact that his hair was so wild and he had an extravagant gold earring in one ear. The man following him wore a hat that had seen better days but still carried three brightly coloured plumes on the side. He also wore long breeches and elaborate cross garters round his knees. Judging by the shine of the satin garters, they had been newly 'liberated'. The last man, much to Nathan's amusement, was wearing half of a priest's cassock as a shirt, torn hose and a pair of fine but scuffed boots. Drake's men were fearsome looking but, to Nathan, these Dutch Sea Beggars looked more like true pirates – shabby, scruffy and desperate.

Visser and Drake clasped each other in the embrace of comrades – an embrace that was repeated when Visser's men produced two silver flagons of wine.

'Come down to my cabin, Visser. We have business to discuss.' Drake was affable. He turned to Nathan. 'Boy, fetch your seasick friend and the Dutchman. We need to parley.'

Nathan reluctantly scampered down below. He wanted to spend as much time as possible in the company of the strange and fearsome Sea Beggars. Pearce was now fully in command of his sea legs again. He asked Marie to fetch Groesbeck and, when she had left, he turned to Nathan.

'How good is your Dutch?' he asked quietly.

'Good,' Nathan replied.

Pearce nodded in satisfaction. 'Then you must tell me if Groesbeck translates my words properly. Speak up if he doesn't. Understand?'

Nathan was puzzled but agreed. *Surely John speaks Dutch as well, if not better than I do?*

Groesbeck arrived and the three of them made their way to Drake's cabin.

The first flagon of wine had already been opened by the time they got there and the sound of merriment filled the air.

'Ah!' boomed Drake as Pearce entered. 'Here is our landlubber. Take a cup of wine, Pearce, if it will not make you puke some more!' Drake's eyes glittered, a half-smile on his face. Pearce did not rise to the bait but merely took the offered cup and drained it dry. The Sea Beggars murmured their approval.

'Now, John Pearce,' Drake said in a businesslike manner. 'Tell us of this gold that Walsingham hinted at, for all the men here are anxious to find it for you.' He winked at Visser, who hunched over the table watching Pearce carefully.

Groesbeck pushed forward and said in his own language, 'Master Pearce will tell you the details and I will translate them into Dutch. That way we make sure that everyone understands fully.' Then he turned to each of the Beggars in turn, shaking their hands and saying, '*Mijn naam* is Jan Groesbeck.'

All the men nodded and Pearce began.

'The Spanish army have not been paid for six months and they are close to mutiny.' He paused while Groesbeck translated. The Dutchmen's eyes lit up.

'Walsingham's spies have told him that a large consignment of gold – one million gold florins – is on its way here from Genoa.'

There was another pause for translation and the Dutchmen banged on the table with approval.

'The problem is that we do not know whether this gold will come by land or sea. Three ships have been spotted loading special cargo and a company of men have started along the Spanish Road, escorting heavily laden carts.'

Everyone nodded sagely.

'If the gold comes by sea, then it will fall to you to capture it. If it comes by land it will be the task of me and my men.'

The man in the priest's cassock interrupted the Dutch

translation to say, in perfect English, 'And if we capture this gold, what is our share?'

Nathan smiled as greed unmasked the pretence of not speaking English.

Pearce looked at each of the men steadily. 'I am authorized by Her Majesty to offer you one quarter of the booty. Two hundred and fifty thousand gold pieces.'

There was a silence as the men looked at their leader, Visser.

'It is a fair price. But . . .' he added, his watchful eyes fixed on Pearce, 'what if the ships we attack do not carry the gold? We will have risked our lives and our ships for nothing.'

Pearce nodded. 'Her Majesty is aware of that and feels that you should have some recompense for your help, whether the outcome is successful or not. Therefore, if the Spanish ships are empty, you shall receive fifty thousand gold pieces.'

There was an explosion of mock outrage from the three Sea Beggars and a torrent of embarrassed argument from Groesbeck, who seemed equally outraged that his fellow countrymen should be so greedy. Nathan's Dutch was not quite up to following a heated argument but he caught various phrases such as 'this is for the benefit of the Republic!' and 'you are nothing but thieves!'

Drake broke into the furore with a loud bellow.

'Gentlemen!' Everyone fell quiet and turned to the Admiral. 'Let us not forget,' he continued, 'that whether the Spanish ships be carrying gold or not, there will be plenty else on board to loot.' He turned to Pearce and said with a sardonic smile, 'I trust that Her Majesty has no feelings one way or the other about these lads helping themselves to whatever they find?'

Pearce shrugged.

'I have no orders to that effect,' he said flatly, thereby giving permission for the Sea Beggars to loot as they pleased.

The Dutchmen seemed satisfied with this and broke out the wine once more.

'Good, good.' Visser nodded happily and winked at Drake. 'We have an agreement, yes?'

'There is just one further matter.' Pearce declined another cup of wine. Nathan sensed that his friend was anxious to reach complete agreement before everyone fell into a drunken stupor. 'Two of my men must stay behind with you, in order either to supervise the transfer of the captured gold straight back to England or, if the ships are empty, to make swiftly for Amsterdam to tell me that we must intercept the gold on land. Is that acceptable?'

Visser stared hard at Pearce.

'So, you do not trust us, Englishman, is that it?' he muttered.

The silence was ominous and Nathan placed his hand on the doorlatch in case they had need of a quick exit.

Pearce spoke slowly and pointedly.

'Not for one minute would I trust a set of vicious cut-throats like you.'

There was a hair's breadth of a pause – just enough for Nathan to draw in a quick anxious breath – then Visser burst into a huge belly laugh.

'Excellent! I would not trust me either!'

He poured himself more wine and raised his cup towards Pearce.

'To the Dutch Republic!' he shouted and everyone who had wine in their hands raised it up and echoed the salute.

'And . . .' he added, 'to Philip of Spain's gold!'

'AMEN!' was the chorus of the sea dogs.

When the laughter had died down Pearce, to Nathan's astonishment, suddenly grabbed Visser's hand.

'I know that ring,' he said, yanking a large silver crested ring from the Dutchman's second finger. 'Where did you get it?'

Visser leaped to his feet, drawing a knife from his belt as he did so.

'From a noble Englishman who displeased me. Now give it back!' His face was full of menace.

Pearce tossed the ring back on to the table with a laugh.

'With pleasure, my friend. I was just admiring it. Tell me . . .' he added casually 'when did this noble English-man displease you?'

'Yesterday. What concern is it of yours?' Visser placed the ring back on his finger and scowled at Pearce.

'As I said, my friend, I know the man it belongs to – and Drake also knows him.'

Drake knitted his eyebrows together and looked at Pearce for enlightenment.

'Lord Harcourt.'

The revelation brought a smile to Drake's face. Nathan saw that, like everyone else at the English court, the pirate had no love for the man who was suspected of being a Spanish spy.

'Visser, you dog!' Drake clapped his pirate friend on the back. 'You have done a good thing!'

Visser smiled happily.

'Then I must rob this Lord Harcourt on his way *back* to England as well!' he announced cheerfully, and everyone raised their cup in approval.

7

'GOD CREATED THE EARTH, THE NETHERLANDERS CREATED THE NETHERLANDS'

*P*earce, Nathan, Marie and Groesbeck stood on the quayside in Flushing, huddled against the cold wind from the North Sea which whipped across the estuary. The Silver brothers, much to their delight, had been left with Drake to await the possible arrival of the Spanish ships. Pearce had given them strict instructions before he left.

'If the gold is on the ships, you help transfer it to Drake's vessel, then you come to find us in Amsterdam. If the gold is *not* on the ships, then you also come to Amsterdam, as fast as possible, by whatever means. Keep your wits about you. When you fight, remember that you are fighting for your lives and not in some fencing tournament. If either of you is wounded then the other must come alone with the information. Trust no one except each other, and stay alert.'

They had just grinned at him throughout his speech and he had reluctantly left them on board, fearing that they would not be up to the job but knowing there was no other choice.

Now they were in Flushing, waiting for the arrival of Samuel Fox and his band of gypsies. Nathan felt sick with anticipation. He had only seen his father three times in the last year. On the first occasion, Samuel Fox had been in his disguise as Stefan the magician, and to Nathan he had been nothing more than a curious entertainer – someone to admire and wonder about. At their second meeting, when his father had saved him from Lord Harcourt's assassin, Nathan had been numb with shock to discover that his saviour was, in fact, the father who he had believed was long dead. The third meeting had taken place after Nathan's tragic first mission, when his heart was heavy with loss; their time together had been short and the parting, when Samuel had to become Stefan once more, had been hard. Since then, there had been nothing. For three long months, Samuel Fox had not made any contact. *Except with Walsingham*, thought Nathan jealously, *to arrange to be part of our mission. Why did he not contact Marie and me?*

The group on the dockside was unusually silent. Nathan and Marie were busy scanning the faces of every passer-by, hoping that the next one would be their father. Groesbeck seemed tense and was uncommunicative.

Pearce was ever watchful, his right hand permanently resting on the hilt of his sword.

Suddenly a cart rumbled through the dock gates, driven by a very large blond-haired man. Seated beside him was a small dark fellow, who looked like a pygmy beside his bulky companion. Behind the cart, trotting amiably, were four saddled horses.

'Samson!' breathed Marie. 'It's Samson and Graco.'

Nathan's joy at the sight of his father's two friends was tempered by a surge of annoyance. *Where is my father? Why is he not here to meet us?*

The cart drew up and Graco jumped nimbly down. Nathan hardly recognized the acrobat without his usual colourful costume. Graco beamed and pronounced Nathan even taller than the last time they met, and he embraced Marie joyously. The giant German, Samson, nodded and smiled shyly at everyone.

'Where is our father?' Nathan asked.

'A thousand apologies to you both.' Graco spoke conspiratorially. 'He thought it best to stay at our camp. Walsingham sent word that Lord Harcourt had set sail for the Netherlands and your father did not want to risk coming into the city.'

'Harcourt has gone to Amsterdam,' said Pearce quietly, shaking Graco's hand.

'Ah, good. We shall take you to our camp now. Let us load up your baggage and be gone before the rain starts up again.'

Groesbeck, who had hung back from the reunion of friends, now introduced himself to the two gypsies and began to help load the cart. Nathan decided to make friends with the horses.

Graco sidled up to Nathan with a grin. 'I chose the brown Ardennes for you. Very hardy breed. Good on the flat and in the mountains. Can go all day without flagging. Good size too. About fifteen hands. Just right for you.'

Nathan smiled gratefully. The horse nuzzled his hand and seemed to say, 'You and I will make a good team.'

'Masters Pearce and Groesbeck, these two Holsteins are your mounts,' Graco said, pointing at the two larger horses. The two men, having finished loading the cart, unhitched the animals and pronounced them good.

'And this one,' Graco winked at Nathan as he unhitched the fourth horse, 'is especially for Mistress Marie. He is a placid, solid animal who knows exactly how to deal with high-spirited females.'

Pearce laughed. 'What is his technique? I should like to know!'

'Why, he just ignores them, my friend!'

Even Groesbeck smiled at the joke. Marie, however, gave Pearce and Graco a stony look as she was helped up on to her horse.

'There is no one who knows more about horseflesh than Graco,' said Samson, his deep voice filled with admiration.

'As we ride, I shall tell you how gypsies buy horses,' Graco announced as he vaulted up into the cart and sat in the back, so that he could spin his yarn to the riders following behind.

It was a tale of barefaced cheek which had them all laughing for the first five miles of their journey. Graco told them how he had persuaded two livery stable owners to part with their best horses at much less than the asking price.

'I told them that your horse had a ewe neck,' he said, pointing to Nathan's mount. '"Her neck is too long and slender," I said. "She will be hard to handle." And *your* horse . . .' he pointed at John Pearce, 'I said it had cow hocks and its knees knocked together.'

And so the tale continued to its conclusion. Four excellent horses bought at knock-down prices, one fine cart bought for a pittance because Graco convinced the carter that the wood was unseasoned, and three honest Dutch tradesmen left very confused and considerably out of pocket. All of the story was acted out with such vitality by Graco that Nathan almost felt as though he had been there.

Graco had now climbed to the front of the cart beside Samson and the party subsided into silence.

Nathan's first impressions of the Netherlands were that it was very flat and very wet. The only signs of life he saw for the next few miles were flocks of geese that made a sound like the far-off babbling of people as they paddled along the estuary banks. The sea seemed every-where, although Groesbeck explained that it was really the mouth of the River Scheldt which had split into two great lakes as it flowed out of the land. The fertile low-lands they were passing were called polders and these lands had been reclaimed from the sea. The water was pumped from the land by the windmills dotted along the landscape. Here and there, the land was criss-crossed by man-made canals to allow water and boats to go where they were needed.

'It has taken centuries to create this,' Groesbeck said proudly. 'We have a saying in my country – God created the earth. The Netherlanders created the Netherlands.'

Nathan nodded and tried to look impressed, but he found talk of farming and land reclamation dull – and the flatness of the landscape was dispiriting. As Groes-beck's hood fell back off his head and his cloak gaped open a little, Nathan saw a flash of the scar on his neck and felt guilty. *The lie of the land does not reflect the spirit of its people*, he reminded himself.

They made good progress inland and in the afternoon came into the province of Brabant. Marie had been chat-tering animatedly to Graco when suddenly she stopped. There, ahead of them, were the burnt-out ruins of a vil-lage. Nathan was shocked. Black timbers stood at jagged, awkward angles, linked together by waist-high charred masses of wattle and daub. Inside each building was a sea of debris from the collapsed roof and walls. The rain dripping from the blackened ends of the timbers seemed like tears falling on the ground. The cart and the riders moved silently down the road, past houses, a smashed church and two mills whose sails had been ripped to shreds and fluttered dismally in the steady rain. *This is the face of war*, thought Nathan. *The price that ordinary people pay for being in the way of an enemy incursion.*

Marie broke the silence.

'Should we look for survivors?' she said anxiously.

Groesbeck was grim.

'You will only find skeletons, if that,' he said quietly. 'This was done over a year ago. The people all fled north.'

'How do you know?' asked Nathan.

'I saw it happen,' was the answer – and he would say no more on the matter.

'We are close to our camp now,' Graco announced, breaking the tension. 'Just another mile or so.'

'The sooner we get out of this province the better,' said Groesbeck. 'It is a battlefield. The Spanish hold the town of Breda, ahead of us to the east.'

'I must meet up with these men, but we will be quick,' Pearce replied.

'Are they coming with us to Amsterdam?' Groesbeck enquired casually.

'Perhaps,' Pearce answered, and Groesbeck asked no more questions.

Samson turned the cart off the road and into a small

area of woodland. Nathan ducked as the overhanging branches brushed his head. He skilfully guided his horse through the thicket until they emerged in a small clearing and there, standing by the fire waiting for them, were Samuel Fox and his companions.

Once everyone had dismounted and all the embraces and hand-shaking had abated, the gypsies burst into a fever of news, gossip, chatter and laughter. Only Nathan hung back slightly. His father had been missing for most of his childhood and Nathan had no personal experience of the gypsy way of life. He had too much English reserve and he watched the animation of his family and friends with more than a little envy. Then he noticed his father's eyes on him – ice-blue eyes which Nathan had inherited. Samuel gave him a small smile and put his arm around him.

'Come with me, Nathan,' he said quietly. 'Let us walk and talk a little.'

Marie glanced at them as they wandered off and gave a small smile of encouragement to Nathan.

The first exchanges between them were awkward. Samuel asked after Nathan's health, Nathan replied that he was well but then showed his father his hand, which still bore a few marks, and told him the story of the queen's teeth. This broke the ice. Samuel shook his head in disbelief and smiled at his son's bravery and his daughter's resourcefulness.

After that, the conversation came easily. Samuel spoke

of his travels in France and the Netherlands, and of how he and his friends had entertained many a group of soldiers tired from the ravages of war. Nathan told his father about his training at Robey's School and the duel staged by the Silver brothers. Samuel listened happily and it was only when Nathan recounted his sighting of Lord Harcourt at the tournament that the light died from his father's face.

'And now I understand that he is here in the Netherlands,' said Samuel bitterly. 'Will I never be free of him?'

Nathan looked at his father with pity. *It is not fair that he spends his whole life in hiding.* He felt a wave of anger that he and his sister had also paid heavily for Lord Harcourt's undiscovered crime. *One day I will make Harcourt pay for what he has done to us,* he vowed.

'Never forget that both you and Marie are in danger from Harcourt as well,' Samuel warned him, as though reading his thoughts.

'Not as much as we were,' Nathan replied. 'Harcourt knows we are protected by Walsingham now.'

His father nodded and Nathan gave silent thanks for England's Spymaster General and his web of agents.

Just then Pearce appeared.

'My apologies for this intrusion,' he began, 'but I need to speak with you both alone.'

Samuel beckoned Pearce to be seated on a nearby fallen tree.

While Pearce explained in great detail about the part

110

that the gypsies would play in the plot to seize the relic, Samuel listened patiently.

'What is this relic?' Samuel asked.

Pearce sighed. 'It is supposed to be the bones of the Virgin Mary.'

Samuel Fox's eyes grew wide. 'The Mother of God?' he breathed. 'We are to transport the bones of the Blessed Virgin?'

'If that is what they are, then – yes.'

Then Pearce told him about the gold shipment and their other mission.

'I am hoping to enlist some Dutch mercenaries to help us take the gold if it comes by land but if I cannot raise enough men, could some of yours help me?'

Samuel smiled. 'My men would welcome a chance to assist you in any way required.'

Pearce shook Samuel's hand gratefully. 'This must be kept a secret between us. Groesbeck knows nothing of the relic and I would prefer to keep it that way.'

Samuel frowned. 'You do not trust the Dutchman?'

'Walsingham has taught me to trust no one unless he tells me specifically that I can.'

When the three of them rejoined the others, the fire had been covered with soil and the gypsies were packing their belongings on to the cart.

'We shall travel with you as far as the city of Dordrecht,' announced Samuel. 'Then we shall take our leave of you again.'

Nathan felt a pang of sorrow that his father was going to disappear once more, but Samuel reassured him that his absence would only be for a short while.

There was so much mystery surrounding Samuel Fox and his gypsies. Nathan wondered if he would ever know the full story. He looked around at the men that he had first met in Plymouth on his last mission – the many-talented Graco; Pepe the fire-eater; Manolo and his brother Pedro, the jugglers; Waldemar the wire-walker; and the huge Samson, whose speciality was feats of strength. *How did all these men come to be my father's friends? Where did he find them all? Why do they travel with him?* So many questions and never enough time for answers.

Groesbeck, who seemed to have accepted that this diversion from their mission was nothing more than a family reunion, mounted his horse and spoke.

'The Spanish are only a few miles away and the border changes daily. We should arm ourselves. We don't want to be picked off by musketeers.'

Pearce agreed and they unwrapped their body armour. Marie sat in the cart with Samuel Fox and the other gypsies and Graco took over her horse. Snaphaunce pistols were offered to everyone and accepted by all except Nathan and Graco, who both elected to arm themselves with bows. Nathan also strapped on, for the first time, the sword that Bardolph had selected for him. It felt heavy on his right thigh and his chest tightened as he faced the reality of being in a strange country, in the middle of a war.

'I will go ahead and scout,' said Groesbeck, once his pistol was primed and his armour was in place. Pearce smiled reassuringly at Nathan and mounted his horse, pistol in hand, sword on hip. He then motioned everyone to move out of the clearing.

'Please sit on the floor of the cart,' he instructed Marie and the others, once they were out on the road. 'I shall ride alongside the big man,' and he grinned at Samson as he eased his horse beside the large gypsy. 'Nathan, ride to the left of the cart and Graco to the right, please.' Marie announced that she was impressed at being surrounded by armed men.

Slowly, they set off once more.

'Keep your wits about you and your eyes open,' commanded Pearce.

Thank God most of the countryside here is flat, Nathan thought – realizing that less than an hour ago he had found that very flatness boring. There were no more woods alongside the road and that gave him comfort. There was less chance of an ambush when they could see for miles in each direction.

Soon Groesbeck came galloping back.

'Good news! The road north is held by patriots. I was stopped by some of them. They will give us safe passage through. It seems there has been little activity by the Spanish troops of late, other than some looting. The fact

113

that they have not been paid for some time is having an effect.'

Pearce smiled broadly.

'Then let us press on! The sooner we put some distance between us and the Spanish army, the better.'

As the cart turned off on to the road that would lead them north, Nathan felt a wave of relief. He knew that he would have to engage in a fight soon but he wasn't happy at the thought of his sister being exposed to such danger. Once Marie was safely ensconced in her Béguinage in Amsterdam, he would be able to turn his mind to men's matters and summon up the necessary mettle.

The Dutch that they met along the road north seemed friendly, although they were a little suspicious of Nathan and his family's dark colouring. One man asked if they were Spanish, or maybe even Italian, but Groesbeck convinced him that they were truly English. The man nodded but was reserved towards them. Nathan noticed, with some surprise, that they did not seem to feel comfortable with their own countryman, Groesbeck. But then he seemed to have lapsed into an uncommunicative mood, so it was no wonder that they did not warm to him.

They left one lot of men behind and progressed on towards the city of Dordrecht. As they passed through various villages and hamlets, all bearing some of the ravages of war, they were always met by armed bands of men, seemingly ready to repel any raids by the Spanish. Women and children rarely appeared, unless Pearce suggested that they stop to water the horses, and then, seeing that their menfolk were engaging the strangers in conversation, they would curiously approach the group.

After several such encounters with the local people, Nathan had learned that most of them had very little food, the Spanish army having made regular sorties to raid farms and capture whatever provisions they needed. When he relayed this to Marie, her generous spirit came to the fore, as usual, and she began breaking off pieces of the loaves she had bought in Flushing and giving them to the children.

'We can always buy more when we get to a town,' she said defiantly to Pearce when he complained about her generosity. 'These people cannot.' Pearce knew better than to remonstrate further. When Marie sucked her cheeks in and set her mouth firmly, he had learned that she would not be crossed.

'Anyway,' she said to Nathan loudly, while fixing her piercing blue eyes on John Pearce, 'I am happy to give to such proud people. Did you notice that in every village we have passed through, not one person came forward to beg from us? I can walk from Shoreditch to the City and encounter more beggars than there are good folk in these villages.' And that was her final word on the matter.

Samuel hugged his daughter and kissed her cheek,

announcing that she put them all to shame. Nathan felt moved to make a similar gesture, so he awkwardly patted her hand. It was the best he could manage but it earned him a smile from Marie.

At one village, during a rare lull in the rain, the men felt the need to stretch their legs and everyone got down from their horses and the carts and either walked around or made for various bushes to relieve themselves. Pedro and his brother Manolo, to the delight of the villagers who had begun to drift into sight, began an impromptu juggling exhibition with several apples from Marie's store. They kept up their skilful display for several minutes before throwing the apples, one by one, to any children they could see in the small crowd. Waldemar, the nimble acrobat, began to walk on his hands, while Pepe balanced Graco on his shoulders and then turned him upside down so that Graco's head was balancing on Pepe's head. When they both stretched their arms wide and stood, with Pepe taking the full weight of Graco, the villagers burst into applause. Samson finished the impromptu performance by lifting up two ample Dutch ladies – one on each arm – and walking around with them, while they blushed and giggled.

'It is good to see the people laugh,' said Stefan quietly to Nathan. 'They have not had much to laugh about in the last few years.'

He nodded towards an animal enclosure. The fences bore signs of recent repair and the only animals inside were two sorry-looking goats. Nathan looked around the village. He could see signs of musket shot in the walls of some of the houses, a cart that had a broken axle and a stone wall that had been knocked down. *What must it be like*, he thought, *to live in constant fear that your village could be raided at any time?* He thought about the tranquillity of his own existence in Shoreditch and how lucky he was to go to bed every night knowing that he would awake safely the next morning.

It was well after dark when they reached the bridge over the River Meuse that would lead them into the province of South Holland and the city of Dordrecht. Nathan saw, in the distance, flickering torchlight on the bridge and the presence of an armed guard.

'We are too late,' said an exasperated Pearce. 'We have missed curfew and they will not allow us to pass into the city tonight.'

'Let's talk to the soldiers and see what they say,' suggested Groesbeck.

Pearce agreed and the two of them set off towards the bridge, leaving everyone else peering after them in the gloom.

'I hope we can find somewhere warm and dry to sleep tonight,' Marie grumbled. 'It hasn't stopped raining since we arrived here and I am soaked to the bone.'

Nathan knew how she felt. Although his breast and back plate had kept him shielded from the cold wind, the rain had trickled down behind his armour and made him uncomfortably damp.

Finally the two men returned and Nathan could see, by the expression on Pearce's face, that they had received good news.

'There is a ruined castle – called Castle Merwede – on an islet outside the city,' he announced cheerfully. 'The soldiers say that it is used as a base by some mercenaries, including Pieter de Ferm. They suggested that we make for there and hope that de Ferm will give us hospitality for the night. So, we have killed two birds with one stone. We have found shelter and our contact. Let's go.'

'Will they let us pass over the bridge?' Marie asked anxiously. 'I would not care to ford the river in the dark, with this cart.'

Pearce laughed.

'Have no fear, my lady. Money has changed hands and we shall be given passage. But I'm afraid that this ruin is in a section of the peninsula which was flooded some hundred years ago and is now dotted with little islands, so we may still have to wade through some water before the night is through.'

Marie pulled a face but Samson merely flicked the reins and turned the wagon towards the bridge.

The soldiers waved them over the bridge with encouraging sentiments.

'God bless the English,' one man called out to them as they passed off the bridge on to the muddy ground.

'It's nice to know that someone likes us,' muttered Pearce drily.

Groesbeck relayed the directions given to him by one of the bridge guards.

'Turn to the left and follow the road for about half a mile. Then you should see a fork in the road. Take the right and follow it until you see the ruins of a castle on the horizon.' He turned his horse towards Pearce. 'If you don't mind, my friend, I should like to go and see my family. They are twenty miles from here, to the north. I haven't seen them for over a year.'

Pearce nodded. 'We will meet you in Amsterdam in two days. Ask at the Béguinage and they will tell you where we are lodging.'

Groesbeck thanked Pearce, turned his horse away and was gone. Nathan peered after him in the dark and felt guilty that during the month he had known Jan Groesbeck, he had not once asked if he had a family. *Perhaps that accounted for his strange mood since we landed in the Netherlands*, he reasoned. *He was anxious to see them.*

Now it was Samuel Fox's turn to take his leave.

'We shall take the cart with all your spare weaponry and armour and we shall head for the countryside surrounding Amsterdam. I do not care to enter any cities now that I know Harcourt is in the country. If your meeting with the freebooters is a success, tell them to come and make camp with us. Then we can all await your instructions.'

119

'Where will you be?' Pearce asked.

'There is an island not far from the city of Amsterdam, called Marken,' Samuel explained. 'We have stayed there before. The people are good. When you come to the mainland shore, find a boatman called Hans Schenck – he is a friend and will bring you to us. If you need to get a message to us, Hans can be trusted.'

Then Samuel turned and hugged his daughter fiercely.

'Be careful and keep that tongue of yours under control, my lady. Perhaps the sisters of the Béguinage will teach you that patience is a virtue. But above all things, do nothing that attracts attention. Amsterdam is a dangerous city.'

Marie nodded, fighting back her tears. Samuel grasped Nathan's hand and then pulled him into a tight embrace.

'Take care, my son. We shall meet again soon . . .' and then he turned away and climbed into the cart. Graco helped Marie back up on to her horse and Pepe handed out various pieces of essential baggage to the three companions. Then Samson gave a flick of the reins and the cart was swallowed up into the darkness. Nathan suddenly felt depressed. *There is never any time to get to know him properly*, he thought as he heard the faint rumble of the cart in the distance.

The trouble with Groesbeck's directions was that they were meant to be followed during daylight. It was almost impossible to see anything in the dark, with the unrelenting rain blowing into their faces. A couple of times, Pearce's horse stumbled sideways into the soft river silt and Nathan had to move alongside his friend and coax his horse back on to firm land.

They managed to find the fork in the road only because the rain clouds decided to part and reveal a full moon which shone its watery light down upon the landscape. But the rain intensified and Pearce urged everyone to dismount and take shelter under a huge tree until the deluge eased.

They stood there, sodden and shivering, as the rain and wind whipped themselves up into a fury; then, as quickly as it had started, it died, and there was a silence.

Nathan stepped forward to comfort his horse but, as his hand touched the horse's neck, he felt the point of a knife press into the side of his own neck.

'Make no move, or you will die,' said a quiet voice in Dutch. Nathan held his breath. Then he heard a small squeal from Marie and the sounds of a brief struggle in the darkness.

The knife point in his neck was pressed a little harder and Nathan realized that they had been successfully ambushed and resistance was not an option.

'ENEMY OR FRIEND – THERE IS NO WAY OF KNOWING'

'And who, may I ask, is the leader of this pack of river slime?' asked Marie in a fury when she was released in front of a roaring fire in the ruins of the castle. Even if none of their captors understood English, they would have little doubt that she was in a very bad mood. Nathan's head slumped forward on to his chest in exasperation at her lack of diplomacy.

A tall young man stepped forward and bowed, a large grin splitting his face. He had fair hair and brown eyes. Nathan guessed that he was in his early twenties but his face bore the lines of a battle-weary soldier. His left arm was roughly bandaged and he seemed reluctant to move it.

'That would be me, mistress. Pieter de Ferm, at your service,' he said in impeccable English.

Marie said nothing for a moment. She just stood in the glow of the fire, her wet hair plastered to her face, her muddy skirt steaming gently in the heat. To Nathan's astonishment, her face softened and she smiled back at de Ferm.

'Then, sir,' she replied coolly, 'as you have forced us to accept your hospitality, the least you can do is feed us. We have come a long way and we are very hungry.'

De Ferm straightened up with a glint in his eye. *Thank God he likes bossy women!* Nathan thought, with a sense of relief.

De Ferm nodded to his men, who immediately released all the captives. Nathan rubbed his thumb across the place where the knife had been pressed into his neck. There was no blood but it was sore to the touch.

'You are the man that we have come to see,' said John Pearce firmly and de Ferm turned towards him with a look of interest.

'And why is that?'

'Sir Francis Walsingham said that you might be able to help us.'

De Ferm laughed. 'I hope the old fox told you that we only help people who pay us!'

Pearce nodded. 'He did.'

'Then we must talk business,' de Ferm turned back to Marie and added pointedly, '*after* you have eaten.'

It was possibly the best stew that Nathan had ever tasted and they sat and ate in silence, savouring the hot food and the warmth of the fire, while de Ferm's men watched them curiously. Nathan had counted thirty faces, possibly more. All veteran soldiers, armed to the teeth and ready for action.

When the last bowl had been scraped and set down, de Ferm spoke.

'What is it that Walsingham wants of us?' he asked Pearce bluntly. 'You can speak freely in front of my men. I trust every one of them and there are not many men in the Netherlands I would say that about in the present times.'

Pearce told him, briefly, of the gold en route to the Spanish army. There was a murmur amongst the soldiers.

'If it comes by land, then we need to stop it before it reaches the Netherlands. It is being escorted by a hundred and fifty soldiers, so we need all the trained fighting men we can get.'

De Ferm looked around at his men crammed into the only part of the castle which still had a roof.

'Odds of five to one,' he said. 'I've known better.'

'We may be able to capture the gold without taking on the whole escort,' Pearce replied. 'It depends when and where we make our move.'

'And what would be our payment for this engagement? My men do not risk their lives for honour and glory, I'm afraid.'

Marie made a tutting noise of disapproval and de Ferm rounded on her in impatience.

'Do not judge us by English standards, my lady!' he

said sharply. 'You, who are safe in your island, protected by the seas. You can afford to be principled about why you are engaged in this war.'

Marie looked at him steadily and her lack of response seemed to irritate him even more.

'Did you pass through any villages on your way here? Did you?' his voice rose to an insistent pitch of anger.

Marie nodded and flushed.

'Then you will have seen the price that the people pay in this country for rebelling against Spain,' he continued. 'Farms destroyed, houses burned, dykes breached and food stolen. Jacob there . . .' he pointed to one of his men in the crowd, 'had his whole family killed in a raid. Willem . . .' he gestured towards another, 'had his farm razed to the ground and his livestock slaughtered. Do you think that, if the Republic wins this war, they will compensate all those who have lost everything? No, they will not. The Republic spends what little money it has on defences and weaponry; there is no money for the ordinary people. If, at the end of this war, there is anything left standing, the only ones who will be able to rebuild their lives will be the ones who have *money*. That is why, my lady, my men fight only for money – not for glory, not for medals, or as a favour to the government. Do you understand?'

Marie nodded slowly and a tear trickled down one cheek. Nathan felt sorry for her but she had asked for it.

If only she would learn to keep her opinions to herself! But you might as well ask a river to stop flowing.

Pearce decided to change the subject and asked if anyone else had come to de Ferm asking to buy his army's services.

De Ferm grinned.

'So, you have heard the stories about us working for the Spanish as well?'

Pearce shrugged. 'Is it true?'

'I never deny the stories,' was the cryptic answer. Nathan felt that de Ferm's anger over the ravages of the war, and the fact that most of his men seemed to have suffered losses at the hands of the Spanish, meant that he would never work for them. But it seemed to suit his purpose to be thought of as a true mercenary.

'In this war, my friend,' de Ferm leaned towards Pearce for emphasis, 'there is no way of knowing who is an enemy or who is a friend. I know Dutch Catholics who fight against His Most Catholic Majesty of Spain. I also know Dutch Protestants who fight *with* Spain. The Spanish army itself is made up of French, Italians and Germans. Many of them have defected to the Republican side. Equally, we have had instances of several noblemen of the Netherlands who have betrayed the Republic and handed their towns over to the enemy. Personally, I no longer follow the whims of politics or religion. We fight for our particular piece of soil, we fight for money and we only trust each other. Isn't that right, men?'

All de Ferm's soldiers rumbled in assent.

'But to answer your question,' he continued, 'no, there has been no one else who recently has asked for our services. Not Dutch, English or Spanish. Now,' he said briskly, with a sideways glance at Marie, 'I believe I was interrupted when I asked how much we will be paid to liberate this Spanish gold for you?'

Pearce offered them the same deal as the Sea Beggars.

'Two hundred and fifty thousand gold pieces, if we successfully capture the gold.'

De Ferm's men shifted with excitement and their leader looked around at them with a smile on his face.

'Some of them are thinking that they can retire after this job!' he said happily. 'What if the gold comes by sea?' he asked, as an afterthought.

'Then you will not be needed. But Walsingham will send you and your men fifty gold pieces each to pay for your silence on the matter.'

'Seems fair, eh, lads?' he asked his men and they murmured in agreement once more.

'Is this your permanent camp?' Pearce enquired.

'No. We rest where we need to. Never in a city or town because the authorities don't trust us and we don't trust them.'

'We shall need you to move nearer to Amsterdam, so that I can easily send word once I know whether the ships are empty or not.'

De Ferm pulled a face.

'Amsterdam! If you are to go there, you had better keep a firm hand on your purse, my friend.'

'And say your prayers very loudly!' called out one of the men, causing much laughter from the others.

'Ah yes, we have just heard that Amsterdam is in the grip of a religious fever,' de Ferm continued. 'The Duke has taken himself off somewhere – no one knows where he has gone – and he has left a man in charge, called Angelo, who has decided to make the people of Amsterdam as pious as possible!'

'He'll have his work cut out!' said another of de Ferm's men and there were roars of laughter from his comrades. Pearce looked bemused.

'A strict Protestant is he, this Angelo?' he asked casually.

The men roared even louder.

'Strict?' De Ferm grinned. 'My friend, you should know that we do nothing by halves in the Netherlands. While we are engaging in a war against the Spanish, the Protestants are waging a war against what they call the "total depravity" of man. If you want to do business in Amsterdam today, my friend, you will have to be "saved" first. There are new "morality laws" in place.' He pulled a face. 'Anyway, enough of that. If we are to head north tomorrow, we shall have to get a good ration of sleep tonight. Come, we shall make some room for you all to rest where it is dry.'

There was a flurry of activity and while some of the

men were posted as sentries, the rest hunkered down where they could to snatch some sleep.

Nathan lay next to Marie but he was aware that she was restless and kept sitting up and looking around at the men.

'Is there a problem?' Nathan whispered.

'Many of these men have ailments that need attention. I must tend their wounds in the morning.'

Nathan nodded and he wondered if his sister was really only interested in one particular man. It was obvious that Pieter de Ferm had impressed her. Certainly he was one of the few men who had got the better of her in an argument. He smiled as he lay in the straw, which was beginning to warm his body, and soon he was fast asleep.

He woke as light was beginning to creep into the jagged ruins of the castle. Mist was swirling through the gaps in the walls and Nathan realized he was shivering with the cold. He felt stiff, so he sat up and began to pummel some life back into his cold legs and arms. The smell of unwashed men hit his nostrils with a vengeance and he wondered how long de Ferm's little army had been living rough. The rain had started again and he cursed under his breath. He realized that Marie was already up.

There was a sweet, hot aroma filtering through the air, so Nathan went to investigate and found that Marie was bustling about. She had been collecting wood and had built up the fire. There was some liquid bubbling in a pot, and Marie was laying out potions on the ground.

Pieter de Ferm was sitting on a rock looking amused by it all. His left sleeve was rolled up and Nathan could see that he had a festering wound on his forearm. Marie was approaching him with a firm look on her face and a knife in her hand. Nathan decided that this could be interesting and he made his way over to them.

'Hold this,' she said to her brother before he could open his mouth and she handed him a bowl filled with hot water. Nathan obeyed while she sprinkled some dried herbs into the water. A strong smell of wild thyme arose.

'This will hurt,' she said matter-of-factly to de Ferm, 'but it has to be done, or you will lose the use of that arm.'

De Ferm winked at Nathan and Marie plunged the knife into the fire, turning it around in the flames.

'Your sister says she is a healer – is that true?' he asked Nathan. 'Or am I about to have my throat cut by a vengeful female?'

Nathan grinned. 'She is a healer; you can be assured of that. In fact, she recently saved the life of the Queen of England.'

'Don't talk nonsense!' Marie snapped as de Ferm gave an appreciative whistle, then she swiftly drew the hot knife across the raised, red wound, making his whistle turn into a gasp of agony. The wound gaped open and discharged its infection like a torrent into the cloth Marie held under it. Nathan curled his lip in disgust and won-dered why his sister derived such satisfaction from such repellent tasks. De Ferm's face went white as Marie probed into his flesh with the point of the knife, scraping away any black pieces of dead flesh that she could see. Then, throwing the soiled cloth on to the fire, she took a fresh one and began to wash the wound with the thyme water. De Ferm said nothing but Nathan could see his eyes were glistening with pain.

Pearce had appeared, obviously under Marie's instruction, and he was shepherding de Ferm's men into an orderly line ready for treatment.

Once she had finished with de Ferm's arm, Marie moved on to the next man, who had obligingly removed his boots. The man's feet were strange. The skin was puckered and lumpy and two of the toes on his left foot were black. As Nathan drew near he was stopped by a smell that almost made him retch.

'Keep back, Nathan,' said Marie anxiously. 'This man has gangrene and I must remove two of his toes. This is not a sight you want to see.' She patted her patient com-fortingly. 'This is what happens when your feet are constantly wet and cold,' she said and then she nodded to Pearce, who put a leather strap between the unfortu-nate man's teeth. Pearce held him from behind, pinning his arms and the upper part of his body, so that he could not move. Marie took another knife, which had been heating up in the fire for some time, and swiftly brought it down on the gangrenous foot. The man screamed and tried to arch his back but Pearce was using all his strength to keep him as still as possible.

'Have courage, my friend, I am almost finished!' Marie shouted to her victim and then, fortunately, the man fainted so she was able to finish her work with more care. Nathan wondered how many more soldiers there were with the foot-rot. *God knows this country is wet enough!*

And so it went on for nearly two hours. De Ferm's men, having been persuaded by their leader that Marie could prevent them from losing limbs, hands and feet, meekly allowed their various wounds and diseases to be dealt with. Pearce assisted if he was needed to help restrain someone and Nathan was given the task of administering a warm herbal drink to each man in turn.

'It will lessen the pain and the shock,' Marie said quietly and then shook her head in despair. 'How these poor souls could have let themselves get into such a state is beyond me.'

De Ferm, the colour now returned to his face, came and sat beside Nathan while he drank the healing brew.

'Your sister is like an angel from heaven,' he muttered, never taking his eyes off Marie as he drank.

'Huh!' was Nathan's response. 'An angel with the disposition of a mastiff!' This made John Pearce and de Ferm laugh out loud. Marie looked up from her work and glared at her brother.

Later that day, as de Ferm's little army and Pearce's

band of agents set off on the road towards Amsterdam, Nathan was highly amused by a request from de Ferm's men. They all wanted a lock of Marie's hair, convinced that it would keep them from harm when they next went into battle.

She declared it was 'nonsense' but Nathan could tell that she was moved and, as they rode along, she periodically sawed pieces of her long black hair off with a knife.

Pieter de Ferm manoeuvred his horse so that he was constantly alongside Marie. He was, he said, attempting to instruct her in the Dutch language and she seemed to Nathan to be a very willing pupil. John Pearce seemed unusually quiet as he rode alongside Nathan but he never took his eyes off the two in front. Nathan wondered if Pearce were jealous, and he also wondered why *anyone* would find his tempestuous sister, with her love of blood and pus, so attractive.

The journey to Amsterdam was long and darkness forced them to make camp for the night. As they sat around the fire gratefully warming their hands, Nathan noticed that de Ferm was constantly watching Marie.

'You like my sister, don't you?' he asked the rebel leader quietly.

De Ferm grinned and looked a little embarrassed.

'I suppose she is spoken for,' he replied casually.

Nathan eye's flickered over to John Pearce. 'Not really . . . but she is interested in someone.'

De Ferm nodded but Nathan was not able to read

anything in the man's face. After a silence, he asked the Dutchman if he had ever been married.

There was a sharp intake of breath and de Ferm said flatly, 'Once, when I was very young. She died.'

Nathan, thinking of de Ferm's speech about the war when they had first met, asked, 'Was she killed by the Spanish?'

The man looked him straight in the eye and said, 'No. It was an English musket ball that killed her.'

Nathan gasped in shock and said, without thinking, 'You must hate the English very much,' but de Ferm just looked into the distance and replied, 'I did once but not any more. Now I just hate the war and I fear that it will go on for a very long time.'

'You are still young,' Nathan persisted. 'You could marry again,' and he looked across at Marie, thinking that de Ferm would probably make the perfect husband for his headstrong sister. But the Dutchman just laughed bitterly.

'None of us can offer a wife anything. We may not be alive this time next year. Sure – if I settled down in one of the cities and became a merchant I could maybe take a wife and raise a family but if all the able-bodied men in the Republic did that, who would fight against the Spanish? If we are to be free then sacrifices have to be made. There is no choice.'

And with that, he returned to the company of his men, leaving Nathan wondering where the glory was in the relentless struggle against a mighty Empire that threatened to swallow up the known world.

The next morning, as they neared Amsterdam, de Ferm and his men parted from them and although those soldiers Marie had tended made a great fuss of her as they left, Nathan noticed that de Ferm had avoided her company and merely nodded as he rode away. Marie had looked a little puzzled at this sudden aloofness.

In the distance, Nathan could see the masts of the ships that encircled Amsterdam, like a forest before the eyes, and his spirits rose a little. He was, he realized, happiest in a big city. He had lived in London all his life and was used to bustle and crowds. A city always promised adventure and Amsterdam looked as though it would fulfil that promise.

'WE HAVE STRICT STATUTES AND MOST BITING LAWS'

A msterdam was not large. Nathan could see the city wall where it turned at either end to encircle the city and he was amazed at how compact it seemed to be. But on their journey he had heard a lot about the life there and how, since the fall of Antwerp to the Spanish, the trade in and out of Amsterdam had become the lifeblood of the Republic.

As Pearce, Marie and Nathan rode in through the main gate, they were confronted by a fight in the street ahead of them, which caused Pearce's horse to rear and backtrack.

Some guards were arresting a large group of women, who were not being led away quietly. In fact most of them were screeching at the tops of their voices and some of them were fighting back. Nathan almost laughed when one of the older women punched one of the guards so hard in the face that he reeled backwards into the crowd with a nosebleed.

'What in God's name is going on here?' shouted Pearce in Dutch as he struggled to control his horse.

One of the guards shouted a reply. 'Back away, sir! It is the orders of Lord Angelo. We are closing down all the bawdy houses. These women are to be locked up!'

Pearce pulled his horse to one side and Nathan followed suit.

'What's to become of us?' screamed one of the women as she clawed at the faces of the guards who tried to restrain her. Then a girl, barely older than Nathan, ran screaming towards his horse and flung herself at his feet.

'This is my fiancé!' she yelled at the guards. 'He will vouch for me!' She dug her nails into Nathan's leg and tried to pull herself up towards him.

'Tell them I'm your fiancé,' she hissed at him desperately. 'Tell them and I will give you anything.' Nathan felt a mixture of dismay and confusion and was about to speak when Pearce dismounted, grabbed the girl around the waist and yanked her off.

'The only thing that you can give my friend is a dose of the pox!' he shouted as he propelled her towards the guards. She kicked and screamed in his grip and, once handed over, she turned on Pearce, her face venomous, and spat at him. Only then did Nathan notice the scabs around her mouth and the hollow shadows in her face. He shuddered. Pearce mounted up again, signalling to Nathan to follow as he urged his horse down a side street.

'Those poor women,' Marie muttered, looking back towards the scene they had just left.

'Their way of life is their choice,' said Pearce flatly.

'Is it?' Marie tried to look into Pearce's face. 'Does any woman enter that sort of life through choice?' But he ignored her and they rode on in silence.

Nathan wondered what his sister meant. Prostitutes were a common fixture around the theatres in which he had worked as an actor. They were part of the underbelly of every city and no one thought of them as human beings deserving of any attention. But the girl who had begged him to save her from prison had been so young and it disturbed him to think about her. *Marie is right*, he thought. *No one that young can have entered such a life through choice.* And he wondered what circumstances had forced her into such a miserable existence.

However, all thoughts of unfortunate women were dispelled as they reached the Béguinage. It was an oasis of calm in the mayhem of the busy city. Through its gates, Nathan could see grass and trees in the centre of a cluster of ancient buildings. There were women, dressed like nuns, hurrying towards the sound of a tolling bell. The medieval walls and the houses beyond gave the impression that time had stopped two hundred years before.

He looked up at the sky. The dull layer of cloud made it impossible to tell where the sun might be at that moment, so he assumed, as his stomach was rumbling, that the bell must be tolling for a noonday mass.

Pearce dismounted, tugged on the rope of the gate bell, and they waited. Nathan looked around at the houses in the street with interest. They appeared to be uniformly made of brick and there were no thatched roofs such as on London houses. *There was a lot in favour of brick houses rather than wood*, he thought to himself, remembering the last time a fire had broken out in Shoreditch and the panic that had ensued as everyone had tried to stop the whole street succumbing to the flames.

The gate was opened by an elderly nun. Pearce stated their business: that they were here to deliver their kinswoman into the care of the Béguinage. The nun smiled happily, ushering them through the gates. Once their mounts were tied to the hitching post, they were shown into a receiving room. There, they would wait for the Grande Dame, who was presently at prayers but would be with them shortly.

Pearce paced the floor. He seemed uncomfortable in religious surroundings and impatient to conduct business and be gone. He turned to Marie and addressed her hurriedly, aware that they might be interrupted at any moment.

'The Grande Dame will tell you if she has any further communication with the owner of the relic. Remember that we shall be in Amsterdam for a short while. If anything happens, then you must send for us. If we are away on our mission, then you must get word to your father. Do not attempt to make contact with the relic owner yourself. There could be much danger involved. Do you understand?'

Marie nodded but looked a little apprehensive. Nathan wondered how she would take to religious life. What once seemed a joke had faded into a concern as he thought about his sister being alone in this place.

The door opened and the Grande Dame entered. She bowed to Pearce, while keeping her arms firmly crossed inside her habit.

'You are the people sent from England by Sir Francis Walsingham?' she enquired softly in English, once the pleasantries of meeting had been conducted.

'Yes, Reverend Mother,' said Pearce, 'I have a letter here,' and he produced a document bearing Walsingham's seal from inside his jerkin.

The Grande Dame took the letter and sat down behind a small table to read. She motioned everyone else to be seated also. When she finished reading she looked up.

'This seems in order,' she said with a note of satisfaction in her voice. 'Sir Francis states that you have apothecary training, my dear,' she said to Marie.

'Yes, Mother. My father taught me well.'

'That is excellent. You shall work in our infirmary with Sister Beatrice. She will be glad of the help.' The Grande Dame turned her attention to John Pearce. 'You understand that I am just a receiver of messages from the patriot who wishes to give this relic to the Queen of England?'

Pearce nodded, and the Grande Dame continued.

'I have no knowledge of when he may be in touch again. It may be some time or it could be tomorrow. Mistress Fox may be here for many weeks.'

Nathan felt a surge of concern and he flashed a look at Pearce, who seemed to read his mind.

'Reverend Mother,' Pearce began hesitantly, 'this young lad is Mistress Fox's brother. He is to accompany me on a task of great importance but this may not be for at least a week. May he be allowed to visit his sister from time to time?'

The Grande Dame smiled at Nathan. 'Of course he may. We are not a convent in the strictest sense. However, we only allow men to visit this room, the infirmary and our chapel, in order to protect our Sisters. Many of them, you see, come to us for sanctuary from husbands, fathers or brothers. Here they can live in peace and without fear. But we do not forbid visits from those who are welcomed by our Sisters.' She spoke directly to Nathan. 'You may also accompany her and Sister Beatrice when they go outside these walls to minister to the sick. In fact, we should be glad if you would protect them in the streets. These are dangerous times.'

The Grande Dame turned to Pearce and her face was concerned.

'The Netherlands is at present in the grip of witch fever. The flames have been fanned by the fact that a new edition of the *Malleus Maleficarum* is about to be published in Frankfurt. Several hundred women have been burnt at the stake in northern Europe this year, accused of being witches. Our Sisters are especially vulnerable, as most are skilled in the arts of healing and are therefore suspect in the eyes of fanatics.'

Nathan and Marie cast anxious glances at each other. Their gypsy heritage meant that they were well-versed in the evils of the *Malleus Maleficarum* – The *Hammer of the Witches*, as the book was known. Written by two Dominican monks about one hundred years before and given a blessing by the Pope, it contained precise instructions on the finding and prosecuting of witches. The *Malleus* was a book that displayed a specific hatred of women – particularly those with special skills.

The Grande Dame continued. 'This places Mistress Fox in particular danger. However, she will have the protection of the Béguinage and, hopefully, this will be sufficient. But, my dear,' she turned to Marie and spoke softly, 'you must take care. Be on your guard and be about your business quietly. Do not draw attention to yourself. That way you should be safe.' She turned back to Pearce. 'So you see, we should be grateful for some extra protection, if possible.'

Nathan was relieved that he would be able to help in such a practical way and said so.

Marie turned the conversation to another subject – one that had been preying on her mind.

'Reverend Mother . . .' she asked nervously, 'will I have to cut my hair?'

Pearce and Nathan smiled and the Grande Dame permitted herself a small laugh.

'Good gracious no! As I said before, we are not a convent and we do not take strict vows. We merely agree to follow God's word in all things. There is nowhere in the Bible that says a woman should cut off her hair or do any of the other things required by the Church of Rome. Such beautiful hair . . .' she added, looking at Marie's tumbling dark curls, 'deserves to be valued but I shall ask you to hide it away under a wimple, in case it should attract too much of the wrong kind of attention. Come now.' She rose and beckoned to Marie. 'We must get you settled. Gentlemen, we bid you good day. The boy may visit each day after noon.'

Pearce and Nathan bowed as Marie was ushered out and when Nathan straightened up, his sister was gone.

'Now, my lad,' Pearce said briskly, 'let's find ourselves lodgings, for you must leave an address here tomorrow for Groesbeck, so that he may find us. Then we must present our papers to this Lord Angelo who seems to be running the city in the Duke's absence.'

As they stepped outside the calm of the Béguinage, Pearce suddenly grabbed Nathan's arm and stopped him in his tracks.

'Maybe this is not such a sanctuary after all.' He pointed ahead to where a steady trickle of people were leaving the Béguinage chapel. There, in the centre of the group, were Lord Harcourt and a young woman Nathan assumed was his daughter. *What are they doing in this place?* thought Nathan, feeling a stab of fear.

The young woman saw them, pointed, and her father spun round, a strange smile playing on his lips.

'John Pearce!' he said with false cheerfulness as he advanced on them both. Nathan fingered his sword nervously. 'And your young servant, Nathan Fox.' Harcourt's smile remained in place but his dark eyes glittered as he looked at Nathan.

'My lord,' said Pearce, giving a small bow of courtesy. Nathan followed suit but was reluctant to take his eyes off his enemy.

'You know my daughter, Lady Catherine, of course?'

'Of course . . . my lady . . .' Pearce took the offered hand and brushed it with his lips. Catherine smiled coyly.

Nathan looked at her. She was about the same age as his sister but not pretty like Marie. She had inherited her father's stockiness and broad face. Her eyes were cold too, like her father's, and they merely flickered across Nathan, registering his existence but no more.

'So you are here on Walsingham's business.' It was a statement from Harcourt, not a question. All of Elizabeth's court knew that Pearce worked for Walsingham. There were no secrets in such a place.

'A small diplomatic mission,' Pearce replied coolly. 'What brings you to Amsterdam, my lord?'

'A few business interests – the wool trade and suchlike,' said Harcourt, his eyes narrowing.

A silence hung over them for some seconds, as everyone struggled to think of some conversation.

Harcourt broke the silence. 'Is there someone else in your party?' he probed, pointing at the three horses they were leading.

'No,' said Pearce flatly. 'One horse is merely for baggage.'

'Ah, I see.' Harcourt did not seem convinced.

There was another silence, then Catherine spoke.

'I wanted to see the Béguinage, and particularly the chapel,' she said enthusiastically.

'Béguinage, my lady?' Pearce pretended to be ignorant of the building they were standing in front of.

'A convent,' Harcourt said dismissively. 'My daughter sometimes has foolish notions that she would like to take the veil.'

'Oh really?' Pearce pretended to be interested. 'For such a pleasant young lady to become a nun would be a great loss to the English nobility.'

'Precisely,' said Harcourt emphatically. 'When the time comes she shall take a husband of my choosing and forget this nonsense.'

The Lady Catherine flushed and looked at the cobbles beneath her feet.

Nathan felt a momentary stab of pity for the girl. *To be a Lord's daughter is no more than just being another of his properties. He will marry her off to some other Lord as a business arrangement and she will have no say in the matter.* He thought how much freedom his own sister had, in that she could choose her own husband if she so wished. And then he thought about the queen, whose only defence from an unsuitable husband was to reject marriage altogether. He could suddenly see the attraction, for some women, of life in a convent, where they were no longer some man's possession to be played like pieces on a chess board.

'Well, no doubt our paths will cross again, John Pearce,' Harcourt stated briskly as he ushered his daughter away. 'And, of course,' he added pointedly, 'Master Fox. Until we meet again.'

Harcourt's last comment sounded like a threat and made Nathan's heart shrivel. Catherine turned slightly as they walked away but it was not Pearce that she looked at – it was Nathan who was the target of those dark eyes, and this made him just as uneasy as her father's words.

Pearce asked one of the many guards roaming the street for directions to the Council Chamber where Lord Angelo conducted his business.

'Past the church of St Nicholas, turn right into the

street of taverns, turn left at the end, go past Weeper's Tower and follow the road round to St Anthoniespoort and you'll see it,' was the brisk reply before the man set off once more.

'I hope you remembered all that, Nathan,' Pearce said with a grin as they turned towards the spire of St Nicholas's church. On their way they passed a livery stable and decided to stable the horses. Trying to press through the crowded, narrow streets leading three horses had proved difficult, but now they were able to make some progress. The city reminded Nathan a little of Venice, where he had undertaken his first mission, in that it was criss-crossed by canals and he seemed to be walking over a small bridge every fifty yards. But Amsterdam had nothing of the space and light of Venice. The houses were thin and tall, making the streets seem narrow and dark. Venice had been warm and sunny. This place was cold and damp.

Pearce and Nathan approached the large church of St Nicholas, and the street was filled with a huge crowd listening to a man preaching up on a platform outside the church. They stopped to listen. Nathan's Dutch was not sufficient to follow every word the preacher said but it was obvious by the expression on his face and the aggressive manner in which his hand punched the air that he was threatening hellfire and damnation to those sinners who stood before him. Some of the crowd looked bored, others looked terrified. One man even attempted to argue with the preacher before several devout crowd members took off their hats and began beating him around the shoulders with them. Pearce tweaked Nathan's cloak and signalled that they should move on. Nathan edged through the crowd, frequently looking at the face of the preacher, twisted as it was with fury.

When Pearce and Nathan reached the Council Chamber and were finally in the presence of Lord Angelo it was plain to both of them why the city of Amsterdam was in the throes of such repression. The man who stood before them was . . . Nathan turned his mind over thinking of an apt description, then he remembered his friend Will Shakespeare once describing a magistrate as 'a man whose blood is very snow-broth'. This Angelo was a perfect example of Shakespeare's poetic description – cold, aloof and emotionless. Nathan guessed he was only thirty, at most. Yet, for one so young, there was no vitality in him. He wore only black, except for a large silver crucifix hanging around his neck. He seemed well suited to a room which looked almost like a chapel. It had a high vaulted ceiling and was surrounded by the sort of screened walls that usually surrounded a Lady Chapel in a cathedral.

Pearce and Nathan watched him conducting various items of business, while they waited their turn. Each task was punctuated by prayer. Before Angelo would give each supplicant a decision, he would fall to his knees, clasp his hands together and his mouth would move silently. Nathan had encountered men like this before. In England, they were called Puritans and they had frequently gathered outside the theatre where he had once worked, to preach against the sin of exhibitionism and to pray for the souls of the shameless actors within.

Pearce moved forward as his turn came and he bowed low, presenting their papers of travel as he straightened. Angelo's eyes skimmed over the documents, pausing only to look at Nathan momentarily, before handing them back to Pearce.

'They seem to be in order, Master Pearce,' he said and he summoned what passed for a smile, a drawing of the lips across hollow cheeks. There was no warmth, or even interest, in his eyes.

'I trust you are not a Catholic,' Angelo added, with a note of warning in his voice.

'Why do you ask, my lord?' Pearce coolly replied.

'Because you should know that our city laws forbid Catholics to worship in public. What they do in private is their business.' The last sentence was uttered with a certain amount of regret, thought Nathan, as though Angelo would very much like to make it *his* business.

'I thank you for your advice, my lord,' said Pearce, bowing again and turning away. 'Let us be gone from here as quickly as possible,' he muttered grimly to Nathan, as they made for the door.

Outside the Council Chamber they both drew deep breaths and looked at each other.

'Pieter de Ferm was right,' said Pearce, 'Amsterdam is a benighted place. I should not care to cross this Lord Angelo in a hurry. It seems this man has a mission to cleanse the world of sin. An easy task when you have no heart beating in your chest!' Pearce gave a mock shiver and drew his cloak tightly around him.

Nathan agreed and he privately hoped that Lord Angelo would never turn his attention to the Béguinage, for then Marie would surely be in grave danger.

Pearce slapped him on the back. 'Come, lad. I suddenly feel the need for a hot meal in a comfortable tavern.'

Nathan smiled. He could always trust John Pearce to get his priorities right.

THE CAT AND MOUSE GAME

*J*he tavern that John Pearce had selected for their evening meal had also proved to be an inn and would serve them well for their time in Amsterdam.

'Our first task is to find out whether the Casados are also in Amsterdam,' said Pearce quietly as they went downstairs to the main tavern room. Nathan wondered how they were going to find out such information but he knew that Pearce already had a plan in mind. He had come to recognize the look on Pearce's face that meant he had worked out the best way to proceed.

The place was full to overflowing with men who, unless Nathan was mistaken, smelt strongly of ripe cheese. As they pushed through the mass, the snippets of conversation he overheard confirmed that these men were here for the cheese and butter market held in a square nearby. Pearce saw the landlord clearing tables in the corner and took him to one side.

'My friend, we are strangers in your country and we

seek some information,' he said quietly, and Nathan noticed that a coin passed discreetly from Pearce's hand to the landlord's, who immediately closed his fingers tight around it. 'Tell me, where would a man go if he wanted to worship in his own way, without attracting any unwelcome attention?' Nathan realized that Pearce was asking where the clandestine meeting places of Catholics could be found and he was impressed by his friend's devious mind.

The landlord grinned as he pocketed the coin in his greasy apron. 'It's an open secret, sir.' He winked at Nathan, enjoying the fact that he had just made some easy money. 'There are several places where a man might go.'

He beckoned them closer and began to speak confidentially.

'In Amsterdam, as you know, Roman Catholics are not allowed to worship in proper churches. So they have set up these churches inside houses. We call them conventicles. Everything is hidden away, so if they have a visit from any officials, there is nothing to be seen. Just a house. There they can worship as they like and good luck to them. The Duke never minded but this piece of upright virtue left in his place, this Angelo, could very well have a purge on all conventicles before the month is out. Mark my words – he has his sights on everyone. Follow me into the back room, sir.'

Nathan and Pearce duly followed the obliging landlord. Once they were in the room, he closed the door and, taking up a quill, wrote several addresses on a piece of paper. 'I wish you luck, sirs, but take care,' he cautioned as he ushered them outside.

'Now,' said Pearce, tucking the piece of paper inside his jerkin, 'we shall go and investigate these places.'

'Do you think that we will find the Casados in one of these conventicles?' Nathan asked in a hushed voice.

'Most of the Spanish agents in Protestant countries are priests. Where Walsingham uses pirates and vagabonds, His Most Catholic Majesty King Philip of Spain uses the clergy. Where there are priests, there we will find the Casados. They will go to their masters for instructions.'

They asked directions from passers-by, being careful only to ask for the street name and not the house, but the first one on the list was shuttered and silent, as though no one had been in the place for months. The next looked hopeful. As they approached, they saw someone knock and look around furtively, before being admitted.

'This looks promising,' muttered Pearce. 'We shall wait and watch for the worshippers to come out. I think it would be prudent to hide.'

They found themselves a place in a nearby alley which had a good view of the door of the conventicle, and waited in the gathering gloom. Nathan gripped his sword comfortingly and began to feel a surge of excitement at the prospect of an adventure.

It was almost an hour later when people began to

leave the house in dribs and drabs. Obviously it was their practice not to draw attention to their activities, so entering and leaving the house was done quietly, again in twos and threes. Eventually, Pearce decided that everyone had left and there was no chance of finding the Casados here. So they proceeded on to the next address.

'How do you know that anyone will be worshipping at these places?' asked Nathan, as they trudged through the streets. He was beginning to feel frustrated at their lack of success.

Pearce laughed and turned to him with an amused look on his face.

'There speaks a true son of the theatre, who has never had time to set foot in a church!' he chided him. 'Do you not know how many occasions for worship there are in a day? Especially for Catholics – they like to keep their priests busy! Aside from the Masses, there is Confession, the daily Eucharist, the Angelus three times a day, not to mention Vespers . . .'

Nathan's eyes widened and he felt a little embarrassed that he had no knowledge of such things. *Does that make me a heathen?* he wondered. But his concern was interrupted as Pearce pulled him roughly into a doorway.

'The house is beginning to empty,' he said, indicating a little way up the street. Nathan and Pearce watched as, yet again, people left the conventicle in twos and threes. Eventually, they were rewarded by the sight of their quarry. Felipe Casado and his son stepped into the street, stopped for a moment's brief conversation and began to walk in opposite directions.

'I shall follow the father and you shall take the son,' Pearce muttered. 'Keep your distance. Do not let yourself be seen. Simply remember where he goes and report back to me at the tavern.'

Nathan nodded and they parted company, each to follow their own quarry.

Carlos Casado was easy to keep in sight. He was a head taller than most of the people on the street and his almost white-blond hair could be seen from fifty feet, even in the gloomy dusk. Nathan ducked and dived in and out of doorways, performing the dual task of following Casado and memorizing the unfamiliar streets around him. Or were they unfamiliar? He began to recognize places that he and Pearce had passed during the day and he wondered where the young Spaniard was heading.

It was now getting very dark but Nathan was relieved to find that torches were being lit on all the small bridges, providing a gentle glow of soft light throughout the busy city. *Yes, they would have to do that,* he thought approvingly, *or they would find that most of their citizens ended up in the canals after dark!* He was thankful that Casado was so fair – he could still see the back of his head in the distance, and he had not once turned around. As Nathan steadied himself against a high brick wall, he suddenly realized that he was back at the Béguinage. Up ahead on his left was the chapel and beyond that the gates that he and Pearce had entered at noon. Casado turned then and entered a house almost opposite the Béguinage gates.

Nathan sat down in a small recess in the wall and waited. He had to make sure that the young Spaniard would not be leaving again. After what seemed like an age, Casado the elder appeared from the other end of the street and also entered the house. Nathan stood up and his heart froze as a hand clutched his shoulder.

'It's me,' whispered Pearce in the darkness.

'You gave me a shock!' Nathan whispered back, drawing in some deep breaths of relief.

'Felipe Casado, as I expected, led me to Lord Harcourt's lodgings. He merely relayed some information to Harcourt at the door and then left. So now we know where both of them are staying and we can keep an eye on them. At least it gives us something to do while we are awaiting Drake's news on the gold.'

Nathan nodded in the darkness and allowed himself to be led towards the glowing lights of the canal torches and back towards their tavern.

He realized, as he sank gratefully into his bed, that it had been some days since he had actually slept in a proper bed, and it felt good. As he was drifting off to sleep a thought came to him with a jolt. *Supposing Harcourt and the Casados are here in Amsterdam to watch us? This is going to be a strange game of cat and mouse.*

The next day, it was obvious that Pearce had had the same thoughts as Nathan and, after they had broken their fast with bread and cheese, washed down with Dutch beer, Pearce reluctantly came to the conclusion that for either of them to shadow Harcourt would be too dangerous, as he knew them both. It would also be impossible for them to watch the Casados, staying, as they were, opposite the Béguinage, at the edge of the city, with no street activity to use as cover. Pearce held out little hope of being able to persuade the Grande Dame to let him use the 'receiving room' to spy on the Spaniards.

'We know that Harcourt and the Casados are in league with each other. The fact that they have arrived in Amsterdam at the same time as us suggests that they know about one or both of our missions and are, possibly, here to intervene. It is too much of a coincidence to be otherwise. The fact that the Casados have taken lodgings opposite the Béguinage, rather than in the centre of the city, also suggests that their prime concern is the relic. Which means, I'm afraid, that they may also know that Marie has taken up residence there and she may be in more danger than before. But there is nothing we can do except wait for them to make a move, be on our guard and go about our business as normal.'

Pearce decided that Nathan would go to the Béguinage at noon to see Marie, while he would go down to the docks to see if any Sea Beggar ships had arrived carrying the Silver brothers. They parted, agreeing to meet at sunset back at the tavern. There was no need for Pearce to tell Nathan to be watchful. They both knew that he had enough experience now to always be alert.

Nathan was surprised to find Marie full of life and enjoying herself in her new environment. He had expected to find her miserable and bored.

'The women in this place are so clever!' she cried when he asked her how things were.

Marie looked strange, almost like a different person, in the simple habit of a Sister. The wimple hid away her luxuriant dark curls and made her face seem younger. She chattered on about how one of the Sisters did the 'most beautiful embroidery' and she was learning some new stitches from her. Then she told him about the infirmary and how she had never been in such a place. 'There are twenty-two beds!' she said with astonishment, and Nathan feigned interest.

'Really? Is that where the nuns sleep, then?'

'No, stupid!' Something of the Marie he was used to shot him a look of scorn. 'The infirmary is where the sick people come to be looked after. Anyway, don't call them nuns. They're not nuns. We are Sisters who follow God's word.'

Nathan noted the use of the word 'we'.

'We all have our own little rooms,' she continued. 'I've made friends with a girl of my own age, called Isabella. She and I are to work together in the infirmary. Sister Beatrice, who runs the infirmary, is going to take me on her afternoon rounds of the city and the Grande Dame wants you to escort us.'

Nathan was led across the grass to a building at the end of the wall and Marie went ahead of him through a door. He noticed that she had, in the space of twenty-four hours, decided to copy the Grande Dame and walk with her hands crossed inside the sleeves of her habit. He began to wonder if Marie was toying with the idea of staying in this place but then dismissed the thought as too fantastic.

The infirmary was, indeed, impressive. It was a large hall and along each wall was a row of wooden pallets which were used as beds. Some of the beds were occupied by men with wounds and disabilities and some were occupied by very elderly men; a young Sister was feeding one such man with some broth. At the end of the room an older woman was busily bandaging a man's foot.

Suddenly a man in a bed near Nathan raised himself up and shouted, 'Mother Lazarus! Mother Lazarus! The Spanish have arrived!' He pointed at Nathan and fixed his glassy eyes on him, his mouth twitching and covered in flecks of foam. The older woman abandoned her bandaging and bustled across to the man in distress.

'Hush now, Hendrick! There are no Spanish here! Be still!'

She wiped his brow with a damp cloth and it seemed to soothe him.

'I'm so sorry.' She turned to Nathan to apologize. 'This man has a fever and he imagines all sorts of things. It's because you are so dark. He thinks you are Spanish.' She smiled at Nathan reassuringly. 'Sister Marie, is this your brother? The brave lad who is to be our protector?'

Nathan flushed and Marie laughed. 'Yes, Sister Beatrice, this is Nathan.'

Nathan was curious. 'Sister Beatrice, I wondered, why did that man call you Mother Lazarus?'

Sister Beatrice pursed her lips in annoyance – not at the question but at the subject matter.

'Oh, that piece of nonsense!' she said with feeling. 'The people around here call me Mother Lazarus because they think that I once raised a man from the dead.'

Both Nathan and Marie opened their mouths in astonishment.

'And did you?' asked Marie in a hushed voice.

'No!' Sister Beatrice was emphatic. 'These people are simple souls and it never occurred to them that he wasn't actually dead in the first place!'

She took a small piece of highly polished tin from the pocket in her habit.

'Look. I carry this with me at all times. It always pays to stick it under the nose of someone who is supposedly dead. If it mists up then they are obviously still breathing. There is no magic involved. The man I supposedly resurrected had had a seizure and he was unconscious for many days. I had him brought back to the infirmary and he eventually came round. But his family were ready to bury him, poor soul.'

'You must have quite a reputation,' said Nathan admiringly.

'Mmm. But not one that I *care* to have,' was Sister Beatrice's answer. 'In these perilous times it is not good to be associated with sorcery. Come now,' she added briskly, 'no more talk of ridiculous nicknames. We must go on our errands of mercy. Sister Isabella, would you finish bandaging that leg? We must go out now.'

The girl who had been feeding the old man stood and came across to them. Nathan found himself staring into the deepest green eyes he had ever seen. They were framed by a pair of pale auburn eyebrows, set in a white heart-shaped face. He imagined that the hair underneath the wimple was probably deep red, like Queen Elizabeth's, and for a moment he was transfixed.

'Sister Beatrice,' the girl said softly, 'shall I make some more medicines while you are out?'

'Yes, child, that would be a good idea, if you have time.'

'Nathan!' Marie interrupted Nathan's foolish stare with a rough poke in the ribs. 'Nathan, this is my new friend, Sister Isabella.'

Nathan opened his mouth to speak but he couldn't say anything more intelligent than 'Yes', nor manage anything more than a nod. Isabella smiled sweetly, while Marie looked amused at her brother's confusion.

Sister Beatrice gathered up two baskets of medications and handed one to Marie. Sister Isabella moved away and Nathan offered to carry both baskets.

'No, no,' said Sister Beatrice briskly. 'They are not heavy and, besides, I would prefer that you kept both hands free for that impressive sword you are wearing, should you need to use it.'

Outside in the street, Nathan shivered against the cold and tried to muster his thoughts. Isabella's pale heart-shaped face kept popping into his mind and he realized that it was the first time he had ever been impressed by a girl, and it made him a little irritable for some strange reason. *I have man's work to do . . . I can't be doing with girls!* And he concentrated on the task in hand.

As they turned the corner and began to walk towards the centre of the city, Nathan noticed with a start that they were being followed. There, fifty yards behind them, trying to look casual, was the young Spaniard Carlos Casado. Nathan gave a grim smile. *He may be the best swordfighter in Christendom but he is a hopeless spy!*

Casado was dressed in the latest fashion, a starched white ruff around his neck and gold thread in his dark red doublet. Nathan's grin became wider. *Talk about showing off his wealth – he'll be lucky if he doesn't get robbed, following us around the city!* Then the grin disappeared from his face as many questions began to rage through his brain. Was Carlos Casado following him or his sister? It seemed to Nathan that the Casados knew that the message about the relic had come from the Grande Dame and, as Pearce had surmised, that was why they were lodging opposite the place. But did they know about Marie's part in the mission? Had someone given them that information in England?

The last question he asked himself was the most worrying. Did this mean that someone who worked for Walsingham was a double agent?

11

'YOUR BROTHER DIES TOMORROW ...'

*I*t had been an uneventful day. Nathan had escorted Marie and Sister Beatrice to various places in the city where they had administered medicine and generally lifted the spirits of needy folk in Amsterdam.

Occasionally, Nathan had looked back and saw that Carlos Casado was still shadowing them. Marie, intent on her work, had been unaware that they were being followed by the young man she had so admired back in London. Nathan had decided to tell her later.

When he could he asked his sister questions about Isabella and had learnt much. She was sixteen years of age; she came from a noble family; she had entered the Béguinage because her father had left only enough money for her brother to live on and there was no money for her marriage dowry. She was very religious and would have become a proper nun, if there had been any Catholic convents left in Amsterdam. This last piece of information had left Nathan feeling downcast and foolish. Being attracted to an older girl who wished to become a nun suddenly seemed the height of stupidity and he resolved to think no more of her.

When the day had finished and Nathan had delivered his charges back to the Béguinage, he left the address of his lodgings with Marie and headed back home, unable to shake off the ever-present Casado until he was within sight of the tavern.

Pearce had not been surprised at Nathan's news. He, too, had been followed by the father, who had stayed at the docks all afternoon and shadowed Pearce back to within sight of home. Nathan shared his fears about there being a double agent in Walsingham's pay who had given the Casados information about their missions back in England. Pearce nodded grimly and said that it looked almost certain.

The next day Groesbeck arrived, looking refreshed and seeming more affable. He was wearing a new set of clothes and a white scarf was tied around his neck. It seemed as though his family had raised his spirits. Nathan asked him how his people were and he replied, 'Well, thank you,' before moving on to the matters of business.

Pearce told him, casually, about Harcourt and the Casados and the possibility that this meant that Walsingham was unknowingly harbouring a double agent. Groesbeck's face clouded.

'So, they are waiting to see what we will do when the message comes about the gold?'

Pearce nodded. 'However, it would seem to suggest that they know the gold is *not* coming by sea. Otherwise, why would they be here, watching us?'

Nathan thought to himself that the Casados might not be interested in the gold at all, merely the relic, but he said nothing, remembering that Groesbeck was ignorant of their other mission.

'Did you find Pieter de Ferm and his men?' asked Groesbeck.

'Yes, we did.'

'And where are they now?'

'I don't know.'

Nathan wondered why Pearce did not trust Groesbeck with the truth.

'They chose not to come into the city,' Pearce added, 'but we can send them a message when we need them.'

Groesbeck nodded and did not press the matter further.

At noon, they went their separate ways again, Nathan to see Marie, while Groesbeck accompanied Pearce back to the docks. As Nathan walked through the gates of the Béguinage, he glanced at the house opposite and saw Carlos Casado's face at the window, and it irritated him. *Why is he so obvious? Do they think they can intimidate us into abandoning our mission?*

Marie was not in the receiving room, so Nathan made

his way across the grass to the infirmary. As he entered, he could hear the sound of weeping and there, in the centre of a small knot of people, was Isabella being comforted by his sister. He rushed over.

'What has happened?'

Marie looked up at him, her eyes filled with tears.

'Isabella's brother, Claudio, has been arrested by Lord Angelo and he is to be executed,' she said, and turned back to comfort her friend.

'What is his crime?'

Isabella indicated a young man who was hovering in the background. 'Luke came to tell me. Claudio has made his girlfriend pregnant before marriage.'

Nathan looked disbelievingly at the assembled group.

'*That* is a crime worthy of execution?' He could not believe it. He had known actors who had got their women with child before marriage. It was regrettable but not, in London, a crime punishable by death. Was Lord Angelo mad?

The last member of the group – a middle-aged Carmelite friar, judging by the white cloak over his brown habit – spoke up.

'For fourteen years, the morality laws of this city have not been enforced – a fault perhaps of the Duke, who was too soft. He has left Lord Angelo in charge and the man simply seeks to bring the people back to a respect for the law.'

Nathan looked at the friar with contempt. *How could*

he justify such tyranny? He found himself distracted by the fact that the man seemed to have recently shaved off a full beard, as the lower half of his face was much whiter than the top half. The friar seemed uncomfortable with such scrutiny and turned away.

'Luke, what shall I do?' Isabella implored the young man who had brought the bad news.

'Go and see Lord Angelo. Plead for your brother. Soften him with your prayers, for he will listen to nothing else. The fact that you are lodged here in the Béguinage may influence him. No man can resist the pleas of a virtuous woman.'

'Marie and I will go with you,' Nathan volunteered, anxious to be of some help.

Isabella nodded gratefully.

'Not before Sister Isabella has taken some calming potion,' said Sister Beatrice sensibly, appearing from the anteroom with a cup which she thrust into the girl's hand. 'What a pretty pass this is! Who is this girl who is pregnant by your brother? Is she of good family? What must they think of it all?'

'Juliet is well-born and my good friend,' Isabella explained. 'My brother would have married her long ago but her parents died and her relatives will not release her dowry.'

Marie tutted with annoyance. 'Why is it always necessary for women to *buy* themselves a husband with a marriage settlement? God's blood, do we not give enough of ourselves to a marriage without having to *pay* for the privilege of being some man's cook and washer-woman?'

'Sister Marie, you have blasphemed!' Sister Beatrice said sharply, then she muttered, 'Even though your words are thoroughly sensible.'

'I'm sorry, sister,' said Marie contritely and Nathan raised one eyebrow – it wasn't often that his sister apologized to anyone.

They spoke little on the walk to the Council Chamber. Nathan could tell that Marie was seething but that she had decided to bite her tongue. What little Isabella said made it clear that she was angry with her brother for being so feckless; she was angry with the law for being so harsh but she was nervous about pleading for her brother's life to this cold tyrant who was now ruling Amsterdam. Nathan felt exasperated knowing that there was really nothing that he could do or say that would make the task easier for Isabella.

Once or twice he looked back and noted that Casado was, of course, following them. He toyed with the idea of fighting the Spaniard, just to make himself feel better, but he knew that John Pearce would disapprove of such childish behaviour just as he knew that Pearce would never have allowed him to become involved in this matter of Isabella's brother. To Pearce, all that mattered was the mission and nothing should ever interfere with that.

When they arrived at the Council Chamber, things were even less encouraging. There seemed to be an endless stream of people leaving the building who had obviously come to plead their cases. Nathan listened to the angry words of the men and the weeping disbelief of the women – it seemed as though the whole of Amsterdam stood accused of immorality. Isabella's pale skin was now so white that she looked like a phantom. Marie put her arm around her and whispered some words of encouragement before they stepped inside the building. As Nathan stood to one side to allow another group of petitioners to pass out of the door, he noticed that the friar from the infirmary was loitering across the street.

Why didn't he come with us? Nathan felt a surge of puzzled irritation. *Why did he not offer to speak on Isabella's behalf and spare her this ordeal?*

'Nathan! Stop dawdling!' Marie's insistent voice brought his mind back to the business at hand and they made their way towards the room where Lord Angelo received petitioners.

Isabella clutched Marie's hand urgently. 'Sister Marie, you must come into the room with me. I cannot go alone!'

'Of course I shall – although I can't be of much help to you as I know very little of your language.'

'It doesn't matter. Just to have you there will be enough.'

Nathan agreed to wait at a discreet distance but he

was downcast that Isabella had not asked him to go into the room as well. Still, there was nothing he could do about it, other than watch the proceedings from behind the latticework screens that ran around the room.

Isabella stated her business to the Provost Marshal and he led them into the room. Nathan walked around the screens and found himself a good vantage point, where he could see, if not hear, Isabella make her case.

Lord Angelo looked up from some papers when the two girls entered and curtseyed. Nathan noticed that his eyes merely grazed across Marie's face but when they rested on Isabella two small crescents of colour appeared on his high white cheekbones.

Isabella knelt down in supplication and Nathan could see that as she spoke to Angelo, pleading earnestly for her brother's life, a single tear was trickling down her pale cheek. Angelo seemed transfixed by her. It was as though his mouth had run dry because every time he answered her he moistened his lips with his tongue. Nathan thought he looked quite predatory.

Nathan saw him shake his head firmly and then turn away from Isabella, who got up from her kneeling position and went over to Marie in some distress. Angelo had obviously refused any clemency for her brother. Marie, however, was not ready to give up. Nathan could see that she was urging Isabella to try again – to be more forceful – and he smiled at his sister's strength and determination. *It's a shame that Marie doesn't speak fluent*

Dutch. If she did, Lord Angelo would be the one on his knees begging for clemency! Fortified by Marie, Isabella turned back to Lord Angelo.

This time she did not kneel. It was as if she had borrowed some of Marie's defiance and Nathan could see that Isabella's face was no longer fearful. Angelo seemed surprised at this display of new-found strength and he began to look at her intently, a smile creeping across his lips. Nathan remembered that he had barely looked at him and Pearce when they had presented their papers.

He likes her! he realized with disgust. *That cold, waxen excuse for a man is attracted to her!*

The interview seemed to have been concluded, as Isabella curtseyed once more, grabbed Marie's hand and they left the room. Nathan continued to watch Angelo, who had now buried his face in his hands, as though he was in despair. Then Nathan was shocked to see Angelo fling himself to his knees and begin feverishly praying as though his life depended upon it. *This man is unhinged!* thought Nathan scornfully as he turned away to find the girls.

Isabella was trembling with relief when they stepped out into the street.

'He said I must go back later!' she said excitedly. 'He is going to think about his decision. Thank you, Sister Marie, for giving me renewed strength. I would have given up if you had not encouraged me to try again. I hope that I can be strong when I go back.'

'I will be there again to support you . . .' Marie began to say.

'No!' Isabella interrupted. 'He said I must go alone this time.'

'When?' asked Nathan.

'At dusk.'

'No. You will *not* go alone!' Nathan's vehemence made his sister look at him questioningly. 'I do not trust that man. I will watch from behind the screens, like I did just now. He won't know that I am there but I am close enough in case there is a problem.'

Isabella looked puzzled, unable to comprehend what possible problem could arise. Marie looked intently at her brother and nodded.

'Nathan is right,' she said quietly to her friend. 'Let him be your hidden protector.' She gave her brother a small appreciative kiss on the cheek which he rubbed away in embarrassment.

When they returned to the infirmary, the friar was there ahead of them, although the boy, Luke, had gone. Sister Beatrice seemed a little put out that she was sharing *her* infirmary with a stranger but it appeared that she had no choice since she announced, to everyone within earshot, that 'The Grande Dame is allowing Friar Lodowick to stay with us for a while.' This seemed astonishing to Nathan as he had understood that the Béguinage rules expressly forbade priests and monks from having any part in its day-to-day business, but he said nothing. He could tell by Sister Beatrice's face that she was not happy with the situation.

Once Isabella had relayed the details of her interview with Angelo, it was time for Sister Beatrice and Marie to make their visits to the sick. Nathan was uncomfortable at leaving Isabella alone with Friar Lodowick and he did not really know why. He had had little conversation with him and had no reason to dislike him but his intuition told him that this holy man was not what he seemed. Reluctantly, he followed Marie and Sister Beatrice out into the street and focussed all his unsettled emotions into one large grievance against Carlos Casado. The Spaniard's continued obvious presence – his arrogance – bit deeply into Nathan. He vowed that, before he and Pearce left Amsterdam, he would settle a score with Casado.

They returned to the infirmary as the dull wintry light began to leave the sky to find Isabella pacing the floor, anxious to go back to the Council Chamber. Marie was insistent that she would also come along and watch proceedings with Nathan, so the three of them set off in a hurry.

There were guards at the main doors but only one man sat, looking bored, in the hallway. While he took Isabella into Angelo's presence, Nathan quietly took Marie to his vantage point of the morning. It was much more difficult to see, as it was quite dark outside now and the room was lit only by a few candles in wall sconces, which made Angelo's bony face look all the more spectral in the flickering half-light.

Isabella sank to her knees again and began to speak. This time Angelo sat in his chair, perfectly still, watching her. Nathan began to feel the hairs on the back of his neck stand up. Angelo was unnaturally still, his deep-set eyes looking like black hollows in his face. Isabella finished her speech and stood up. Then Angelo rose and walked over to her. As his hand reached out and stroked Isabella's face, Nathan's hand tightened around his sword hilt and Marie let out gasp. Angelo spoke urgently, his face very close to Isabella's, and she seemed to sway but he grasped her arm and steadied her. As Angelo raised his head, Nathan could see that his eyes were shining and there was an excitement in his face. Isabella's face, on the other hand, looked drained of everything. White – deathly white – and expressionless – her face seemed to float, disembodied. Every sinew in Nathan's body wanted to run into that room and impale Angelo to the wall with his sword – but he could not move.

Isabella turned, saying nothing, and left the room. Nathan heard Marie's skirts swish as she hurried to be at her friend's side but he just stood there, watching Angelo, who had sunk to his knees in prayer – this time with a radiant smile on his face.

'Nathan!' Marie hissed from the darkness of the

175

corridor and the sound made Angelo turn from his prayers. For a moment, the man who held all the power in Amsterdam seemed to lock eyes with the boy spy from England, although all that Angelo could have seen in the gloom was a vague shape beyond the latticework. A questioning look sprang into his eyes but then Nathan was gone, moving silently down the corridor like a ghost.

Marie and Isabella were outside, on the front steps. Isabella, despite the relentless sleet and cold wind, had slumped down on to the steps and seemed unwilling to move.

'What happened? What did he say?' Nathan asked desperately.

Isabella lifted her white face upwards and let the cold, wet ice flakes spatter on to her skin.

'He said that he would spare my brother's life . . .' there was a moment's pause while she struggled with the words, '. . . if I would become his mistress.'

Nathan felt numb. Marie's face was like stone. Isabella continued, half-laughing and half-crying.

'I misunderstood at first. I thought he was asking me to become his wife. But then I realized that he was not talking about marriage. He was talking about an . . . arrangement. My body in return for my brother's life. As simple as that. All over the city he is arresting people for committing mortal sin outside of marriage but he wants me to do that very thing!' Her whole body shook with the horror of it all.

'I must get her back to the Béguinage. She is in shock,' Marie muttered.

Nathan, who had been in shock himself, now felt as though he was going to explode.

'You hypocrite!' he shouted at the closed doors of the Chamber. 'You damned hypocrite!'

'Nathan! There is nothing you can do. Stop it!' Marie pulled her brother round to face her. 'We must take Isabella back home and speak with the Grand Dame.'

Nathan nodded, but he still seethed with rage.

They hurried back through the dark, wet streets. It was slippery underfoot and Isabella seemed to have lost the will to walk properly. Nathan took off his cloak and placed it over hers. No one spoke.

In the warmth of the infirmary, Isabella was wrapped in dry blankets by Sister Beatrice and the friar while Marie relayed, in a hushed voice, what had happened. Friar Lodowick seemed almost as affected as Nathan and stood quivering with suppressed rage.

'It is as I suspected. Dress a man in a little brief authority and it changes his soul,' the friar muttered, almost to himself, which made Nathan look at him with renewed curiosity. Friar Lodowick then spoke softly to Isabella.

'We shall help you, Sister. Never fear.'

Isabella looked at him.

'How?' she said brokenly. 'How can anyone help me?

Who can I complain to? Who would believe me? It is Lord Angelo's word against mine! He is the law in Amsterdam. Everyone believes him to be pure, perfect, almost holy. Who would believe that he is a wicked hypocrite? Who?'

No one could answer her question and Nathan, no longer able to bear it, ran from the room, out into the cold air.

Out in the street, partially hidden in a doorway, stood Carlos Casado, and at that moment, he became the focus of all Nathan's hatred and frustration.

'You! Casado! Come out, you dog! Stop hiding away like a grass snake! Come out and face me!'

Confused, the Spaniard stepped out into the light from the frozen moon that hung overhead, and tentatively drew his sword. Nathan strode across the street and drew his. He wasn't going to give the Spaniard the chance to fight like some dainty courtier. Nathan was going to fight on *his* terms. Brutal, hard, street fighting – like Robey had taught him.

His last few strides turned into a run and Nathan's sword slashed through the air like whipcord, making the Spaniard leap out of the way, but not before the edge of the sword caught his sodden hose and slashed a gaping slit in the fabric on his left knee.

Casado's sword flashed through an arc, down on to Nathan's sword, smashing it on to the cobbles – but it did not break. Then the fight began in earnest.

What in God's name am I doing? thought Nathan in a moment of lucidity. *This man is one of the best swordsmen in Europe!* But then he was once more overtaken by a surge of white-hot rage. In the moonlight Casado looked surprised, almost shocked, at the intensity with which he was being attacked. This had not been part of the plan.

Nathan was slashing indiscriminately and Casado used his skill to dodge and parry the blows. Then, as the rage began to work itself out, Nathan began to realize that he had started something that would only end badly for him unless he began to fight properly.

The rhythm of the swords changed. Nathan slowed his pace and began to target his blows more carefully. Casado sensed this adjustment of pace and smiled. Now he started to do more than fend off blows and he began to test the full extent of Nathan's capabilities.

Casado started to make his attacks wider by springing back a few paces and taking advantage of his greater sword arm length. Nathan began to flag but then he remembered Robey's words,

'Every swordsman has a weakness – some part of him that will give you an opportunity to overcome him.'

As the swords clashed and clanged in the half-light, Nathan realized that Casado still had his right wrist bound up – a legacy of when he fought Robey in Black-friars and the Master had dislocated his wrist. *So,* Nathan reasoned, *it must still be weak.* He began to execute manoeuvres that required Casado to fully flex his wrist in order to parry Nathan's blows. He made the Spaniard swing first to the right and then to the left, over and over, until he was sure that the wrist must be aching from the exertion. Then, using all his strength, he engaged Casado's sword, ran forward along its length until the hilts of both swords clashed together and, with split-second timing, brought up his other hand on to his sword hilt and pushed with all his might, forcing the Spaniard's hand sharply over to one side. Casado yelled with pain, brought up his left hand and punched Nathan hard in the side of the head. Both of them slumped to the ground – Casado clutching his right wrist and Nathan swaying nauseously on all fours from the knockout blow to his temple.

'For God's sake, what was the point of all that?' It was Marie's voice but to Nathan it sounded far away, as though she was shouting from the end of a long tunnel. Then his face hit the cobbles and he heard no more.

'...A REMEDY PRESENTS ITSELF'

*H*e had no sense of being carried to the infirmary, only at some point in the strangeness of his condition, he did register being laid on something soft – but all the time he was falling . . . falling . . . down and down and hearing voices through the void.

'This is a bad thing you have done, Nathan,' said Pearce.

Then Walsingham said something – *or did he*?

The Spaniard, Casado, spoke. 'Will he recover? It was only a glancing blow.'

And woven through them all was Marie's voice. 'How could you be so stupid, Nathan? . . . so stupid . . . so stupid . . .'

He awoke with a start, breathing heavily and feeling sick. Marie and Sister Beatrice were bending over him.

'How could you be so stupid, Nathan?' said Marie crossly.

'He'll have a great bruise on the side of his head, I

shouldn't wonder,' said Sister Beatrice, placing some-thing very cold on his temple which made him wince with pain.

His head was throbbing and his right cheek felt as though it didn't belong to him. Also, the vision in his right eye was limited and it felt as though the eye was closing up.

'I think you cracked your cheekbone when you fell on the cobbles,' Sister Beatrice continued. 'It will be swollen for some time and you have a black eye coming.' She sounded almost gleeful as she bustled off and Nathan glared at her.

'What possessed you to attack Señor Casado?' Marie said over her shoulder as she walked away from the bed. Nathan struggled up on to one elbow and saw that she was going over to apply wet bandages to Casado's wrist. The Spaniard grinned at Nathan and winked.

'He wash following ush,' was Nathan's mangled reply. He put his hand up to his mouth and discovered that the right side of his top lip was puffy and distorted.

'The boy sees ill intent where none existed, Sister,' the Spaniard replied smoothly in perfect English. 'It was just a coincidence that I was walking the same streets – noth-ing more.' He looked intently at Nathan as if to remind him that the spying business was private and not to be discussed with women. Nathan slumped back on to the bed in irritation, which just caused his head to throb more.

He watched Marie through half-closed eyes as she bandaged the Spaniard. Some of her dark hair had escaped from the wimple and Casado was watching her appreciatively. Marie was aware of this scrutiny, and occasionally she looked at him and smiled prettily. Nathan closed his eyes in disgust but the resulting dizziness made him open them again quickly.

Sister Beatrice returned with a foul-tasting herbal brew she insisted that Nathan drink and some salve which she applied to the right side of his face. Whenever he cried out in pain, she would tut and tell him that if he wanted to brawl in the street he 'should take the consequences like a man'. Casado laughed and Nathan scowled at him.

A bell tolled, signalling that it was time for evening prayers for the Sisters, so Marie and Sister Beatrice left. Nathan raised himself up again and looked around. There were only two other occupants of beds on the other side of the room and Friar Lodowick was tending to them. Casado sat at the table in the centre of the room and looked at him.

'That was some punch you gave me,' said Nathan grudgingly.

Casado nodded in agreement. He pointed to his temple. 'Didn't they teach you that if you hit a man there – just there,' he pushed back his hair and put his fingers on a point just up from the side of his eye, 'you will render him unconscious?'

Nathan shook his head, which made it throb even more. Casado walked over and sat on the edge of his bed.

'But, my friend, I think you did the most damage when you hit the street. Now, are you going to tell me why you called me out to fight?'

Nathan had been foolish and he had to admit it. 'I was angry about something else and you were just there. I can't explain it,' he mumbled.

'Ah.' Casado seemed to understand. He leant forward conspiratorially. 'You and I both know this covert game we are playing. I watch you and you watch me. We serve our masters. But you have broken the rules by attacking me. I do not think that your partner – this John Pearce – will be very happy when he finds out. Do you?'

Nathan said nothing, so Casado continued.

'However, you have done your masters one small favour. You have removed me from the game altogether. My wrist will take a long time to heal. I cannot afford to go into a situation where others may rely on my swordsmanship. So now I must stay in Amsterdam, kicking my heels. Congratulations, English spy. You have done your job well.'

The Spaniard did not seem unduly bothered that Nathan had bested him. *Perhaps he is pretending to be gracious in defeat*, Nathan thought, but in any event, he admired his cool demeanour.

Casado continued, 'You use a sword very well, but

then I understand you were trained by Señor Robey, the man who damaged my wrist in the first place.'

Nathan nodded.

'Then he has trained you well. Once you have learned not to fight in anger then you will surpass even your teacher.' Casado smiled. 'This dark-haired one who bandaged my wrist, she is your sister, yes?'

Nathan nodded. 'Marie. Her name is Marie.'

'Ah.' The Spaniard seemed to be committing it to memory. 'And when you leave Amsterdam soon, as we both know you will, she will be left alone here?'

'If you touch her . . .' Nathan rasped loudly, making Friar Lodowick look up from his work.

'No, no, no – be still!' The Spaniard was smiling. 'You mistake my intentions. I was merely wondering if I might be of service to you, since I shall be stuck here with nothing to do. I was offering to watch over your sister, to protect her – nothing more.'

Nathan looked at him warily as he turned the proposal over in his head. *Would there be any harm in Casado watching over Marie? She would be well protected. It is obvious he likes her.* There was something about the Spaniard which Nathan admired. He seemed to be straightforward – honest even – and yet he was the enemy. Nathan's head throbbed and he felt confused.

'I'm sure she would be grateful of your protection,' he said slowly.

'Good,' was the brisk response. 'Then when you leave

I shall offer myself as a replacement escort to the Sisters when they go to minister to the sick. But now, I shall return home. Adios, English spy. Until we meet again.'

After Casado left, Friar Lodowick came over to Nathan with some hot broth which he painfully and slowly ate, dribbling half of it down his jerkin. The friar watched him silently which Nathan found rather irritating. *Who is this man and why did he follow us to the Council Chamber?* There were lots of questions Nathan would have liked to ask but there was an aloofness about the friar which signalled that he would not get any satisfactory answers.

Friar Lodowick spoke at last.

'Sister Isabella has gone to visit her brother, Claudio, in prison,' he said, opening the conversation.

'Alone?' said Nathan in alarm.

'No. The boy Luke came to escort her. He is a friend of her brother's.'

'What will her brother say?' Nathan knew that if it were Marie who was in Isabella's situation, he would be very angry.

Friar Lodowick sighed. 'I know something of Claudio. He will probably ask her to do as Angelo desires to save his own skin.'

What sort of brother could do that? thought Nathan angrily.

'It's all the Duke's fault!' he said vehemently. 'How

could he go away and leave such a tyrant in charge of his people?'

Friar Lodowick turned away for a moment and cleared his throat. 'Perhaps the Duke had some purpose that no one knows about.'

'Like what?' said Nathan scornfully.

'Amsterdam is in the process of changing from a Catholic city to a Protestant one,' he explained, still not looking properly at Nathan. 'This process throws up many extremists, in both religions. Some of these extremists, who have converted to the new Protestantism, hold positions of power in the government of the city. They need to be removed but the Duke could not do that purely on the grounds of someone's religion. Perhaps he was hoping that such men would, once given a little power in his absence, tie the noose around their own necks by their actions.'

Nathan struggled to understand what Friar Lodowick had just said. 'So, what you are saying is that the Duke left this Angelo in charge so he could prove himself to be a criminal and then the Duke would have good reason to get rid of him when he returns?'

Friar Lodowick nodded. 'Exactly.'

'But that doesn't help Isabella now, does it?' Nathan continued contemptuously. 'Or the dozens of others who have been imprisoned by Lord Angelo. It seems to me that this Duke is something of a coward, leaving other people to do his work for him.'

Friar Lodowick's face tensed into a mask of misery. 'Perhaps there is a way to help Isabella now. I may have a remedy.'

'What?'

'I had a very good friend once . . .' He looked off into the distance, as if trying to remember his friend's face. 'Frederick. He was a great soldier in the Netherlands but he died in a shipwreck and all his worldly goods and money went to the bottom of the sea with him . . .'

There was a pause and Nathan waited impatiently for the point of this story.

'His sister, Marianne, was betrothed to Lord Angelo – they were to be married as soon as her brother arrived in Amsterdam – but when Angelo discovered that Marianne had been left penniless by her brother's death, he refused to marry her and abandoned her to loneliness and poverty.'

Nathan gasped. 'How evil is this man? What happened to Marianne?'

'She still lives near the city – alone – and she still loves the despicable man who cast her aside.'

'So what does this have to do with Isabella?' Nathan asked, having failed to see the point of the diversion.

Friar Lodowick looked thoughtful. 'I am not sure yet. Just be reassured that I will not allow Isabella to come to any harm. Neither will I let her brother die, if I can help it.' He seemed quite firm in his intention but Nathan wondered how a humble friar was going to outwit the unpleasant Angelo.

The Friar patted Nathan's arm. 'Be assured that I shall remedy the situation while you are away from Amsterdam.'

'What makes you think I'm going away?' asked Nathan suspiciously.

'Your friends told me, of course! They were here earlier, while you were out with Sister Beatrice and Sister Marie ministering to the sick. I told them that you had some extra business to attend to and they said they would return tonight.'

Nathan leaped out of bed in alarm, which made him sway unsteadily and he momentarily on to the bed for support.

'Why didn't you tell me earlier?' he said in panic.

Friar Lodowick shrugged. 'I was not here when you returned with the Sisters and you had left for the Council Chamber by the time I got back. There has been no opportunity.'

Nathan's mind was racing. *What am I going to tell John Pearce? Please God, don't let him be so angry that he sends me home!*

As if on cue, Pearce strode through the door at that very moment, followed by Groesbeck and the two newly returned Silver brothers. The wide grins on their faces disappeared as they were confronted by a swaying Nathan, one eye fast closing up, a cheekbone that was swollen, red and grazed and a purplish colour gathering around the right side of his face.

'Holy Mother of God, what happened to you?' Pearce's face was a picture of disbelief.

Nathan's throbbing head seemed fit to burst as he struggled to find the words.

'I'm afraid I've done something really stupid,' was the best he could manage.

NO MORE FOLLY

*P*earce insisted that they all adjourn to the receiving
room where they could air their various pieces of
news in private.

He escorted Nathan in silence, his face betraying no
emotion, which only made Nathan more fearful. Once in
the room, he sat him down and looked at him more carefully.

'What a sight!' said Toby Silver, attempting to prod
Nathan's cheekbone and being pushed away.

'I'd like to see the state of the other party to this fight,'
said George Silver, winking at his brother, while Nathan
scowled at him.

'And just who was that other party?' asked Pearce
coolly, in a voice that silenced everyone.

Nathan swallowed hard. 'Carlos Casado.'

There was a pause during which Nathan felt a bead
of nervous sweat trickle from his hairline down to his
eyebrow.

'Casado.' Pearce was quite calm. It was not a question, it was just a statement but it held a note of disbelief in it. 'Did you kill him?' he asked, quite matter-of-factly.

'No.'

'Pity,' was the surprising response. 'It would have been one less of the enemy to worry about.'

Nathan looked up, a half-smile on his face, but if he imagined that Pearce was about to forgive him, he was mistaken. The look on his friend's face was one of extreme disapproval.

'I think that you had better tell us the whole story, before we tell you our news,' said Pearce, drawing up a chair.

So Nathan began explaining the story of the unfortunate Isabella. Pearce raised the occasional eyebrow; Groesbeck made a few comments about the level of corruption in the city; and the Silver brothers, much to Nathan's annoyance, smirked throughout. When Nathan had finished Pearce's eyes were as cold as steel.

'Groesbeck, George, Toby, leave us,' he barked, without taking his eyes off Nathan. 'Go back to the tavern and we will join you there later. I need to speak to Nathan alone.'

Without a word, they obeyed his command and left. Nathan's lower lip trembled.

'Please, please don't send me back to England,' he said hoarsely, desperately trying not to cry with frustration at his own stupidity.

Pearce looked at him angrily.

'What use are you to me, looking like that?' he hissed and he turned away and slammed his foot into the door in anger. Then he took a deep breath and turned back to Nathan.

'Nathan, when you took on this work, you were told that it must come before *everything*. Before family, before religion, before . . . personal relationships. I thought you understood that.'

'I do.'

'Then why did you allow yourself to become involved in the plight of some young girl who had taken your fancy? Why did you lose your temper and place your life in danger, unnecessarily, by fighting with Casado? Why?'

Nathan had no answer and he hung his head.

Pearce sighed. 'You are so talented and I sometimes forget that you are so young.' He sat down and placed a reassuring hand on Nathan's shoulder. 'And I have been doing this work for so long now that I have almost forgotten what it is like to have feelings for someone.'

Nathan looked at Pearce and was rewarded with a small regretful smile.

'The trouble with you, lad, is that you have too much honour,' Pearce continued. 'You cannot jeopardize your missions by rescuing damsels in distress every five minutes.' He slapped Nathan on the back. Then he stood and paced the room for a little while.

When he turned back to Nathan, his eyes held a

warning. 'What you do not realize is that you have unwittingly played into Carlos Casado's hands. I am almost certain that he and his companions are here, not to save the gold shipment, but to find the relic. That is why the Casados took lodgings opposite the Béguinage and that is why Carlos Casado so generously offered to escort Marie and Sister Beatrice in your place. Today, while you were away on your private business, there was another development. Lord Harcourt's daughter, Catherine, was admitted to the Béguinage as a temporary guest. Their plan is, I would imagine, to watch and wait from both inside and outside the Béguinage, for news of the relic. Nathan, Marie may be in great danger and I must warn her.'

Nathan felt sick. 'Did *I* put Marie in danger by fighting with Casado?'

Pearce shook his head. 'Not really, but you have made it easier for him by introducing him into the infirmary. Do you see now that our actions, no matter how small, can affect the whole outcome of these missions? You must never deviate again from the orders that you are given – no matter how hard it seems. We have tasks to complete and nothing must get in the way.'

Nathan swallowed hard. It had been a bitter lesson to learn.

There was a knock at the door and Marie entered. She smiled when she saw Pearce but then she looked concerned at Nathan's obvious misery.

'Is he in trouble?' she asked Pearce.

'Most certainly,' he replied firmly.

'Will you send him home?'

There was a pause and Nathan held his breath.

'No. Much as I am tempted, I need him too much.'
Nathan exhaled with relief.

Pearce turned his attention to Marie. 'We shall be leaving tomorrow,' he explained and the corners of her mouth turned down immediately. 'And you must know that you are now in a dangerous position.'

'If you are going to warn me about Catherine Harcourt, I already know. The Grande Dame introduced me to her before prayers. She is a sly one, I can tell that. It is obvious that she is here to watch me.'

Pearce agreed. 'But there is another who will be watching you. The Spaniard, Carlos Casado. He intends to offer to take Nathan's place as your escort each day. Both of them, I have no doubt, have been instructed to find out anything they can about the whereabouts of the relic—'

'But none of us know that,' Marie interrupted. 'The Grande Dame has received no message. I asked her today.'

'If a message should come while we are away, you must explain to the Grande Dame that nothing can be done until we return. The Dutch patriot who holds the relic must be persuaded to hold on to it safely until we come back to Amsterdam.'

'I understand.'

'I hope that you do, Marie,' said Pearce gravely. 'I would not like to think that you would be tempted to take action on your own. Your life would be put in very great danger.'

'I would never do such a thing!' retorted Marie, her eyes flashing with defiance.

'Your brother did,' Pearce reminded her, 'and you are even more headstrong than he is.'

'You may be sure, Master Pearce,' she said acidly, 'that I would not dream of doing anything without your express permission.'

She gave him a final glare, then kissed her brother lightly on his undamaged cheek, urged him to take care of himself and swept out.

Pearce allowed himself a small smile.

'There is no doubt that she is someone a man would never forget,' he said softly to himself.

Now that Nathan was reassured that he would continue to be part of the mission, he allowed himself to think once more about the plight of Isabella and he felt some distress that he would not be able to help her in any way.

'I just have to fetch something from the infirmary,' he said quickly, 'some salve that Sister Beatrice prepared for my injuries.'

'Make haste then,' said Pearce. 'I will wait for you outside the gates.'

Nathan hurried across the dark quadrangle to the infirmary and was relieved to find that Friar Lodowick was still alone with the two patients.

'I have to leave now,' Nathan whispered urgently. 'I am being called away from Amsterdam. Friar Lodowick, promise me that you will help Isabella – promise me.'

The friar looked solemn. 'I swear to you by all that is holy, I will save Isabella and her brother from harm. Do not worry. When you return, all will be remedied.'

Nathan gave him a grateful nod, grabbed the pot of salve from the table and left.

In the cold night air, the sleet had turned to snow, gently powdering John Pearce's head and shoulders. As Nathan approached his friend, he saw a figure scurry out of a doorway towards Pearce. It was Marie. He saw her hand rest lightly on Pearce's arm – she said something – he said something – and then Pearce lightly kissed her cheek and she scurried off once more. Nathan grinned. He knew that his sister could never part with anyone on bad terms, especially someone as important to her as John Pearce.

'So,' he said casually to his friend, as they set off down the street, 'Marie found it in her heart to forgive you then?'

He couldn't see Pearce's face in the dark but he heard his friend laugh.

'Like I said, Nathan, no one would ever forget someone like your sister.'

*

The snow fell softly and quietly, tiny powdered flakes that rested on eyelashes and eyebrows and refused to melt. Nathan found the soft coldness comforting on his battered face as they walked through the silent, white streets.

The warmth of the crowded tavern felt good. They had arrived just in time, before curfew was sounded, and the main room began swiftly to empty as men made their way back to their homes before they fell foul of the law. The Silver brothers and Groesbeck were seated near the well-banked fire, so Pearce and Nathan gratefully joined them. Some good Dutch beer was ordered, along with some bread and cheese. By now, there was no one else in the tavern. Even the landlord had taken to his bed. So Nathan settled happily back to hear the story of the attack on the Spanish ships by the Sea Beggars.

Exactly five days after Pearce and his companions had departed for Flushing, the Spanish ships that Walsingham's spies had spotted loading 'special cargo' in Genoa arrived on the horizon, three of them, sails full of the heavy wind that was whipping across the North Sea. Drake brought the *Elizabeth Bonaventure* about and the Sea Beggars' flyboats formed up on either side of him. They had chosen to line themselves up on the north side of the mouth of the River Scheldt because the Beggars' leader, Conraadt Visser, did not want to be south of the Scheldt in case the Spanish sent reinforcements down the river to attack them from the rear.

Drake's ship stood higher in the water and had the bigger guns, so the *Elizabeth Bonaventure* hung slightly back from the Sea Beggars' vessels and was the first to fire on the three approaching Spanish ships as they bore windward towards the Scheldt.

There had been a half-hearted response from the Spaniards, which made Drake immediately suspect that they were not carrying anything of worth. The first salvo from the *Bonaventure* brought down the mainmast of the leading Spaniard, leaving it to drift aimlessly, while a shot from one of the Beggars' flyboats breached a second Spaniard below the gun deck, causing it to list in the water.

In all, the engagement took no longer than an hour from start to finish and when the Dutch and English sailors boarded the Spanish ships they met with very little resistance. It had been a disappointment for the Silver brothers, who had been hoping for a serious battle. Drake's mood got blacker. The man had a nose for treasure and his instincts told him that these ships were nothing but decoys. He was proved right. A thorough search of all three ships found nothing of great value – just provisions for the Spanish troops in Antwerp, which the Sea Beggars gleefully 'liberated'. There was enough food and wine to keep them at sea for another six months.

Drake's mood improved when he found the priest attached to the expedition, who had in his possession several gold chalices, one large solid gold altar crucifix and several small gold crucifixes. Then he discovered that the captain of one of the ships had a private cache of gold coins. Finally, he assembled the crews of the three ships and his men parted them from all their valuables – rings, earrings, rosaries, crucifixes – anything that looked as though it were made of gold.

'The thing is,' said Toby Silver, 'that almost all of the crews had served their time in the New World and they all had more gold jewellery about them than most men see in a lifetime.'

So Drake was mollified by his modest haul and the Sea Beggars merely shrugged off the disappointment of the encounter.

Drake sailed back to England that day, leaving Conraadt Visser to do as he pleased with the Spaniards. It pleased Visser to place all the crews in longboats, giving them the choice of a long row back to Spain or death, while he scuttled all three ships. Toby and George had been transferred to one of the Beggars' ships but were refused passage to Amsterdam until the Beggars had enjoyed the sport of sitting on deck, drinking their newly acquired Spanish wine and watching the three ships sink slowly beneath the waves, while shouting derisory comments to the fleet of longboats slowly disappearing into the distance.

So that was it. No gold on the ships. It was no surprise to Pearce.

'Tomorrow,' he announced, stretching and yawning, 'we shall rendezvous with Pieter de Ferm and his men. I have purchased some more horses for our two mariners here,' he winked at Toby and George. 'We shall be quite a little army on the march.'

'Where will we intercept the gold?' asked Groesbeck.

'I haven't decided yet,' said Pearce dismissively. 'I shall have to send scouts on ahead to find out where the gold actually is on the Spanish Road, before I make any more plans.'

'I could scout for you,' Groesbeck volunteered.

'No,' Pearce replied. 'My Dutch is not as good as it should be. I need to have you by my side. Now, we must all get some rest.'

When Nathan lay in bed, gingerly applying Sister Beatrice's salve to his cheekbone, he wondered why John Pearce had lied about his Dutch being poor. He knew that Pearce always mastered fully whatever language was needed for his missions. Yet again he was displaying mistrust of Groesbeck. *Does he know something about him? Or is he just being cautious?*

AN ARMY ON THE MOVE

*J*he next morning, Nathan found a note pushed under his door. Pearce had gone on ahead and was now asking Nathan to assemble the others and meet him on the road outside the nearby town of Hilversum. Nathan was instructed to say nothing about the gypsies' refuge on the Island of Marken. Despite the curfew, Nathan suspected that Pearce had slipped away under cover of darkness.

Groesbeck was surprised that Pearce was absent. He seemed annoyed that he had been left in sole charge of three boys – and said so. Nathan felt insulted by this. True, the man had once been their tutor and the Silver brothers had not impressed him with their feeble book learning but Nathan felt that the three of them were just as skilled as the Dutchman when it came to a fight. So, after they had broken their fast, the four of them retrieved their horses from the livery stable and set off in an atmosphere of resentment.

Nathan was glad to be reunited with his spirited Ardennes. He never felt more comfortable than when he was on horseback and this particular horse had, indeed, been chosen well by Graco. Rider and horse were superbly matched and it gave Nathan a feeling of omnipotence.

Sleet had started up as soon as they had left the city gates and this made it slippery underfoot for the horses. And it was cold – bitterly cold. The sky was a leaden grey but with that tinge of yellow that promised snow. Nathan shivered. As they passed through the flat countryside he could see that some of the irrigation canals were completely frozen over. People were sensibly staying indoors in such weather and, eerily, it seemed as though they had the whole of the Netherlands to themselves.

Twice they stopped to water the horses. Groesbeck would break the ice on a village horse trough and their animals would reluctantly drink the cold water. Nathan filled up a leather water carrier and strapped it to his horse's side, figuring that the warmth from the animal would warm the water, so that her next drink would be easier on her belly. *It is a bad thing for sweaty horses to drink ice-cold water*, he fretted.

Finally, ahead of them, under a small copse of trees, stood John Pearce and what seemed like a small army. Nathan eagerly scanned the sea of faces and then his face dropped. *Where is my father?* Disappointment was replaced by irritation, which in turn was replaced by anxiety. *Is he hurt? Is he ill?*

They dismounted and Nathan faced a barrage of questions about the state of his face.

'Look at you!'

'What a bruiser!'

'Did you get in a fight with your sister?'

Nathan told them, sarcastically, that they were all *very* funny. In truth he realized that he had almost forgotten about his injuries, such was the effectiveness of Sister Beatrice's salve. What he did not realize, however, until he looked into the clear ice of a puddle, was that the salve had lessened the inflammation but brought the bruise out more, so now he looked even more awful. Almost half of his face was various shades of purple and blue.

Introductions were made and Nathan fancied he saw something flash through Pieter de Ferm's eyes when he shook the hand of Jan Groesbeck. It was fleeting, whatever it was.

Upon being introduced to the Silver brothers, de Ferm said, 'The English seem to like their agents young, I see,' and he playfully punched George Silver's shoulder. The Dutchman seemed buoyant, as though he was eager to engage the Spanish.

'Your father has stayed on the Island of Marken,' murmured Pearce softly, answering Nathan's unspoken question. 'It was too dangerous for him to accompany us.

We do not know if Harcourt or Felipe Casado are shadowing our every move.'

Nathan nodded, swallowing his disappointment, and Pearce gave him an understanding look.

'Besides,' Pearce added, 'I have set a courier service in place between your father and your sister. Should she need help, she can contact him. He can send someone to escort her to Marken, if there is a problem.'

That news gave Nathan an unexpected sense of relief. He had been feeling tense since they left the city and he had not realized that he had been so worried about Marie until Pearce mentioned it. Now he felt that he could turn his attention fully to the mission ahead of them.

Pearce summoned de Ferm, Groesbeck, Nathan and the gypsy Graco to the back of the gypsies' cart. Pushing aside some of the armour, he produced a piece of charcoal from his sleeve and drew a basic map on the wooden floor of the cart.

'We are here,' he said, scrawling a cross. 'We need to travel across country to Arnhem – avoiding any English garrisons, since we do not want word to get back to the Earl of Leicester that we are here – then we shall travel by barge down the river Rhine to the Palatinate Forest. The rulers there are hostile to Spain and have blockaded the Rhine against any Spanish troop movements. We shall intercept the gold right there, in the forest. The Spanish have had problems in the past getting their consignments through that area. There are people there who will hide us, if necessary.'

'It will be difficult getting into Arnhem,' said de Ferm.

Groesbeck agreed. 'The Spanish hold almost all the towns surrounding it. Arnhem is like a sealed fortress because of the activities of the Spanish raiding parties.'

'We'll have to deal with that one when we get within striking distance,' said Pearce, resuming his explanation of the plan. 'If the squadron left four weeks ago, then it will just about be struggling through the snowbound Vosges Mountains at the moment. We need to be there soon.'

Everyone murmured their understanding of the situation.

'Who is going to scout ahead and find out the true position of the consignment?' Groesbeck was anxious to know.

'The gypsies,' replied Pearce, clasping Graco by the shoulder. 'Who better than a travelling band of entertainers?' he added and Graco grinned in agreement.

'But,' Pearce added, 'they shall not go ahead until we have established a base in the Palatinate. Now, let us be on our way before we are frozen to the spot!'

Pieter de Ferm laughed. 'If you think this weather is bad, my friend, spare a little pity for the Spanish soldiers who are, as I speak, struggling through the waist-high snow blizzards in the Vosges!'

Everyone who was mounting up enjoyed the thought

of a small section of the Spanish Army trying to dig themselves out of snow drifts, and it made for a merry start to their journey.

They were, indeed, a small army on the move. De Ferm had mustered twenty-nine men, plus the six gypsies, Pearce, Groesbeck, Nathan and the Silver brothers – making a grand total of forty.

'The odds are better,' said de Ferm, easing his horse alongside Nathan's. 'Now we are maybe three to one, which is good odds for an ambush.'

'Also, the Spanish soldiers will be weary, having travelled so far,' Nathan reminded him and de Ferm agreed.

'Have you ever been up into the Vosges Mountains?'

Nathan shook his head.

'Ah. The air is so good.' De Ferm smiled at a pleasant memory. 'For a lowlander like me, the mountains are exhilarating. And how is your sister?' he said, almost as an afterthought, but Nathan smiled, knowing that the mercenary had really wanted to ask that question first.

'She is well. She likes it in the Béguinage.'

De Ferm laughed. 'The thought of your sister in a Béguinage . . .' He left the rest of the sentence unspoken. 'Still, at least she is safe,' he added, almost to himself. Nathan could not mention the fact that Marie, too, was on a mission. No one, except Pearce and the gypsies, was supposed to know about the relic.

The rest of the day was spent in idle chatter as the men

rode along. Groesbeck remarked at some point that it was remarkable that the Silver brothers had managed, in one short day, to pick up more of the Dutch language than they had in a month under his tutelage. He also noted, with disdain, that most of the words they had learned were curses and blasphemies. He further remarked that while he had no doubt that they would find such words extremely useful at some point, they would do little good in battle. George and Toby merely laughed and when Groesbeck had urged his horse ahead of them, they made rude gestures behind his back.

Most of de Ferm's men, despite their hard lives fighting a never-ending war, living out in the open and having suffered terrible personal losses, seemed good-natured. They were certainly tough and uniquely skilled in survival. Nathan was aware that, now and then, individual men would separate from the group and go off into any woods they could find, only to gallop back sometime later with a pair of dead rabbits or pigeons slung over their shoulders.

When the army stopped for the night to make camp, it was the turn of the gypsies to demonstrate their talent at turning the day's kill into a succulent meal. The rabbits were skinned and each gypsy wrapped a carcass in wet clay, and then placed it in the glowing, spitting fire that de Ferm's men had built.

'When the clay is baked, so are the rabbits,' announced Waldemar, to no one in particular.

After they had eaten the sumptuous feast and pronounced it very good indeed, Graco, who seemed to be the unofficial leader of the gypsies when Samuel Fox was not around, organized an entertainment. Manolo and Pedro juggled daggers, which was very impressive; the giant Samson lifted George and Toby Silver above his head – one in each hand; Waldemar rigged up a rope between two trees and proceeded to walk over their heads; Pepe ate fire, which caused at least three of the Dutchmen, unused to such magic, to make a sign to ward off the evil eye, and Waldemar dragged Nathan up from his contented spot by the fire to put on a display of his diabolo skills. Between them, Graco and Nathan tossed the diabolos from one to the other, catching them on the strings with breathtaking speed.

'I had no idea you were so talented,' remarked de Ferm after Nathan had flopped down on the ground, sweaty from his exertions. 'Obviously a talented family.' Nathan knew the Dutchman was thinking of Marie again.

John Pearce interrupted. 'Any more evenings like this and the men will be getting soft,' he said with a grin, before wrapping himself up against the cold and selecting a place near the fire to sleep.

Next day they awoke almost buried by snow. In fact, the snow had provided an extra warm blanket – it had been such a dry, soft fall during the night. As Nathan sat up, the snow cracked apart and fell off the rise of his legs like the shell of an egg. For the first time since he had landed in the Netherlands the sun was shining, and he walked out of the camp and looked across the vast acres of silent whiteness glittering in the morning rays. He had always found snow exhilarating. To him it made the world look new and fresh, and the cold air tingled in his throat.

He surveyed the camp – men coughing and spluttering as they eased their aching bones into movement – and felt a surge of camaraderie. Belonging to such an army, however small, gave him a feeling of pride. Being accepted by them made him feel as though he had become their kinsman and he understood why de Ferm's men had all chosen to become mercenaries. Better to be a band of brothers than to be alone in times of war.

The Netherlands that they passed through over the next few days was a very different country from those lands that lay further south. Not only had the flatness of the estuary areas given way to soft hills and forests but here there was little evidence of Spanish incursion. The villages they passed through seemed more prosperous and the people gave them curious looks but not fearful ones.

So far they had followed the curve of the great inland sea the Dutch called the Zuider Zee but now they swung southwards towards the city of Arnhem and the frontier of the Spanish Empire and its allies. Pearce insisted that they pause and put on armour. De Ferm's men permanently wore an assortment of breastplates and helmets they had retrieved from enemy sorties but now many of them chose to stop and prime their pistols in readiness for action.

De Ferm sent two of his men ahead to scout while the rest of the army proceeded watchfully. Soon the men came back and announced that there was a Spanish contingent – not many men, about twenty – encamped by the side of the road just outside Arnhem. Pearce immediately detailed de Ferm, Nathan, the two scouts and five more of de Ferm's men to follow him and deal with the Spanish, otherwise they would not be able to pass through to Arnhem. Groesbeck's expression showed that he was upset at being left out, until Pearce pronounced him 'in charge' while they were away. This seemed to mollify him but the Silver brothers were not happy. While Nathan was being issued with a pistol he could see their annoyance that he had been chosen over them. It bothered him to be the object of their jealousy but he reasoned that even though he was some three years younger than them, there was no denying that he had more experience in the field.

The ten of them rode swiftly until the two scouts signalled it was time to hide the horses and proceed on foot. They tethered them in a shady copse and gathered around Pearce.

'We must advance very slowly and quietly. No sound at all. If we carry on through these trees we shall come

211

around the back of the Spanish. Wait for my signal. Do not waste powder and shoot unnecessarily. You know how to ambush by stealth. After all, is that not how we met?' He grinned, remembering how de Ferm's men had captured Nathan, Marie and himself outside Dordrecht. The men all grunted in agreement.

Slowly they made their way through the trees, taking care not to make a sound. The fall of snow made it easier, since everything was wet and there was no risk of snapping dry twigs underfoot. Nathan could smell the smoke of the Spaniards' fire and the aroma of warm bread. He could hear the men talking amongst themselves. Idle soldiers' chatter. They suspected nothing.

Pearce dropped down behind a tree and everyone else followed his example. He signalled to them to fan out, so that they formed a semi-circle around the Spanish encampment. Then they watched for a little while, in silence.

The Spaniards looked grizzled and tired. Several of them had some days' growth of beard and most of them were wrapped up against the cold in strange patchwork garments made of animal skins. Pearce had identified the leader as the man sitting with his back to them, hunched over the fire – the one to whom all the others came for instructions and advice. None of them was armed or even watching the road for any signs of activity. *This is a poor way to run an army unit*, Nathan decided.

Pearce passed a whisper along the line that he would

step out and take the leader and everyone else should step out at the same time and aim their weapons at the nearest man. Nathan adjusted his grip on the unfamiliar gun in his hand. There was no doubt that pistols made him nervous and he hoped that he would not have to use it.

In a flash, Pearce stood up and leaped out of the woods and, before the rest of them had got into position, Pearce's gun was pressed to the back of the leader's neck.

'Say your prayers, my friend,' said Pearce in faultless Spanish, while nine other pistols were raised at the rest of the Spaniards.

Nathan almost laughed at the expressions of surprise on the Spaniards' faces. It was so unexpected that no one made a sound or moved.

'What do you want?' the leader asked wearily.

'We are Dutch mercenaries, and we want safe passage into Arnhem.'

The Spaniard laughed. 'You need not fear us.' He turned and looked Pearce straight in the eye, an expression of unconcern on his face. 'Until we are paid we will not fight.'

Pearce nodded. He could see from the state of this ragtag band of men that it was some time since they had had the basic comforts most soldiers purchased with regular pay.

'We shall stay here until our people have safely passed. Just in case you change your minds.' Pearce nodded to one of de Ferm's men and instructed him to ride back to the others and tell them to proceed. 'Here we have a good example of what months without pay does to an army,' Pearce said in English to de Ferm.

'I thought you said you were Dutch?' Apparently the Spanish leader spoke almost as good English as Pearce spoke Spanish.

Pearce grinned. 'Dutch, English, what does it matter? To you we are all the enemy.'

'That may once have been true,' the Spaniard shrugged amicably. 'But now our enemies are the cold, starvation and lack of gunpowder. Until His Most Catholic Majesty King Philip of Spain sends us money and supplies, we live as best we can and . . . how do you say? We fight for whoever pays us.'

Pearce raised his eyebrows.

'And how many Spanish units are doing the same as you?' he asked.

The Spaniard shrugged once more. 'Many,' he said. 'Soon more will come here to join us to . . . to . . .' he struggled again and lapsed back into Spanish, 'to lay siege to the city of Arnhem and make them give us food and drink.'

De Ferm hung his head in despair at this piece of information. 'When the Spanish Army is well fed it fights the Dutch people like tigers and when its miserly king makes it starve, it takes the food from the mouths of the Dutch people. What justice is there in that for my country?' His voice had risen to a bitter angry rant and he stepped forward to shove his gun angrily against the temple of the nearest Spanish soldier. There was a movement of concern amongst the other Spaniards.

'Back off, de Ferm!' Pearce barked the order and looked steadily at the Dutchman. 'Now is not the time to settle grievances.'

De Ferm gave Pearce a murderous look and stepped back two paces. Nathan could see that he was having difficulty controlling his impulse to kill every Spaniard in front of him. Nathan looked from Pearce to de Ferm anxiously but the Dutchman nodded slowly and spat on the ground in contempt.

The clatter of horses and wagon wheels defused the situation. Nathan watched as the rest of their comrades passed by on the road, gazing in wonderment at the tableau in front of their eyes.

'That is one clutch of sorry-looking Spaniards, captain!' shouted one of the men on horseback to de Ferm and several of the others laughed.

One of the Spaniards could not stand the dishonour and screamed, 'Protestant scum!' to which Graco shouted back, 'Go to the Devil!' and de Ferm's men laughed raucously, joining in with a few insults of their own.

Pearce silenced them all with his own shout. 'Graco! Give these Spaniards some bread and cheese.'

There were some disbelieving murmurs of protest from the Dutch.

'Are you mad?' said de Ferm angrily.

'No,' replied Pearce coolly as the gypsies scurried over to them carrying armfuls of the requested food. 'You may have forgotten, de Ferm, that we have to come back this way – hopefully with a laden wagon. There will be more of these starving Spanish outside the city walls and we will need their goodwill in order to pass through.' Nathan admired Pearce's tactical skills. *He is always in command – always thinking further ahead than those around him. I have so much to learn from someone like John.*

Pearce turned to the Spanish leader, at whom he was still pointing his gun.

'What is your name?'

'Corporal Pedro Salinas,' the man replied.

'Well, corporal, my men and I have some business to conduct and when we return we will give you more food and maybe a little money if you give us safe passage through again.'

The Spaniard agreed and looked around at his men who were happily munching away on the bread and cheese.

'Gracias, señor. You ask for me when you return.'

'That I will do. Adios, amigo,' and Pearce signalled to all his men to mount up.

As they rode away, Pearce sidled his horse up to de Ferm and put his hand on the Dutchman's shoulder.

'Forgive me, Pieter, that I did not allow you to take a few Spanish lives back there. But I am a diplomat above all else and if there is a way through a problem without shedding blood, I will always take it. Content yourself with the great victory you will strike on behalf of your people when you take that gold home to the Republic.'

De Ferm stopped scowling and offered his hand in friendship and they shook on it. When Pearce had urged his horse ahead and Nathan came side by side with the Dutchman, de Ferm grinned sheepishly, nodded towards Pearce's back and said, with a wink to Nathan, 'Don't you get tired of him always being right?'

15

WITCHES AND SIRENS

Arnhem was a city at prayer. Behind its heavily fortified walls every street corner played host to a preacher addressing a fretful crowd. The tone of each one of them was accusatory. The city was about to be punished for allowing evil in its midst. It was only two years since Arnhem had been a Spanish stronghold and the legacy of the Inquisition still hung about the place like a shroud. Now the Spanish were back outside the walls, about to lay siege and, said the preachers, someone had called down this evil upon them. By the church of St Eusebius men were laying down bundles of wood around hastily constructed platforms and wooden stakes – enough stakes for eight people, maybe more if they were tied up in twos.

Some of de Ferm's men crossed themselves and their leader made his feelings clear by snarling, 'Religious madmen!' The gypsies looked fearful and Pearce muttered, 'The sooner we leave here, the better.'

Nathan, in horrified curiosity, asked Groesbeck, 'Witches or heretics?' and the Dutchman gave the curious answer 'Is there a difference?', earning him a strange look from de Ferm.

As they were now forced to travel by water, the cart was swapped for some indifferent horses for the gypsies, much to Graco's annoyance, and all the travelling paraphernalia – the herbs, the spices, the juggling pins and diabolos, the ropes and tricks – were distributed amongst the troupe.

Two flat-bottomed boats were purchased and all the men, weaponry, baggage and horses were loaded up. Nathan, Graco and the Silver brothers had the job of tending to the horses. Each was tied to the side rails of the boats – twenty horses to each vessel, ten horses either side. Graco and Toby took one boat, Nathan and George the other. George Silver remarked that he thought it would be a rather easy job until Nathan presented him with a shovel and told him that their main task was to shovel horse dung into the river and keep the deck clear. Graco, having arranged his own team of horses to his satisfaction, came aboard Nathan's boat to arrange the rest of the horses according to temperament.

'It is important', he said, untying two horses and moving them in between two others, 'to put the highly strung ones in between the placid ones. It will reassure them and stop them rearing every time the boat moves under their hoofs.'

He shifted the horses about the boat like chess pieces until he was satisfied that he had done his best. Then he made the sign of the cross, murmured a prayer and took Nathan to one side.

'You know I am a true-born gypsy,' he whispered, 'a Gitano from Spain, and . . . we do not like to cross water . . .' he looked at Nathan apologetically and received a sympathetic grin in return.

'I know, I know.' Graco raised his hands in a defensive action. 'I have been to sea many times with your father but . . .' he looked around furtively and brought Nathan closer to him, 'this river is *enchanted*.' He said the last word with a kind of horror and Nathan looked at him, startled. Graco continued, 'Yes, yes – the River Rhine has dragons and sirens – things that lure men to their deaths. Believe me; we must protect ourselves at all times.' With that he pressed a small pouch on a leather thong into Nathan's hands.

'Wear this around your neck. It is a potent charm.'

Nathan looked at the departing Graco with disbelief, and then he opened the pouch. It contained a collection of small shells, nothing more, but he could see Graco signalling to him from the other boat, so he tied it around his neck to placate him.

Pearce was on Nathan's boat, along with Groesbeck, half of de Ferm's men, Manolo, Pedro and Samson. De Ferm, the rest of his men and the rest of the gypsies were on the other one. Fortunately, all the Dutchmen were expert sailors. The sails were broken out and quickly flapped in the stiff river wind, which made some of the horses agitated, forcing Nathan and George to scurry from one animal to another to calm them down or fit them with blinkers, so they could not see the movement of the sails.

'We have to travel over two hundred miles down this river,' Pearce told Nathan, 'but this is the only part where we can use the sails because the river is wide and the land either side is flat. We can use the wind – even though we are travelling up river, against the currents. Once we reach Cologne, the river runs through steep gorges in the mountains and we shall have to be towed or punt the ships ourselves.' He looked a little pale but Nathan guessed that Pearce was better able to tolerate river travel than the open sea.

The horses were calm now, all staring out at the water as though transfixed. Nathan and George joined them, gazing in companionable silence at the wide, grey expanse of the river. The land beyond was white with snow, although none had fallen since last night and Nathan could see that some of the shallow reed beds at the water's edge were frozen solid. The wind was like a knife and many of the horses bowed their heads behind the ship's rail to keep it out of their eyes. *Sensible animals,* thought Nathan, drawing his cloak further around him and feeling the gypsy charm around his neck. He shared some of Graco's anxiety about this voyage – not because of dragons or sirens but because the river was so cold and grim that he reckoned any man who fell into the Rhine would last no longer than five minutes at this temperature.

They made good passage to Cologne. There had been a handful of islands to negotiate but de Ferm's men seemed able to handle whatever hazard the river might throw up. Nathan and George had kept themselves warm by shovelling dung. They had moored the boats overnight, fed the horses, eaten their own evening meal, slept as best they could, and pressed on for Cologne at dawn the next day. Fortunately, the wind had not abated during the night and they had been able to continue under sail.

Nathan felt cheered at the sight of the great city of Cologne, its massive cathedral towering above the river, but there was no time to stop. They were able to continue under sail for a few more miles until the river began to narrow and the land either side began to climb steeply upwards. The wind was then cut off and they were forced to punt until they could find some available towing.

Two men, one either side of the bow of the boat, put great long poles into the water until they found the river bed and then they pushed with all their might. But the river was getting deeper and punting would soon not be an option. Fortunately, shouts from the river bank signalled that a man was offering his massive draught horses for hire and both boats were manoeuvred towards the bank so that they could be tethered to the horses on the towpath.

Nathan had never seen such massive horses. They were bigger than plough horses – over eighteen hands. Each boat was tethered to a pair of these beasts and, as they walked stolidly along the path, they gave the impression that they were pulling nothing more than a handcart.

Groesbeck came to Nathan's side, amused at the look of wonder on the boy's face.

'We are easy boats for them to tow,' he remarked. 'We have no cargo to speak of. These horses are used to towing many more tons than we are carrying.'

'What breed are they?' asked Nathan.

Groesbeck struggled to recall the name. 'Mmm . . . I know they are native to the Netherlands . . . now what province is it that they are named after? Ah, yes – Brabant. They are called Brabançons. They are bred for towing vessels along canals and rivers. They are too heavy even for field work. The farmer would not be able to turn them easily in front of a plough. Besides, if the ground was too soft, they would just sink in!'

Nathan laughed and nodded. The giant gypsy, Samson, joined the group.

'I think that even *I* would be hard pressed to lift one of those beasts,' he growled in his deep voice.

The river took on a new personality as the boats

slowly progressed. The land either side grew more and more mountainous. Steep, forbidding rocks loomed above them and equally forbidding castles perched high on their summits. Manolo pointed out Castle Drachenfels, on the opposite bank, supposedly where a fire-spitting dragon had once lived. Nathan judged it to be a fine castle but it sat quietly on the hilltop, giving no impression that it harboured anything other than noble folk who were probably hunched sensibly around a warm fire at this moment. He smiled to himself at the thought that perhaps they had a tame dragon in the cellars who obligingly breathed on some kindling wood every morning.

De Ferm's men were forced to use the punting poles against the craggy rocks to keep the boats from grazing their sides. No one spoke. Any sound seemed to echo around the gorge and the horses began to whinny and snort nervously. Nathan became aware that most of the men were silently arming themselves and he knitted his eyebrows into an unspoken question to Pearce.

Pearce pointed silently ahead and Nathan saw, with a lurch in his stomach, that a large group of Spanish soldiers were standing high up on a ridge on the opposite bank of the river. The boats passed them by with agonizing slowness but not one soldier moved a muscle. They just watched in silence as the boats ploughed through the water.

'It seems,' muttered Pearce quietly, 'that like their

compatriots at Arnhem, they are in no mood to fight unless they are paid.' Nathan, struggling with two of the most restless horses, murmured a quiet prayer of thanks.

When the tow horses came to the end of their owner's allotted route, another man's horses were hitched up. By night they moored as best they could and hunkered down against the cold. Pearce told Nathan that it would take another night and a day to reach their final destination – the city of Mainz.

The river became considerably narrower and, consequently, colder, since sunlight barely found space to shine on to the water. The appearance of castles became more frequent until they seemed so thickly clustered either side of the river that George Silver wondered aloud if anyone in this part of the world lived in normal houses.

The river began to swirl with strong currents and the men struggled to keep the boats from turning into the rocks. The great draught horses began to stumble as the weight of the boats pulled them sideways but they carried on with dogged determination. The gypsies began to cut pieces of sacking from the flour bags and stuff them in their ears. Then, one by one, they dropped to their knees and began to pray.

'Cover your ears, boys!' Samson urged Nathan and George. 'It's the siren's rock!' and he pointed ahead to where a massive jutting stone loomed high above the river.

Nathan decided that if there was anything to hear, he wanted to hear it, and he ignored the gypsy's advice. Slowly, the tow horses, men and boats struggled against the currents to get past this section of the river. All available men were now assisting Nathan and George with the horses, which had become unusually restive. The gypsies remained immobile in the centre of the deck; eyes closed in prayer, they would not be budged.

'Such foolishness!' said an irritated Groesbeck, struggling with the horse next to Nathan's.

'What is the legend of the rock, then?' Nathan asked as the mountainous structure loomed closer and his neck ached from staring upwards.

'Something about a nymph called Lorelei, who, because her heart was broken by some lover, killed herself by jumping off that rock. She was then, apparently, turned into a siren that sings and lures boats to crash on to the rocks.' His words were full of scorn. 'It has more to do with the hidden reefs and rapid currents in this stretch of the river than any so-called siren,' he added emphatically.

Nathan was not so sure. Something of the gypsy in him made the hairs on the back of his neck stand up and he strained to see if he could hear the siren singing. But there was nothing – only the gurgling of the water and the keening of the wind – but he could see how some superstitious sailors might mistake that for a siren's call.

Once the Lorelei rock had passed, the river took a

sharp turn to the left and they passed several towns all showing normal commercial activity, with boats loading and unloading at the quaysides. The silent, ominous face of the Rhine was no more. It had suddenly widened once more into a flat, smooth waterway and everyone on board the boats relaxed. Even the horses tossed their manes, as if to toss away the memory of the last day's journey, and George Silver hugged Nathan spontaneously when Pearce announced that they were almost at their destination.

When they arrived at Mainz, the first boat had already docked and unloaded its restless horses. Toby Silver and Waldemar were shovelling the last of the dung overboard and both of them looked up and grinned when George gave a piercing whistle. Nathan saw how desperate George was to see his brother so he generously urged him to disembark, saying he would clear up after the horses himself.

Pearce said that tonight they would camp outside the western walls of Mainz. Nathan looked enviously at the warm taverns and cosy houses as they rode through the streets of the city but Pearce reminded him that no one would be able to find beds for forty men. Such an army must behave like an army and billet itself where it could. Luckily, Sir Francis Walsingham had provided him with a contact – a good farmer, loyal to the Republican cause – and that night they were offered the sanctuary of a big warm barn, filled with hay, which they gratefully accepted.

'Get a good night's sleep, Nathan,' said Pearce cheerfully. 'Tomorrow, I want you to accompany the gypsies and scout for the Spanish squadron.'

Nathan was overjoyed. 'Really?' he asked, a grin splitting his face from ear to ear.

'Really,' Pearce confirmed. 'You shall be the messenger. Take note of the countryside and the route that you take because, when the squadron is found, I want you to ride like the wind back to us here, to show us the way.'

Nathan nodded happily. It was an important job and he knew it. To be a scout was dangerous but vital work. But to be the messenger who relayed the information of the location of the enemy was the most important job of all. Best of all it gave him the chance to ride fast and hard – the thing he loved most in the world.

He fell asleep almost immediately and his imagination took him in his dreams to the top of a mountainous rock where Isabella sang to him beautifully while he gazed into her sweet face.

PIECES OF WORTHLESS PAPER

*R*iding along with his father's gypsy friends was proving very interesting indeed to Nathan. It was while riding through a dense forest, so thickly populated by trees that very little snow had made its way to the forest floor, that Nathan learned where each man had come from and how he had become part of his father's troupe.

Graco, as he had already said, was a Gitano – the name given to the gypsies of the Andalusian region of Spain. He had been a horse trader and, therefore, was accorded a degree of protection from the Inquisition not usually given to many gypsies. But, one day, an army captain who had bought a high-spirited horse from him that was proving hard to handle had accused him of 'bewitching' the animal and Graco had been arrested. After he had been beaten to within an inch of his life, the Inquisition had left him face down on the cathedral floor to do penance. Stefan (the men always called Samuel Fox

'Stefan' because they had never known him as anything else) had rescued him – taken him away and tended to his injuries – and Graco had rarely left his side since.

The two juggling brothers, Manolo and Pedro, were also from Spain, but they were 'Hungaros' or, as a playful Graco chose to call them, 'gypsy scum' – which earned him the usual kick from Manolo. The Hungaros, being nomadic drifters, fell foul of the authorities regularly. As Pedro explained, most Hungaros' principal occupation was begging and because this was usually accompanied by offers of good luck or curses, the Hungaros were the first in any community to be accused of sorcery. Both brothers readily admitted that they had been thieves in their time and both of them credited Stefan with changing their lives. They had drifted across Europe, entertaining and thieving, until they had wound up in England. This was where Stefan had found them – languishing in the stocks in a north-country marketplace, being pelted with rotten vegetables for their misdeeds. Despite many protests from Graco, Stefan had taken the two brothers into his band and they had been so astonished that someone would actually *want* their company, they had become reformed characters.

'We don't steal any more,' said Manolo.

'Except when we are asked to,' added Pedro.

'And except from the Spanish,' added Graco.

'True,' Manolo confirmed.

Pepe, the fire-eater, and the darkest-skinned of the

men, was a Tsengui – a gypsy from Turkey – who had ended up in Portugal as part of a travelling entertainment troupe. There had been a fight between Pepe and another man over one of the dancing women, and Pepe had accidentally killed the other man. His neck had broken when Pepe knocked him over. So he had to go on the run and that was when he met Stefan, Graco, Pedro and Manolo.

Waldemar, the nimble wire walker, was a gypsy from Bohemia who had gone to France and, unbelievably, ended up as an entertainer in the king's court. He had no dramatic story to tell.

'I was well paid; I had a fat French girlfriend; I had no troubles,' he said to Nathan. 'But, my friend, I was dying of *boredom*. Everyone in the court of the King of France was bored. Even the *king* was bored!' The expression of distaste on Waldemar's face made Nathan laugh.

'Then,' he continued, 'your father came along – and his pack of rascals – and I thought, "Yes! This is what I want!" Companionship, the open road, new sights, new sounds, new people . . .'

'And new women . . .' said Graco drily.

Waldemar shrugged. 'Can I help it if the women of Europe find me so attractive?'

Everyone groaned.

'And what about you, Samson?' Nathan turned his head to look at the blond giant who, although he had been given the largest horse, still looked as though he was perched on a small donkey.

Samson hung his head. 'There is nothing interesting about me.' Nathan shot a puzzled look at the others.

Graco looked exasperated. 'What he means is that he is not a gypsy and he's ashamed of it.'

Nathan laughed as he looked at the big blond man. The fact that he was no gypsy was hardly a surprise. The fact that he was *ashamed* of not being so was ridiculous. Most people would be glad not to be a gypsy!

Then Nathan's mouth dropped open when Graco told him that Samson was only eighteen.

'But . . . but . . . that's only four years older than me!' Suddenly he felt very puny beside this massive man with his deep voice. Nathan reckoned that his own thighs were probably smaller than the muscles at the top of Samson's arms. *How could he be only eighteen?*

Graco told him the story of Samson's lonely childhood in a village not far from where they were at the moment. The youngest of five children – and the largest – he had grown and grown beyond any normal child until he was viewed by his village as being a monster. Gentle though he was, they still treated him as though he were the Devil's spawn and rumours abounded that his widowed mother had got him through some unnatural alliance with the forces of evil. The family were hounded out of the village and took to wandering the countryside, unable to find a place that would allow them to settle.

Then Stefan and his troupe had come along and they took pity on the boy, who was then fourteen. Stefan paid his mother some money and promised to look after him well. His given name of Manfred was abandoned in favour of the name Samson, after the biblical strong man, and the boy found himself the object of admiration instead of curses. He had also found himself a new family.

The sentimental gypsies all had tears in their eyes after Graco finished the story and Samson had turned a deep shade of embarrassed pink.

So now Nathan had heard all their stories and now he knew how his father had become the head of such an assorted group of men – through kindness. He swallowed hard the bitter realization that these men enjoyed being more of a family to Samuel Fox than ever he and his sister could. But although he envied them he did not feel spiteful jealousy. A second realization had followed the first, and that was that these men were also *his* family. They were like a strange pack of kindly uncles who would lay down their lives for the children of their brother Stefan and that made him feel good.

Occasionally, the dense forest would give way to valleys with villages. Graco would casually ask if anyone had heard that a Spanish Army supply squadron was heading this way and he was usually met with hostility, and sometimes horror. Although he was at pains to reassure the villagers that the squadron was not hostile – not as far as he knew – he still provoked the same reaction.

Finally they arrived at a small town and, being weary and cold, they took themselves off to the nearest tavern for some wine. As it was dusk, the tavern was almost empty – most folks had gone home to a warm fire and supper. The innkeeper seemed friendly enough. When they were settled in a corner with a flagon of wine, he came over to talk to them.

'Fighting men, are you?' he enquired, eyeing the bulk of Samson and the state of Nathan's face.

'No,' answered Graco in a friendly manner. 'Horse traders. On the lookout for any good mounts we can buy for our clients.'

The innkeeper looked impressed. 'You won't find much in this town,' he volunteered helpfully, 'but I hear there are some good horses being bred near Haggenau.'

Graco thanked him and said they would be sure to go that way. Then he hesitantly asked if the innkeeper had heard that a Spanish supply squadron was headed this way and to his surprise the man said, 'Yes. It's about a day's march away. God rot them!'

'You don't like the Spanish then?'

The innkeeper snorted. 'I would if they paid their bills!'

'Oh?' Graco shifted in his seat with excitement. Nathan sensed that Graco felt that an opportunity was about to present itself.

'I'll show you something,' the man said, and disappeared into the back room. The gypsies looked at each other and grinned. The innkeeper reappeared with a sheaf of papers which he slammed down on the table.

'Look at those!' he said with feeling, and Graco picked them up and scanned them.

'Requisition slips?' Graco asked, knowing the answer.

'Yes. Bloody requisition slips. Can you see the date?' He jabbed at them with his finger and without waiting for an answer, continued, 'Two years old! They come to this town, they strip the place of all its available provisions and then they bugger off – leaving us with worthless pieces of paper. There's *supposed* to be a District Inspector,' he continued sarcastically, 'who comes round and pays the bills. But we haven't seen one for two years! The Council has sent letters to Spain asking to be paid but we never get any reply. And now, in the middle of winter, when we've got scarcely enough food for ourselves, there's another bloody pack of Spanish soldiers going to descend on us. What are we going to do? I ask you. What are we going to do?'

All the gypsies murmured in sympathy, then Graco stood up and put his arm around the innkeeper's shoulders.

'We are no lovers of Spain,' he said quietly, 'and we may just be able to help you out of this predicament.'

'Oh yes?' said the innkeeper, looking suspicious. 'And just what do you have planned?'

'A little deception – no more. All that you would be required to do is lend us a cart, and some empty barrels and sacks, and we will return with them full of provisions for you.'

'Lend you a cart? Do you think I'm soft or something? How do I know you won't run off with it?'

'Because, sir, we shall leave you our dear friend Waldemar here as a hostage.'

Waldemar smiled pleasantly and gave every impression that he did not mind at all being left behind in this warm comfortable inn. The innkeeper peered at him.

'Hmm.' He was still not convinced. 'And what do *you* get out of all this?'

All we would ask, my friend, is that when the Spanish come to you to requisition your provisions you . . . how can I put it? . . . *delay* them a little . . . take your time getting the stuff together?' Graco looked at the innkeeper and winked.

'I don't want no trouble,' the man said, but Nathan could see that he was warming to the idea. 'Let me get this straight.' He needed to go over it once more. 'I give you a cart, some empty barrels and some empty sacks. You go off and leave your friend here with me as surety . . .'

'Right.'

'. . . You return with provisions and give them to me.'

'Right.'

'When the Spanish come, I let them have the provisions but I take a couple of days getting them together.'

'Right.'

'But I don't make any money out of it?' There was the flaw in the plan as far as he could see – but Graco had an answer.

'You might do . . . we'll see. But you certainly won't *lose* any money.'

There was a pause and then the man nodded.

'I must be mad but I'll go along with it. When do you want the stuff?'

'How about now?' Graco said energetically. 'Might as well strike while the iron is hot. You said that they are about a day's march from here. Then we need to be on our way!'

The wine was downed and they all trooped out the back of the inn to hitch up the cart and horses and load up the empty barrels and sacks.

'Just one more thing,' said Graco, before they had finished. 'I need to buy – *buy*, mind you – a cask of your best wine.' Pearce had given him some money before they set out, so he flourished a full leather purse at the innkeeper who instantly located a cask, which Samson loaded. Graco removed a phial from one of his bags and, while the innkeeper was kept busy by Waldemar, he took out the bung in the cask and poured all the contents of the phial into the wine.

'Couldn't you leave me the big one, instead of him?'

237

asked the innkeeper hopefully, pointing at Samson. 'He would certainly be useful around here.'

'Sorry,' said Graco, climbing up into the wagon. 'We need him. He's an important part of the plan.' Then the others mounted up and they all clattered out of the courtyard, leaving Waldemar and the innkeeper in each other's company.

'Just what *is* the plan?' asked Nathan curiously, once they had left the inn.

Graco winked. 'We are going to steal the Spanish provisions and give them to our friend the innkeeper, so that he can sell them back to the Spanish, without them realizing they are buying back their own stuff. And we are going to make sure that the Spanish are held up for a few days while we prepare an ambush.'

'And just how are you going to do that?'

'You'll see,' answered Graco mysteriously and the other gypsies just grinned at Nathan.

The light was beginning to fade very quickly and Nathan feared that he would be unseated from his horse by a tree branch because he could no longer see.

'Get into single file behind the cart!' called out Graco. 'These horses seem to know this road blindfolded. It must be a regular run for them.'

So everyone gradually fell into a line and they trundled on through the dark.

Eventually, they smelt smoke and heard men's voices up ahead. Then, through the trees, they saw a great fire blazing and smelt roasting meat. As they came into the clearing, Nathan could see that they had found their Spanish squadron sooner than expected. The innkeeper had said a day's march but they were less than two hours' cart ride away.

To call it a *Spanish* squadron was something of a misnomer. Almost all the men were Italian, having been recruited in Genoa and, although they swore allegiance to the Spanish Empire and wore the red sash of the Spanish Army, Nathan could tell, just from the briefest of acquaintances, that their hearts and souls were not in this job. It was cold, hard work and these Italians wanted to be in their warm homes with their warm women – so, when the gypsies approached them, they were accepted into the camp with pleasure and allowed to entertain the soldiers. It was with even greater pleasure that they accepted, for the price of a few pennies each, a cup of good Rhenish wine from the gypsies' cask and they invited the men to sit and eat roast pig with them after they had done a bit of juggling and fire-eating.

The captain in charge *was* Spanish and he seemed to be a conscientious individual, although Nathan thought he looked very young for the task. He tried to protest at the entire squadron drinking wine but his objections were ignored. He seemed to have very little authority amongst the Italians. Nathan supposed that for a fine young Spanish officer, being asked to nursemaid supply wagons along the Spanish Road to the Netherlands, in winter, must be a rather ignoble job. Graco had noted that the captain had a particularly fine horse – a Spanish Jennet – which he greatly coveted. His present horse, bestowed upon him at Arnhem by John Pearce, was adequate but nothing more than that. Graco was very discerning about horses and he had pointed out many times that it pained him every time he mounted up.

But, for the moment, there were other matters to attend to. 'You see that there are three wagons,' murmured Graco to Nathan, as they both filled up cups from the cask. 'Two wagons filled with food and one to carry the gold.' He pointed to the third wagon, which was reinforced with steel bands and sat heavier in the snow than the other two.

'Why don't we steal the gold *now*?' asked Nathan.

'Because there are not enough of us to steal the gold *and* keep it safe. No, no. Our job is to delay these men and send you for reinforcements.'

The wine cask was soon emptied, so Graco and Nathan put on a display of diabolo work. As they did so, it was evident that the audience was gradually becoming quieter. After about fifteen minutes every soldier in the camp was asleep. Soundly, deeply asleep and snoring.

The gypsies stood in the middle of the camp and looked around, half-smiles on their faces.

'Right!' said Graco quietly. 'These men will now sleep for at least eight hours but we must move fast. Samson,

240

start unloading their provision wagon and transferring their stuff into our friend's barrels and sacks. Manolo and Pedro, I hereby give you permission to relieve the sleeping men of any money or jewellery. Pepe and Nathan, I want you to go round every man and cut up the soles of one boot out of every pair . . .'

'Why not both boots?' asked Pepe.

'Because it would take you twice as long! Anyway, the idea is to slow them down by making their journey awkward. Not even I would be so cruel as to strand a man out here in the snow without any boots at all. Where is the sport in that?'

So Nathan and Pepe set about ruining the soles of one boot on each man. Nathan followed the example of Pepe, who was slicing each left boot in a cross shape, so that the leather would split after a few hundred yards of walking.

Graco began to assist Samson in his work. The blond giant picked up each Spanish barrel – bearing the Genoese crest and the insignia of the Spanish Army – as though it were a small fluffy kitten. Some of the barrels contained Italian wine, which had not travelled well, judging by the face Graco pulled when he took the bung out of the first cask.

'Pure vinegar!' Nathan heard him comment. 'No wonder they were so eager to drink the wine we brought.'

The Italian wine was poured into the empty barrels

241

provided by the innkeeper. Other Spanish barrels contained salted pork and the contents, again, were transferred into the innkeeper's empty, unmarked barrels. Flour was transferred from marked sacks to unmarked and so on, until the job was completed.

Manolo and Pedro had performed their task with great speed and thoroughness and they laid before Graco two small mountains of gold jewellery and leather purses filled with coins.

'Excellent, excellent!' beamed Graco. 'Now, we must take both the Spanish food wagons and their empty containers. Manolo and Pedro, tie your horses behind one; Pepe and Nathan, tie your horses behind the other. Samson and I shall take the innkeeper's cart. The gold wagon shall stay with the squadron and we shall liberate it later. And . . .' he darted nimbly to the corral of horses belonging to the sleeping squadron, 'I shall give this beauty a new master,' and he untied the pretty Spanish Jennet and led her to the cart. Everyone else grinned and Graco made a face of mock astonishment. 'I am doing the captain a favour!' he protested. 'This horse is much too high-spirited for such a young man. I shall give him the Flanders carthorse in exchange.' Nathan wished that he could see the captain's face when he woke in the morning.

That task completed, Graco boarded the front of the innkeeper's cart and Samson led the way back through the dark wood, with the Spanish wagons following behind. Fortunately there was a full moon which shone intermittently through the thick forest and made the snow on the road gleam. The journey back to the small town seemed easier and they were soon in the innkeeper's yard, where a patient Waldemar was curled up asleep on a bale of hay. The innkeeper, unsure of when they would return, had gone to his bed and Graco decided not to wake him. The innkeeper's horses were unhitched and the cart, fully laden with the Spanish Army provisions, was pushed into a corner of the stable.

Graco divided the gold jewellery and coins into three piles.

'One portion is for us – to help pay for our travels this winter.' He winked at Nathan and continued, 'One portion is for John Pearce, to do with as he wishes, and the third portion is for our friend the innkeeper,' and he handed that over to Waldemar, with instructions to tell the innkeeper in the morning to keep his side of the bargain and keep the Spanish squadron in town for at least two days.

The gypsies were now going to take the Spanish wagons and hide deep in the woods until Nathan came back with the mercenaries. Waldemar would stay until the squadron was ready to resume its journey and then he would come and alert his friends.

'How will he find you?' Nathan asked Pepe, as they set off on the forest road, back towards Mainz.

'Gypsy signs,' said Pepe. 'Graco will leave them on

trees when we leave the road and go into the forest. He will make marks that are secret and known only to gypsies.'

After a few miles the first wagon stopped. Graco climbed down and came back to Nathan.

'Here is where we part, young Master Fox,' he said jovially. 'You will now take your excellent horse – that I chose for you – and you will ride as hard as you can to fetch the others. Tomorrow, at this time, one of us will be here, at the edge of the road, watching out for you. If the Spaniards should make a move early, then we will come to meet you. But they won't.' He laughed at the success of his plan. 'By the time they have woken, cold through to the bone, discovered that they have no food and drink and have hobbled into the town, they will not want to leave for at least two days. I would stake my life on that. So,' he added, 'ride swiftly but do not overtire your horse. Let the animal drink, but not eat, during the journey and allow at least two hours' rest before you return. Take care, my friend, and tell John Pearce that we shall have everything prepared for a most excellent ambush.'

Nathan nodded, mounted his lively horse and began to trot around the wagons. Graco climbed up again and Nathan turned to see them disappearing slowly into the forest until all that was left was a faint cry of 'Take care, Nathan Fox – we shall see you soon!'

PREPARATION

$\mathcal{I}$t was not possible to ride at full pelt. There had been a fresh fall of snow during the night and the morning sun was making it softer underfoot, so Nathan rode his horse as quickly as he could without putting either of them in danger of slipping. More than once, the animal lost its footing and slithered to a halt, making Nathan dismount and walk alongside to reassure it before he could continue once more.

Nathan realized, during the journey, that it had been a long time since he had been completely on his own and he was not happy without company. Unwelcome thoughts continually crept into his mind. He began to remember Isabella's face and, for the first time in several days, his bruised cheekbone began to ache in the cold wind as though sensation in that part of his face was linked to the memories he was now dredging up. He wondered if Friar Lodowick had kept his promise to save Isabella and her brother from the evil Angelo.

All efforts to push her out of his mind only resulted in the thoughts being replaced with worries about his sister Marie and his father. *If the owner of the relic made contact with the Grande Dame would Carlos Casado harm Marie? Or would he keep his promise to look after her? Would his father be safe, all alone on the Isle of Marken, or would Lord Harcourt find out where he was hiding and go after him?* All these concerns kept nagging at him and, try as he did, he could not think of anything else.

So, it was with great relief that, as dusk was beginning to fall, he saw in the distance the barn where his comrades were housed. He spurred his horse into a gallop.

The snow had muffled his horse's hoofs, so when he opened the barn door, there was an immediate sound of drawing steel and the cocking of pistols. He stood, rigid with shock, hoping no one would accidentally shoot him, and for a few anxious seconds there was silence, until the men burst into loud, appreciative pandemonium as they realized Nathan had returned.

The Silver brothers flew at him, almost knocking him over – they were so glad to see him. From their garbled sentences Nathan gathered that Groesbeck had whiled away the time forcing them to have more Dutch lessons. Pearce strode up with a mug of mulled ale in his hand and proffered it to his friend.

'Please tell me that you and the others have been successful,' he said with a grin. 'After all this waiting, we are desperate to complete the mission.'

Nathan took a large grateful gulp of the warm ale and felt it travel, like a ball of fire, down to his belly. This set up a fearsome growl from his gut and George Silver sniggered.

'Yes, we were successful,' said Nathan, happy once more to be in the company of his friends, 'but please can I have some food before I tell you everything!'

One of de Ferm's men brought him some thick soup and large chunks of fresh bread and he sat and ate as fast as he could, while all the men in the barn watched him in silence. The only sound to be heard was the occasional chuckle from the Silver brothers and Nathan found it difficult to eat while being the object of such intense scrutiny.

As he wiped the last of his bread around the bowl, he belched loudly and settled back with a grin to tell his story. When he got to the part about Graco drugging the Spanish squadron, some of the men gave whistles of loud appreciation. De Ferm and Pearce laughed out loud when he told them about stealing the soldiers' provisions and giving them to the innkeeper so that he could sell them back to them when they hobbled into town. Groesbeck tutted when Nathan produced a cloth parcel full of gold jewellery and coins and explained that the gypsies had kept some of the booty to 'finance them through the winter'. This earned the humourless Dutchman a glare from de Ferm and a raspberry blown by Toby Silver.

Pearce was very pleased and said so. Nathan told him of Graco's promise to prepare an 'excellent' ambush and Pearce was even more satisfied.

'Our friends have done well, and since the Spanish Army will take at least two days to re-equip and have their boots mended, we can afford to let you and your horse rest before we set out in the morning.'

Nathan gladly ate some more soup as he elaborated on some of the details of his adventure to the Silver brothers, who kept plying him with questions.

Before he settled down for the night, he went into the adjoining, smaller barn and made sure his horse had eaten well. He stroked the nut-brown face and the animal nuzzled his cheek appreciatively. Graco was right – they made a good team and he would be sorry to part company with the horse when the mission was completed.

She was a responsive mount, always receptive to his unspoken commands – no more than a light pressure with his thighs would make her speed up and a gentle tug on the reins would make her slow down. 'You are a queen amongst horses,' he murmured in her ear and she replied with a soft whinny of appreciation.

There had been no further falls of snow during the night and the sun was shining weakly when they all saddled up in the morning.

The farmer who had given them refuge came out to

see them off. Pearce rewarded him with some gold coins and he, in turn, presented them all with parcels of bread and sausage to sustain them for the journey.

They set off silently, cloaks drawn around them against the cold, and many men had hats pulled over their bald heads or scarves wound around their necks and mouths. It was a jaw-numbing cold and Nathan's battered cheekbone began to ache once more.

They made good time. Nathan led the way, flanked on either side by the Silver brothers, who spent the journey vowing revenge on Groesbeck, who had now assumed the role of 'official torturer' in their eyes. *It is a shame,* he thought, *that Jan Groesbeck cannot see that George and Toby have learned more Dutch from idle chatting with de Ferm's men than ever they have in his tedious lessons!*

Again, it took the best part of a day to reach the forest road where Nathan had parted from the gypsies. Once they had entered the mighty Palatinate Forest, the road and the trees were featureless and Nathan began to panic about finding the exact spot. Pedro had mentioned 'gypsy signs', but he had never shown Nathan any of them, so he had no idea what he was looking for.

Suddenly, a disembodied voice called out, 'It's about time, Nathan Fox! We thought you would never return!'

The small army of riders pulled up sharply and scanned the trees on either side of the road for any signs of life, but there were none.

'Look upwards, my friends!' said the voice, with a laugh, and they all looked up into the grey sky.

There, hanging on an almost invisible rope, like a monkey, was Graco. He let go of the rope with one hand and saluted cheekily. The rope was strung between the trees above the road, very high up. Another rope was strung about five feet above the first. Graco swung athletically around the lower rope, moved hand over hand to its end and climbed down the tree.

'How high is that rope?' whispered Toby Silver nervously to Nathan, who smiled, remembering that both the Silver brothers had no head for heights.

'About twenty feet,' Nathan answered casually and he saw Toby's Adam's apple move up and down the full length of his neck in a frightened gulp.

Graco strolled over to Pearce and shook his hand.

'We have spent the last two days constructing this network of ropes.' He made a great sweep with his arms and Nathan noticed that the trees on either side of them also had hidden rope constructions in the branches. 'Tomorrow, at dawn, we will show you how it all works, so your men can position themselves for the ambush.'

Pearce nodded happily and slapped Graco on the shoulder with approval.

'Waldemar has not yet appeared from the town,' Graco continued, 'and we do not expect him until at least noon tomorrow. So your men can come and camp with

us in the woods and at first light tomorrow we shall prepare everything.'

Graco gave a low whistle and the Spanish captain's
horse trotted obediently out of the woods to allow her
new master to vault into the saddle. Nathan marvelled
at Graco's talent with horses. In two days he had made
the horse his own and she was now trained to obey his
every command.

Graco led the way through the forest, which was
almost pitch black now that the sun had fully set, but he
had brought a glass lantern with a lighted candle inside,
which he held aloft, so that everyone could follow safely.
Eventually they came to a small clearing where the
gypsies had built a roaring fire and cleverly constructed
a large tent using the sides of the Spanish wagons as the
back and the oiled cloths that had been in the wagons as
a roof and two sides. Everyone dismounted and tied
their horses to the trees around the clearing and then
they crowded into the tent to eat their supper and settle
down to sleep.

Men huddled together, sharing cloaks and body
warmth in an attempt to get some sleep. De Ferm's men,
used to the rough outdoor life, soon began to snore,
while the others found it more difficult. Nathan, George
and Toby clung to each other in a corner of the tent and
were rewarded by being offered the broad back of the
giant Samson to lean against. It was like having a warming pan against their bodies and they soon began to feel

drowsy. Groesbeck, Nathan noted, preferred his own company, which was just as well, since none of de Ferm's men offered him a place in their huddles.

Pearce and Graco sat apart from everyone, by the fire, their cloaks wrapped around them, talking earnestly and occasionally drawing diagrams in the snow by their feet. Nathan felt reassured that the two cleverest men he knew – apart from Walsingham and his own father – were planning tomorrow's ambush.

18

AMBUSH

*I*t was agreed that the gypsies and Nathan would position themselves on the tightrope across the road. No one else was keen to go up that high, apart from John Pearce, and he was needed at ground level. Some of de Ferm's men were happy to be on the rope structures within the trees at either side of the road. This meant that they would only have to climb up to branches which were, at most, about eight feet from the ground.

The object of Graco's 'spider's web' was to allow the men to swing out on the ropes and knock the squadron off the backs of their horses – and this had to be practised. Graco was adamant that, if possible, no horses should be hurt. This was for several reasons, he explained: firstly, he disliked the business of putting maimed horses down and, secondly, he would sell the horses in Mainz for a tidy sum. *More for the gypsies' 'winter fund'!* thought Nathan, with a smile. There was also a firm instruction given that no one was to yell as they swung out on their ropes because this would make the horses rear and make the likelihood of hitting a horse, rather than a man, more probable.

So they had to practise. Therefore, Samson was recruited. The amiable giant, who was roughly the same height as the average horse's head, would trot towards the ambush point and the men would swing out and attempt to vault over his head, as though they were flying over a horse's head and their feet were making contact with a soldier's chest. This seemed to Nathan to be a risky proposition for Samson. On the first attempt Nathan swung out from the tightrope and duly arched his back to sail over Samson's head. However, he misjudged and clipped the giant's shoulder as he went past. As he hit the ground he decided that making contact with Samson was rather like striking a brick wall. He resolved that his next attempt would be better judged and he limped back towards the trees to climb aloft again. The gypsies had no such trouble and Nathan wondered if they had ever done this kind of exercise in one of their entertainments. One by one, they sailed over Samson's head, let go of their ropes and landed firmly on their feet.

Then it was the turn of de Ferm's men to practise their ambush. Their aim was to swing out and clasp Samson round the chest with their legs. This proved difficult for de Ferm's men and caused great hilarity amongst the gypsies. Again Samson trotted along the road at a horse's pace (which Nathan thought was a comical sight in itself) then the men, one by one, were supposed to swing out of the trees, legs wide open to grasp the giant. This tactic was abandoned when three of the men sustained painful injuries to their groins and had to lie face down in the snow to relieve the pain.

Graco, unused to people who were not acrobatic and could not control the velocity of their bodies in mid-flight, devised another exercise. This time, the men had to judge Samson as the head of the horse, and swing out the split second he passed, with their legs together, the theory being that they would knock off the rider on the horse's back. This was more successful. Toby and George Silver, who had volunteered for this job, proved to be surprisingly adept at picking the right moment, so that, in the end, they were actually brushing Samson's back as he passed. Everyone else – Pearce, de Ferm, Groesbeck and the rest of the men – would step out of the trees with pistols cocked and swords drawn, when the bulk of the riders had been felled.

They practised the ambush for a couple of hours until Graco called a halt. The biting cold was making it difficult for even gloved hands to grasp the ropes prop-erly. Then, as if he were possessed of some sixth sense, Graco turned and said, 'Waldemar is coming. Everyone to their positions! Warm your hands and get ready!'

Pearce had given them a talk before they had left the

camp that morning and Nathan remembered the instructions as he climbed up to the tightrope once more.

'I would like you all to reflect that there is no valour in unnecessary killing,' had been Pearce's surprising opening remark and Nathan had seen de Ferm raise a puzzled eyebrow.

'If we can take this gold without shedding too much blood, then it will be to our honour,' Pearce had continued. 'Her Majesty is most anxious that no act of brutality is laid at her door. If we can take the gold and leave the squadron alive to report back to Philip of Spain, then I would deem it a personal favour.'

De Ferm's men merely shrugged. De Ferm spoke up for them.

'We have all had our fill of killing in this war. It will be an interesting challenge to leave the enemy with a bloody nose and no more.'

So it was to be a fight but not to the death – unless it was unavoidable. No problem for those who had been taught by Master Robey. Nathan remembered his first lesson at the School of Defence, where the Master had taught him all the different ways to maim, but not kill, an opponent in a sword fight. Whether de Ferm's men would be able to exercise such control was another matter.

By the time Nathan reached his position on the tightrope, Waldemar was galloping up to Graco and breathlessly reporting that the squadron was no more than half an hour behind him. He and his horse were spirited away, and within seconds Waldemar, the agile wire-walker, positioned himself in the previously empty space alongside Nathan with a broad grin on his face. Men were checking their belts to make sure that their pistols and swords were firmly in place – for once they had swung out on their ropes and knocked off a rider, they would be in hand-to-hand combat.

There was a noise from below and Nathan realized that Graco and Pearce had devised a sure way to make the squadron stop. The Spaniards' own wagon, the one that the gypsies had stolen from them, had been stripped of its tentage and was being trundled out into the middle of the road, just behind the tightrope array. The soldiers would see the wagon and slow down – then the mercenaries would, literally, swing into action.

The next half an hour seemed like an eternity to Nathan, standing twenty feet up, balanced on the rope. The arches of his feet began to ache and the cold was beginning to seep into his bones. All the men who were to swing out on ropes were unable to wear any loose clothing, such as cloaks, and so they were feeling the cold more than the others.

Finally, they heard the sound of many horses' hoofs thudding on the frozen earth, and then, around a bend in the road, came the Spanish captain and his Italian soldiers. Nathan felt a surge of excitement and his breath began to shudder a little in his chest. Closer and closer the squadron came, thankfully not looking up into the trees – although Graco had sited the tightrope array so that it was just before another bend in the road and the men aloft were camouflaged by the treetops beyond. The captain then caught sight of his stolen wagon and his horse faltered a little, before he spurred it on to a trot and his men followed at the same pace. As they came within range, every muscle in Nathan's body was taut, waiting for the signal – a whistle from Graco, who was two men away from him on the tightrope. When it came, Nathan vaulted off the rope and swung his lower body through 180 degrees at tremendous speed. As his feet came level with his waist he saw the terrified face of his target. The man just had time to open his mouth in horror before Nathan's feet skimmed over his horse's head and hit him full square in the chest, knocking him backwards off the horse. Nathan let go of the rope and with two feet together he jumped on to the horse's rump and immediately off again on to the road. The dazed soldier sat upright for a brief moment before the toe of Nathan's boot made sickening contact with his jaw and he slumped back unconscious.

The ambush had degenerated into a free-for-all. There were men on the ground who had been laid out either by contact with the road, or by an ambusher's boot, or by the butt of a pistol. Many of them were in danger of being trampled to death by the horses that were rearing and backtracking in terror.

'GET THE HORSES OUT OF THE WAY!' Nathan screamed at the top of his voice, grabbing two horses by their reins and dragging them to the side of the road. Those who had heard him began to follow suit and soon there were fewer hoofs flailing about in the melee of men in the centre of the road. As Nathan turned back into the fray, an Italian soldier lunged at him with a knife and although Nathan ducked swiftly, the knife caught his arm, ripping his sleeve. He charged at his assailant, head-butting him in the stomach and sending him crashing to the ground, winded. Then he grabbed the man's head by his hair, lifted it up and swiftly applied the lesson he had learned from Carlos Casado – a hard punch to the temple. The man's head lolled backwards and fell from Nathan's grasp, which allowed him to momentarily nurse the hand that had delivered the punch. Casado hadn't bothered to tell him that punching a man's head would hurt like hell. He flexed his fingers and was relieved that none were broken.

Toby Silver had also punched a soldier, who reeled backwards, where he flipped over the still-kneeling Nathan. The soldier attempted to scrabble to his feet but Nathan decided to administer another kick and the man only made it to his knees before being knocked out. *Yes, a much better way of laying a man out than using my fists,* he thought with satisfaction.

Samson was busy going up behind soldiers and banging their heads together, while Graco was creeping up behind any other soldiers who were still standing and calmly pressing his thumbs hard into the neck area under the ears, making them black out. De Ferm's men seemed to be having a good scrap with all their chosen opponents. Nathan assumed that they were enjoying themselves, as most of them had grim smiles on their faces, even though all of them seemed to have bloody noses, black eyes or fat lips. Pretty soon they were the only men still fighting, a small knot of activity in what seemed a sea of groaning bodies.

Pearce, De Ferm and Groesbeck had been surplus to requirements. No weaponry had been used, save for the odd pistol butt against a soldier's head, so they began to drag the bodies over to the side of the road. Nathan was collared by Manolo, who wanted his help to dismantle the tightrope, and soon the gypsies were swarming all over the trees, throwing ropes down to the road.

'Well,' said de Ferm heartily, slapping Pearce on the back, 'a squadron of unconscious soldiers and miles of rope. I wonder what we should do next?'

Pearce laughed and they set about dragging the soldiers upright and tying them to the trees by the road. De Ferm's men made short work of it and soon every tree for a hundred yards, on each side of the road, boasted a soldier decorating its trunk. Not one man had been killed.

Groesbeck had busied himself with trying to open the two chests of gold that were strapped to the wagon, before Samson pushed him gently aside and pulled the locks apart effortlessly with his bare hands.

Everyone gathered around, stared silently at the gleaming gold coins and smiled. Nathan's mouth dropped open at the sheer brilliance of the newly minted gold and he could not resist stretching out a hand and running it through the top layer of coins to hear the satisfying chink of so much money.

'You will die for this! King Philip will send a whole army after you now. You will never leave this country alive!' a voice croaked in desperation from one of the trees. The Spanish captain had revived.

Pearce walked up to him and spat on the ground.

'Philip could send a hundred armies after us, my friend, but if they are all like you, we won't lose any sleep worrying about it!' The gypsies, and those of de Ferm's men who spoke Spanish, laughed loud and hard and the captain glared at them, unable to do anything else.

Pearce then gave instructions for the squadron's horses to be rounded up. All the soldiers' horses had leather saddlebags, which Pearce decided would be transferred to their horses and the gold coins would be split up, so that each man would carry a load.

Once again, the gypsies climbed aboard the two provision wagons and took charge of them. Nathan laughed and pointed out to the Silver brothers that Graco and his friends were stealing back the provisions that they had stolen originally, then given to the innkeeper, who had then sold them to the soldiers.

'They can sell them again!' crowed Toby Silver ecstatically but Pearce shook his head.

'No, I have plans for those,' was his enigmatic reply.

As they set off in the direction of Mainz – the small army of mercenaries, plus two wagons and a drove of captured horses – Waldemar called out to the tree-tied soldiers, 'Don't worry, my friends! The innkeeper is coming this way tomorrow to go to market. He will rescue you. You will only have to spend one night in the cold!'

The chorus of laughter from the gypsies and their comrades drowned out the curses emanating from the men they were leaving helpless and humiliated with only the trees for company.

A BITTER PARTING

*J*he mood was one of jubilation as they rode along the road back towards Mainz. Nathan felt the satisfying weight of the gold in the saddlebags behind him and laughter bubbled in his throat. Toby and George were full of themselves, constantly recounting to each other the blows they had struck and the blows they had dodged. Each telling of the stories became more and more elaborate as the journey progressed.

De Ferm and his men seemed happier than they had been for a long time and de Ferm himself confessed to Pearce that there had been great satisfaction in taking the gold with no loss of life. It had been a greater humiliation for the Spanish captain, and this had added to his enjoyment. Pearce just nodded contentedly. Nathan had become used to Pearce's lack of emotion when he was on a mission. *He prefers to focus on the task at hand,* thought Nathan.

Only the gypsies seemed a little subdued, and Nathan

found this puzzling. Whatever was troubling them was, perhaps, none of his business but in any event he did not want to spoil their little army's mood of exultation.

It was dark when they arrived back at the barn where they had rested before. The farmer was pleased to see them – even more so when they offered him the pick of the horses they had 'liberated' from the squadron – and soon, men and horses were feeding handsomely in their allotted quarters.

It was then, after they had eaten, that Nathan realized what was troubling the gypsies.

Samson, accompanied by Graco, approached John Pearce with a request.

'Samson wants to visit his family,' said Graco. 'They are not far away from here and he is a little homesick. He would like to pay them a visit and meet up with us later.'

Nathan could tell by the set of his face that Pearce was not happy with this.

'It is not convenient,' he said, shaking his head.

Samson hung his head and looked miserable.

'It is only one man – what difference would it make?' said Graco with anger in his voice. All the other men in the barn were listening but pretending not to, their heads bowed to some imaginary task. *Surely Pearce will let him go*, thought Nathan.

Pearce spoke calmly. 'Samson is worth ten men if we find ourselves in a situation where we need brute strength. We have this gold to get back safely to Amsterdam. I cannot afford to let him go off on some sentimental jaunt.'

The last two words were spoken with contempt. *It is unlike John to be so harsh!* Nathan was embarrassed for Samson.

Graco's eyes glittered. 'We have made the capture of this gold easy for you, my friend,' he reminded Pearce coldly, 'and we have done you good service in all other respects.'

Pearce nodded his head. 'I do not deny that your work has been invaluable. But the mission must come before all personal considerations.'

'We are not Walsingham's paid lackeys!' Graco hissed venomously. 'You have no power over us. We do what we do for our brother Stefan and his family. What do we care for your English queen and country? Neither welcomes the gypsy brotherhood.'

Nathan knew Graco was right.

'Nevertheless—' Pearce began.

'The boy is going to visit his mother,' cut in Graco. 'He will take a barrel of flour and a barrel of wine. These are our share of the provisions. There will be no further discussion.' Graco turned to the gypsies. 'Come!' he barked. 'We will sleep with the horses tonight.'

With that the gypsies stood and left the barn. Nathan was mortified and he decided to go out to the gypsies and apologize to them, but Pearce swiftly crossed the barn and blocked his exit.

'Go back to your place, Nathan,' he said quietly.

'I want to talk to my friends.'

'Go back to your place . . . that is an order.'

Nathan looked at Pearce, hardly able to recognize him. He hesitated but Pearce's eyes never wavered from his face.

'You *are* in the employment of Sir Francis Walsingham and therefore you *will* obey me.'

Nathan flushed an even deeper red and unwillingly went back to his place by the Silver brothers. They looked at him with wide eyes, astonished by the argument between him and Pearce. No one could think of anything to say and it seemed as if the happy mood of the day had been lost forever.

Nathan lay down in the straw, his heart thudding with confusion and anxiety. He thought he *knew* Pearce. He never would have imagined his friend would risk losing the respect of those he worked with. He had a momentary surge of hatred towards Groesbeck when he heard the Dutchman mutter, 'It's about time those gypsies were put in their place.'

All Nathan could think about was the injustice of it all. *Pearce would never have been able to take the gold without Graco and the others preparing the way*, he thought. It seemed so stupid to be stubborn about such a little thing as Samson visiting his family. Perhaps Pearce was tired and the strain was beginning to tell. He looked over to where Pearce was sitting – hoping that he would make eye contact and receive some reassuring sign – but Pearce had rolled over on to his side with his back towards Nathan and there was no reassurance to be had.

In the morning Samson had gone. He had taken one of the wagons, a barrel of flour and a barrel of wine, as Graco had promised – no more, no less. The gypsies had saddled up their horses and were sullenly waiting for everyone else to get ready. Nathan caught one defiant look that passed between Graco and Pearce but there were no words spoken. He went towards Graco but was sharply called away by Pearce, who seemed determined to keep him from speaking to the gypsies.

When they arrived at the quayside in Mainz, the two boats were still moored where they had left them, but now they had more horses to transport, Graco having insisted that the squadron's horses would fetch a better price in the Netherlands. Pearce decided that all the horses would go in one boat with the remaining wagon. The gypsies and Nathan were to look after the horses and two of de Ferm's men would be their mariners. Everyone else would go in the second boat.

This caused Groesbeck some concern and he took Pearce to one side.

'Is it wise to put all the gold in the boat with the gypsies? Let me go and guard it.'

Nathan, who overheard this remark, was about to protest at the implication that the gypsies would steal the gold, when he felt Pearce's hand close around his wrist like a vice – a warning to be silent.

'Nathan will be there to guard the gold. In any event, the gypsies are on a boat, in the middle of the river. How are they going to steal anything?'

Groesbeck looked doubtful and gave Nathan a suspicious look. *He's thinking about the fact that I am also a gypsy.* Pearce's grip on Nathan's wrist tightened, so he contented himself with giving Groesbeck a baleful look and the man obviously thought better of making any further comment and turned away.

Pearce released Nathan's wrist and looked at him steadily.

'Well done,' he said, and they both knew that he was referring to the fact that he had kept his mouth shut. 'Now go and do your duty on the boat.'

Nathan scanned Pearce's face, hoping to see a glimmer of his old friend and confidante, but Pearce remained impassive. *This mission has changed him*, he thought bitterly as he turned away to board the boat.

The journey back down the Rhine to Arnhem was less dramatic than before. The Lorelei Rock seemed nothing more than a rock and there were no Spanish soldiers standing menacingly on the cliffs.

When they came to the part of the journey where they were once more towed by the giant Brabançon horses, Nathan remembered that he and Samson had stood together watching the horses on the journey up the river.

'Will we see Samson again?' Nathan asked Waldemar, who was standing alongside him at the rail.

'For sure!' Waldemar seemed astonished that Nathan could think that Samson was gone forever. 'Samson is happy with us. Happier than he has ever been in his life. We will see him again when we reunite with your father.'

The mention of Samuel Fox made Nathan's stomach flip over. Suddenly he felt concern for all those they had left behind in the Netherlands – his father, Marie and Isabella. *Were they safe?* Then he felt guilty that he had not given them any thought at all in the last few days. There was something to be said for being dispassionate like John Pearce.

When they stopped for the night and attempted to get some rest, Nathan tried to talk to Graco about the bad feeling between him and Pearce but Graco refused to be drawn.

'You are not responsible for other people's words or actions, Nathan, so stop worrying about it,' Graco wisely counselled. 'None of this affects the friendship between you and me, so just leave it be. Gypsies never get involved in other people's disputes if they can help it. We have enough troubles of our own. Remember that.'

The next day, the river became grey and flat and widened out. There was enough wind to use the sails and they began to pick up speed. If they could make Arnhem before curfew, they would be able to moor at the quayside and get some hot food at the nearest tavern.

This was their plan, but as they approached the city, the wind brought them the unmistakable odour of burning flesh. Nathan began to feel like retching and the gypsies all fell to their knees and began to pray. The horses became agitated and their prancing made the boat sway furiously in the water. There was a glow beyond the city walls which signalled that the fires that they had witnessed being built when they last passed through Arnhem were now burning fiercely. In deadly silence they threw lines to the men on the quay for tying up.

The smell was unbearably putrid and everyone was holding their cloaks or pieces of cloth over their faces. It was unspoken amongst them but there was no desire to stay in Arnhem. Although it was dark, Nathan just wanted to pass through the horror and get away.

Pearce ran to Nathan's boat and shouted, 'We have less than one hour to get everything off the boats and through the city. It is almost curfew. Move swiftly, for God's sake!'

Once they had disembarked the horses and the wagon, they set off through the city. The streets were deserted. Nathan supposed that the population, having worked themselves up into the frenzy of a witch hunt and the hysteria of the burning, had now taken to their beds, doors and windows shut tight against the acrid smell of their terrible deed.

There was no other way to go through the city, other than past the green by the church of St Eusebius and the burning fires. They passed in silence and watched as the blackened forms that had once been human beings slumped, one by one, into the flames. The stakes had burnt through and, as the terrible structure collapsed into the fire, it sent a shower of sparks into the air which frightened the horses even more.

As they reached the gates of the city, Nathan realized that the wind was in their favour and the terrible smell was being blown out towards the river. At last he was able to breathe without wanting to vomit.

The gates opened and the long train of horses clattered out on to the road. When the last man had passed through the gates, they were closed behind them with a finality and the church bells began to ring out the signal for curfew.

They had come through a vision of hell and each man slowed his horses and gave in to a fit of coughing, weeping or retching.

But ahead of them, in what should have been darkness, were more fires. Not, this time, the fires of a witch hunt, but the fires of hundreds of Spanish mutineers who were laying siege to the city of Arnhem and, as each man on horseback recovered and looked up, he found himself looking at a sea of bedraggled soldiers which stretched as far as the eye could make out in the light of the campfires.

20

DOUBLE-CROSS

Jhe Spaniards looked grim. Their ragged clothes, their makeshift boots made from animal skins and, most of all, their eyes, spoke of a desperation beyond comprehension. For a brief moment Nathan felt compassion for these men, all but abandoned in a cold and wet foreign country by a king who expected them to fight for his Empire without payment or food. Then his compassion was swiftly replaced by fear. Such desperation bred evil acts. He began to notice that the sea of eyes before them were changing subtly from wariness to resolve. Men began to move their hands towards their weapons.

Suddenly a voice rang out from amongst the Spaniards.

'Stay your hands! I know these men!' And from the crowd stepped the Corporal, Pedro Salinas – the leader of the group that Pearce had so wisely helped at the start of their journey.

'This man saved my life and gave my men food,' Salinas explained, pointing to John Pearce, and then he strode up to Pearce and shook his hand.

The Spaniards visibly relaxed – but not for long. Before Salinas could speak further, a horse broke away from the train and rode towards the congregated mutinous soldiers. They scattered as the horse wheeled round and came to rest, its rider now facing towards Nathan and his comrades. It was Groesbeck.

'My friends, these men are your enemies,' he said in perfect Spanish. 'They carry the gold which King Philip sent to pay his army in the Netherlands. They stole it from the squadron that was delivering it!' Then he put his hand into his saddlebag, stretched out his clenched fist and allowed a shower of gold coins to fall to the ground. As they fell, glinting in the firelight, the men around his horse began to scrabble on the ground for the coins. His horse reared and some man cried out in pain, his hand crushed under a horse's hoof.

The look on Groesbeck's face was one of pure triumph. Nathan's own face had frozen in shock. *So he is the double agent!* The shock was replaced by pure anger. No one moved. Even the horses were strangely immobile.

Then there was a sound of pistols being cocked and Nathan realized that both de Ferm's men and a large number of the Spanish soldiers were now pointing weapons at each other. The danger was that someone would start firing indiscriminately and there would be nowhere to hide. His stomach ached with terror and his eyes darted to Pearce's face.

'Put up your weapons! All of you!' Pearce barked in English. Then he repeated himself in Spanish. There was an uncertain pause and Pearce shifted in his saddle to face the men behind him.

'Put up your weapons and throw your saddlebags towards the Spanish.' The tone of his voice was strange – calm but firm, reassuring even. Nathan was confused. *Please God, don't let John Pearce be a double agent as well.* He couldn't face that betrayal.

De Ferm was the first to unhook his saddlebags and throw them on to the ground. His face was impassive and his eyes never left Pearce's face. Nathan knew that if Pearce was a traitor then de Ferm would not let him live. The pain in Nathan's stomach was now so great that he wanted to die – anything to make it stop.

One by one, the others followed de Ferm's lead and soon the saddlebags were piled high on the ground in front of Groesbeck's horse.

Pearce dismounted and addressed Salinas. 'Open them,' he said. He stood quite still while the Corporal walked over to the bags and picked one up. He looked in it and then swore. He turned it upside down and what fell out was not glittering gold but dull, grey pebbles. There was a murmur of disgust from the Spaniards and several of them ran to the pile of bags and began to drag the contents out. More pebbles ... and more. The murmur grew to a howl of rage which found its focus in Groesbeck, whose face seemed to have drained of blood. The Spaniards dragged him from his horse and hauled him up on to the gypsies' wagon. Three pistols were at his throat. The gypsies were pushed off the wagon and the horses were pulled until the wagon was under a tree. Then a rope was produced. The sight of it brought a scream from Groesbeck the like of which Nathan had never heard a human being utter, and at that point he slid off his horse on to his knees, and brought the contents of his stomach up.

Exhausted from retching, his forehead pressed against the ground, Nathan heard Pearce shout 'STOP!' and he raised his head to see Pearce stride over to the wagon and vault up to stand beside Groesbeck.

'This man is a traitor to both England and Spain,' and he pulled the scarf away from around Groesbeck's neck to reveal his scar. 'This scar was not won in battle. It is the scar made by a Dutch rope when the people of Antwerp tried to hang him as a Spanish spy during the Great Siege. His real name is Jan de Groot and he works for whoever pays him. The only gold you will find here, my friends, is the gold paid to him by the Spanish ambassador to France. It is blood money.'

There was a roar from the Spaniards and Groesbeck, or de Groot as they now knew him, buckled at the knees, only to be dragged upright again by Pearce.

'Hang him again and do it properly this time!' shouted a voice from amongst the Spaniards.

But before anyone could act, there was the crack of a pistol shot and Groesbeck's face contorted – his mouth opened in shock – and then he fell face forward, revealing his assassin, Toby Silver, who had crept round behind the wagon and fired at point blank range into the Dutchman's back.

'*Dubbelhartig verraderachtig stuk a braaksel!*' he said, in Dutch, his face twisted into a vengeful smile.

'What did he say?' Nathan asked one of de Ferm's men as he hauled himself up from his knees.

'Double-dealing, traitorous piece of puke,' the man obligingly translated and Nathan almost laughed at Toby's mastery of the language Groesbeck had tried so hard to force into him.

There was now an impasse. The Spaniards had lost the focus of their hatred and Pearce knew there was a real danger that they would turn on the rest of them. It was time to save their skins. He raised his hands and his voice for attention.

'My friends, the dead spy was lying about the gold. We passed the squadron carrying your pay. They are maybe three days' journey away and they will be here soon. Let us pass through safely and we will give you this wagon of food as payment.'

The Spaniards looked to Salinas and the Corporal repeated that Pearce had saved his life and was therefore a man to be trusted. So the bargain was struck. The wagon and its provisions, plus the gold in Groesbeck's saddlebags, were handed over in return for safe passage. The gypsies mounted some of the spare horses and slowly the Spanish army parted to let them through. Pearce disarmed Toby Silver and dragged him back to his horse. Nathan realized that if Toby was to receive any punishment it was tempered by the fact that many of the Spaniards shook his hands as he passed through and called him *'valiente'*, *'valeroso'* and *'un hombre honrado'* ('Courageous', 'brave' and 'a righteous man').

As they rode in silence along the moonlit road, Nathan's mind was in turmoil. *Where is the gold? What has John Pearce done with the gold?*

De Ferm was obviously tormented by the same questions because once the Spanish campfires were left far behind, he pulled his horse over to the side of the road and dismounted, signalling to his men to do the same. Pearce slowed his horse to a halt in front of them and looked at de Ferm with a smile playing about his lips.

'Where is it?' asked de Ferm flatly.

Pearce raised himself up on his stirrups and scanned the dark woodland ahead. Finally his searching gaze stopped and he grinned broadly before sitting down in his saddle again.

'Up ahead, a couple of miles in the distance, you will see the faint glow of a fire,' he answered. '*That* is where you will find the gold and, unless you want to forgo your share of the booty, I suggest that you and your men mount up and make haste.' Pearce urged his horse on and left de Ferm and his men in confusion.

The mercenaries mounted and followed.

'If you play any more games with us we shall have to kill you, John Pearce!' de Ferm shouted in annoyance.

'My games have saved your life, de Ferm, remember that!' Pearce called back from the darkness up ahead.

'My gratitude knows no bounds,' de Ferm muttered sarcastically under his breath but he shot a quick glance at Nathan, who was riding abreast with him.

'Did *you* know that Groesbeck was a Spanish spy?' he asked Nathan accusingly.

'No, I did not!' replied Nathan firmly. 'Neither do I know what John did with the gold. In fact, I don't know anything any more!' He was beginning to feel hurt and excluded. *Why wasn't I party to John's plans? Doesn't he trust me?*

The glow of the fire began to loom large on the horizon and the pace of the riders quickened as they were all anxious to have a satisfactory outcome to this puzzle. Nearer and nearer they came to the fire until they could make out the dark shape of someone hunched in front of it. As they jostled their horses into a semi-circle, some yards from the fire, they found themselves looking at the beaming face of the giant Samson.

'What kept you?' he said jovially and suddenly they all understood.

The men erupted into a frenzy of back-slapping and hugging. Pearce and Graco, who had not spoken since leaving Mainz, were clasped in a congratulatory embrace and Nathan was dragged off his horse by Waldemar, who danced him round in a little jig near the fire.

Once the jubilation had subsided, Samson hauled the huge 'barrel of flour' off the back of the wagon and removed the top to reveal that it was tightly packed with gold coins. The barrel of wine, however, was real, and the bung was swiftly knocked out to toast their successful theft of the Spanish gold.

As they sat round the fire, Pearce and Graco, taking it in turns, told the rest of them how they had hatched the plot to ensure the safe passage of the gold the night before they had actually ambushed the squadron. Samson was chosen to play the homesick boy who needed to visit his mother.

'Didn't you actually visit your mother, then?' interrupted a guileless George Silver.

'My mother lives in Hanover with her second husband!' laughed Samson. 'I saw her only three months ago!'

Despite feeling a little resentful at not being in Pearce's confidence, Nathan began to smile at the inventiveness of the plan.

Graco had decided to create the dispute between himself and Pearce as a means of removing the gypsies from the main barn and allowing them to transfer the gold from everyone's saddlebags (except Groesbeck's) into the empty flour barrel.

Pearce had been thinking ahead. He knew that the Spanish soldiers they had encountered on their way to Arnhem were expecting to be joined by other mutineers and he knew that Groesbeck would pick that moment on the return journey to expose them.

'How long have you known that Groesbeck was a Spanish agent?' asked Nathan.

'From the very beginning. Walsingham's agents in France knew that de Groot had been paid by the Spanish Ambassador to draw us into a plot to steal the gold. De Groot had approached Walsingham pretending to be a Dutch patriot and telling him of the gold shipment and, at the same time, offering his services for the mission. Robey knew he was a spy and so did his men. The only people who did not know were you and the Silver brothers. We did not feel that you were ready to deal with a double agent without showing your true feelings.'

Nathan felt stung by this remark but he knew it to be true. He would not have been able to take lessons with Groesbeck and to behave naturally around him if he had known that the man was a traitor. Even less so in the case of the Silver brothers. Toby's instinctive execution of the spy when he was exposed had demonstrated that.

So Samson had taken the gold by road, which was, in fact, a quicker route than by river. But, as Pearce explained, one man and a wagon of flour and wine would not be stopped in what was, effectively, Spanish-held territory, whereas a small army of mercenaries would have had to fight its way through every province.

It had been a clever ruse. Very clever. Now they had the gold at least one of their missions had been success-ful, reasoned Nathan. The wine hit his empty stomach and his head began to swim. Back in Amsterdam, maybe Marie would be waiting for them with a message from the mysterious 'patriot' who wanted to give England the precious holy relic. Maybe.

DIABOLIC FORCES AT WORK

*I*t had been a tense journey back from Arnhem. Even though they were a considerable force, knowing that they carried six months' back pay for the Spanish army in the Netherlands caused them some anxiety.

Conversation was limited and this gave Nathan time to dwell upon what might await him when they returned to Amsterdam. During the return journey on the River Rhine he had almost persuaded himself that his infatuation with Isabella was stupid. Although he felt a flutter in his stomach every time he pictured her face, it made him resentful. Over the last week or so he had enjoyed the company of men, with its promise of adventure and drama. He never felt so alive as when he was in the midst of a fight or some other escapade. Affairs of the heart seemed, in retrospect, like a living death. The moping and the sleeplessness, the foolishness of being tied to such emotions made him squirm now, when he thought of it.

As they drew nearer to Amsterdam, Nathan began to feel the pressure of his worries about his sister, his father and the unresolved situation with Isabella. It made him feel grumpy – this gradual facing up to his responsibilities. He supposed that it was the reason that so many men – like Pearce, de Ferm and Casado – seemed to prefer a life without any attachments. It was easier. *So confusing! All these decisions!* He decided there and then that he would exercise better judgement regarding girls in the future. His cheekbone was aching again, as if to remind him of his past folly, and he tried, in vain, to think about something else.

The exuberance seemed to have evaporated from most of the men by the time they were hugging the shores of the Zuider Zee once more. The sky was a leaden grey and the men drew their cloaks around them, lost in their own thoughts. *Perhaps this is how it always is,* thought Nathan. *After a great victory there is always a low period.* Will Shakespeare and his other actor friends always used to feel down after a successful play. They would spend a whole week with their nerves taut and their minds racing, lapping up the applause from the audiences and congratulating themselves in the tavern every night. Then, at the end of the week, they would become sombre. The play was over and there was a lull before the next one went into rehearsal. Marie always said that it was the body's way of making you rest after so much excitement.

Marie. Every time Nathan thought of his sister he had a vague feeling of uneasiness which he could not shake off. They had often known when the other was in trouble. It was a measure of their closeness, and Marie always maintained that it was their gypsy blood. Their mother had had the second sight. Marie said that she had not inherited the gift – but she had always turned up at his school or the theatre, unbidden, when she had sensed that Nathan was in trouble. And she had usually been right. Nathan was less gifted than Marie. A typical boy, he usually gave very little thought to his sister. She put food on the table, she washed and mended his clothes. He took her for granted. But sometimes – just now and then – he would feel something. He was feeling like that now – the uneasiness – but he kept shrugging it off as no more than exhaustion and the cold. But still it kept nagging at him.

Finally, they were nearing the Isle of Marken and everyone visibly brightened. De Ferm's men began to talk of the pleasure they would have telling their wounded comrades about the capture of the gold and how it would all be equal shares, whether the men had languished on Marken or fought the Spaniards. Nathan thought that this was fair and he gave de Ferm an approving smile.

The gypsies were anxious to be reunited with their leader again, and Graco called out to Nathan, 'Soon we shall have our spirits lifted by your father! No one can make a herbal brew to revive the spirits like he can!'

Nathan nodded and smiled again. He was beginning to share the gypsies' need to see his father. He wanted reassurance that Marie was safe.

A shout went up from the gypsies and Nathan raised his head. There, up ahead, standing next to a man on horseback, was his father. Samuel Fox had hold of the horse's bridle and his body was arched as he looked up at the man. Then a cart appeared trundling down the road and ... Nathan peered at the black silhouettes against the snow-filled sky ... it was being driven by a nun! His chest tightened, the feeling of uneasiness grew, so he kicked his horse hard into a gallop. The sleet drove into his face. There were others behind him, he could hear the pounding of hoofs and he supposed it was the gypsies. Then he heard his father shouting, 'Nathan! Thank God! John Pearce! God be thanked that you have come at this moment!'

Nathan pulled his horse up sharply to a halt and looked at his father's anguished face. Then he registered that the man on horseback was Carlos Casado and he was bleeding from a wound to his head. The nun in the cart was the Grande Dame.

'What is it? What's wrong?' he asked breathlessly.

'Marie has been denounced as a witch. Sister Beatrice too. They have been taken to Oudewater.' The Grande Dame was frantic.

Casado looked miserable. Nathan turned on him impatiently.

'How did this happen? You were supposed to be looking after her. How could you let this happen?'

'Nathan, for shame!' His father's voice was harsh and near to breaking. 'Can you not see that this young man has been injured trying to protect Marie? Learn the full story before you accuse someone!'

'What has happened to Marie?' Pearce and de Ferm spoke over each other, their concern evident to all. Casado looked at them jealously.

'We're wasting time!' Nathan howled in anguish. All he could see in his mind were the blackened stumps of corpses in Arnhem – the poor devils accused of witchcraft and burned at the stake.

'Nathan!' His father's voice rang out again to silence him.

Nathan slid down off his horse and embraced him. For a moment they stood, father and son locked together in joint misery, and Nathan felt the salt of his father's tears sting his wind-burned cheek.

Samuel Fox held his son at arm's length and looked at him steadily. Then he spoke with great difficulty. 'Marie has only just been taken away. We have time to dress this young man's wound and to listen to explanations. The more we know, the better we are able to deal with the problem.'

Such wisdom brooked no argument and Nathan

nodded in agreement. Then Samuel Fox moved swiftly. Carlos Casado dismounted and sat on the back of the Grande Dame's cart while his wound was quickly cleaned and dressed. By now, the rest of de Ferm's men and the gypsies had ridden up and had formed a solemn wall around the cart, sensing that something was wrong.

'My lady, tell us everything,' Fox said as he worked, and she began her tale.

'It was that terrible girl, Lady Catherine Harcourt, that I foolishly took in as a guest, believing her to be a pious and worthy child. I did not know that she was sent to us to spy and cause grief . . .'

Nathan looked at Casado, who returned his look with an unspoken plea for silence in his eyes. *If only the Grande Dame knew that she had more than one spy in her house of refuge.* He thought about exposing the Spaniard but decided it would be a waste of effort at the moment. Nathan turned his attention back to the story.

'. . . It was on the fifth day, yesterday, that she absented herself from the Béguinage, saying that she wished to visit her father. This she did, apparently, but then they went to Lord Angelo and denounced both Sister Beatrice and Sister Marie as witches. Today, the city guards went to where the two Sisters were ministering to the sick and arrested them. There was fighting – apparently many of Sister Beatrice's patients tried to save them – and this young man –' she pointed to Casado – 'fought valiantly and only just avoided arrest himself. Then he came to me.'

Casado interrupted. 'I wanted to go to Oudewater straight away, to rescue the women, but the Grande Dame persuaded me to come here, with her. She said that there would be more men here who could help release the two Sisters.'

Pearce stepped forward at this point. Nathan could see that the mind was working behind the impassive face. *He is wondering if this is a trap. I know now that he sees what the rest of us cannot.*

'Where are Lord Harcourt, his daughter and your father?' he asked Casado sharply. Samuel Fox paused in his tending of Casado's wound to await the answer.

Casado looked uncomfortable.

'I will speak only in front of you and the boy,' he said quietly.

'And you will speak to me as well,' Samuel Fox said grimly.

Casado nodded and Pearce asked everyone else, including the Grande Dame, to move away. Only Pieter de Ferm stood his ground. Pearce looked at him questioningly.

'Since I shall be part of the rescue party, I want to know everything,' he said stubbornly.

'Who says you will be part of the rescue party?' Pearce sounded aggressive.

'I do. Marie saved my life. I shall save hers. Do you have a problem with that?'

For a moment the two men faced each other and Nathan wanted to shout, *'This is not the time to fight over my sister!'* But sanity prevailed and Pearce just said, 'No, I don't have a problem with that. Stay.' Then he turned back to Casado. 'Well?' he said.

'Harcourt and his daughter have gone to Oudewater to testify against the women. Catherine Harcourt is doing this partly because her father wants to flush Samuel Fox out – and partly because she is jealous of Marie.'

'Why is she jealous of Marie?' Pearce asked suspiciously.

'Because of me,' was the barely audible answer.

There was a sound of de Ferm cocking a pistol and everyone looked at him with surprise.

'If you have been forcing your attentions on Marie, I shall blow your brains out right here,' the Dutchman said savagely.

Pearce looked exasperated and grasped the pistol barrel.

'Shut up and put it away. If you knew Marie Fox a bit better you would know that *no one* forces their attentions on her – not unless they have a death wish. Carry on, Casado . . .' He gave de Ferm a withering look and turned back to the Spaniard.

'Catherine Harcourt tried to force her attentions on *me*

and I rejected her,' he seemed almost embarrassed to relay this information, 'so she therefore assumed that I must be interested in someone else and that "someone" was Marie.'

'You still haven't told us where your father is.'

'He's gone back to England. He is one of Spain's most experienced agents and we . . .' he paused for a moment and then reluctantly continued, '. . . were sent here to retrieve the Spanish gold, if you had managed to take it. But Harcourt made it plain that he was pursuing a personal vendetta against Samuel Fox and he had no interest in our mission. My father told him he wanted no more to do with it. He left on the morning tide. He wanted me to go with him but I refused. I said I would follow when I had rescued the Sisters and when I had . . .' Casado trailed off.

'When you had what?' Pearce was suspicious again.

'Delivered them safely back to the Béguinage, of course.' It was a lame response and Nathan suspected that he had stopped himself before he had mentioned the holy relic. The story about retrieving the Spanish gold sounded false to him. Pearce had said, in Amsterdam, that he believed Casado's mission was primarily to find the relic, and Nathan felt that Pearce was probably right.

The wound was dressed and they were ready to leave. Pearce assembled everyone and stood on the back of the cart to address them.

'We now have two tasks to perform. One, we must

rescue Marie Fox and Sister Beatrice from the fanatics who want to burn them as witches and two, we must guard our precious cargo until it is ready to be sent to England.'

Pearce continued. 'Nathan, de Ferm, Samson and Graco will come with me to rescue the women. The rest of you will go over to the Isle of Marken to be with your comrades and mount a twenty-four-hour guard on our cargo. Understood?'

'I shall come with you,' announced Samuel Fox.

Pearce shook his head. 'Too dangerous. Harcourt is waiting for you.'

'All the better,' replied Fox firmly. 'Now I can settle matters with him.' Pearce looked uncertain so Samuel added, 'You cannot expect me to wait here while my daughter's life is in danger!'

Reluctantly Pearce agreed. Then the Grande Dame spoke up.

'I shall go too.'

'Reverend Mother,' said Pearce in a patient but exasperated voice, 'I appreciate your concern for Sister Beatrice but we shall be riding hard and fast and you will only slow us up.'

'I can ride as well as any man!' she retorted scornfully. 'If I had had a decent horse spare I would have ridden here faster than Carlos Casado. I *will* accompany you and I shall take *that* horse!' She pushed past the men and grasped the bridle of Graco's prized Jennet.

291

'For the love of God, Mother! Not *my* horse!' Graco looked around, pleading for support. Everyone just grinned.

'Here, take mine.' Waldemar brought his own horse forward and patted Graco's back in consolation. 'Never argue with a nun, my friend.'

'We shall need spare horses each so that we can change mounts halfway, and we shall need two spare horses for Marie and Sister Beatrice.' Pearce directed the men into action.

The two largest horses were walked forward for Samson and everyone began to mount up. An extra horse was found for Casado. Nathan's eyes widened as the Grande Dame sat astride her horse like a man. She meant business. Not for her the delicate side-saddle position of a lady. Pearce walked her horse away from everyone and engaged her deep in conversation for some minutes. *What is he plotting this time?* Nathan was watchful. Never again would he be caught unawares by John Pearce.

As the rescue party assembled and bade farewell to those waiting for the ferry to take them to the Isle of Marken, Nathan looked at his father, in the saddle, eyes closed, lips moving in silent prayer. He wished he knew him better and he wondered if he had the gypsy gift of second sight, like Marie. He suspected that he did. If anyone had the power to send Marie a message of comfort, and tell her that help was on the way, it was Samuel Fox.

THE WITCH TRIAL

*J*he Grande Dame led the way in a ferocious gallop. Nathan, who still had many unanswered questions, urged his horse on until he was neck and neck with her.

'WHY OUDEWATER?' he shouted across at her. She shook her head, unable to get her breath.

'SLOW DOWN!' he shouted at her. 'THE OTHERS CAN'T KEEP UP!'

With a look of triumph she began to rein in her horse until it slowed to a fast canter.

Nathan kept pace. 'Why Oudewater?' he repeated.

'The town was granted a charter by Emperor Charles, to be the place where suspected witches are weighed.' Her breath came in short gasps.

'Why do they weigh them?'

'Witches are supposed to be very light so they can ride broomsticks – don't you know that, child? If a person has a normal weight then they are not a witch.'

Nathan drew comfort from this. He had lifted Marie

293

out of the saddle or from a cart often enough to know that she was a normal weight.

The Grande Dame continued, 'But the men who do this weighing are not above bribery. And I have seen such evil, as I never thought to see, in the last few days, that I fear for my Sisters.'

She was right and Nathan felt a sickening lurch in his stomach. Lord Harcourt would make sure that Marie and Sister Beatrice were found guilty. He knew that.

The others were catching up with them, and Pearce called out, 'Is there a problem?'

'None at all!' was the spirited reply from the Grande Dame and she urged her horse onwards.

On and on they rode – south, the way they had come from Flushing when the mission had first started. Sometimes they stopped in a village for the horses to get water and, at each place, Samuel Fox asked if the two Sisters had passed through. Always the answer was yes and always the arrival and departure had been the same. An Amsterdam guard would ride into the village first and read a proclamation.

'We are bringing through this village two women who are accused of witchcraft. Do not look upon these women, lest they give you the evil eye. If you know these women, or have any information pertaining to their trial, leave your house and tell the Captain of the Guard. If there are any malevolent forces at work in this village that you wish to be rid of, tell the Captain of the Guard, and such persons will be arrested and taken to Oude-water.'

All the villagers Samuel Fox spoke to had taken refuge in their houses and had not come out until the guards and their prisoners had passed through. One other piece of information he had gleaned, which gave Nathan hope, was that the two women were being trans-ported in a caged-in cart, so their journey would be slower than their pursuers'.

They were about thirty miles from Oudewater when Graco counselled that the horses were near total exhaus-tion and they must change mounts. When they were doing this, Pearce took the opportunity to get Nathan and his father into a huddle.

'There is another reason why Harcourt and his daugh-ter chose this moment to denounce Marie,' he muttered, looking about him carefully to ensure that de Ferm and Casado were not within earshot. 'The Grande Dame received a message from the mysterious patriot regard-ing the relic. Marie committed it to memory but the Grande Dame has the original piece of paper with her. I think he may be hoping to strike a bargain with us.'

Nathan and Samuel nodded with relief. This gave them further hope that Marie could be saved.

They left their spent horses with a villager, who was paid by Pearce to take care of them until they returned. Graco said a fond farewell to his beloved Jennet and Nathan, likewise, to his faithful Ardennes.

They were only a few miles from Oudewater when Samuel Fox suddenly clutched his chest and they all pulled up, concerned because he had walked his horse to the side of the road and was lying over the horse's neck.

Nathan hurtled from his own horse and over to his father.

'What is it? Father? Speak to me! Are you ill?' He was frantic.

Samuel Fox lifted his head from the horse and his long grey hair fell back. Tears were streaming down his face.

'Father! For the love of God, what is it?'

'Marie . . .' was all that Samuel could manage to say.

Pearce had now arrived at Nathan's side, looking worried.

'What is it?' he asked with concern.

'He knows something about Marie.' Nathan was beside himself.

'How?'

'He feels something. He has special instincts, like Marie. It's a gypsy gift. Father, is Marie dead?'

Samuel Fox shook his head slowly and Nathan almost cried with relief. Still the tears coursed down his father's face. Finally he spoke.

'She is not dead, I know that. But she is terribly distressed. Something has devastated her. Perhaps the other woman is dead. Perhaps that is why I feel her tears. Bitter tears.'

Pearce found all this gypsy intuition unfathomable. All he knew was that they needed to get to Marie and get there fast.

'Sir,' he said firmly to Samuel Fox, 'If you are not ill, then I urge you to ride again with us. Otherwise we shall have to leave you here. We must go!'

Samuel Fox nodded and struggled to compose himself.

'Go! I will follow! Go!'

Nathan and Pearce raced back to their horses and kicked them into a gallop. As he looked back, Nathan could see that his father was walking his horse back on to the road and he knew that he would follow as fast as he could. Whatever had happened to Marie, she had called out in her distress to their father. *What could it mean?*

The town of Oudewater was in sight and the riders slowed down. People were thronging into the centre to see the latest witch trials and it was a slow business trying to push the horses through the crowds. Eventually, when they could see the platform on which they assumed the trial was to take place, they tied the horses to some trees and made their way on foot. The Grande Dame stayed to guard the horses and Pearce signalled to Nathan to climb up a tree which was to the side of the square.

'Be on the lookout for Harcourt,' he muttered. 'He will be here somewhere.'

297

A man walked on to the platform and lifted up a piece of parchment. He began to read.

'Let all be witness that on the 7th day of November in the year 1587, two women stand accused of being witches. One Sister Marie and one Sister Beatrice, known also as Mother Lazarus, both of whom profess to be Sisters of the Béguinage in Amsterdam.'

There were cries of 'For shame!' from the crowd and sundry other expressions of outrage that the Devil's minions should be hiding in a holy place.

'It just goes to show that the Devil can hide these witches anywhere,' said one man loudly just beneath Nathan's tree. Nathan wanted to kick him.

The man on the platform continued.

'These women have been examined and all magical properties have been removed from them. Salt has been laid upon this platform to protect all those present from malefice. You are urged to pray to Almighty God for deliverance from evil before we bring the accused forth.'

At this point a priest stepped up on to the platform and led the crowd in the Lord's Prayer. Nathan pretended to pray but he was busy scanning the crowd for Harcourt. All the time he kept thinking, *What magical properties have they removed from them? What does that mean?* His mouth was dry with anxiety.

Finally, the prayer finished and they brought the accused out from the Council Hall to the platform. Their heads and faces were covered with hoods. They could see nothing and both of them stumbled as they were hauled up the steps. Then a man stepped forward and held up two great handfuls of hair – one was black, lustrous and curly, the other was long and grey. Nathan's heart stopped. The crowd roared its approval. The hoods were pulled off and the two women stood there – pale, defiant, with completely shaved heads. Nathan felt a tear roll down his cheek and a terrible ache in his chest that his sister had been parted from her beautiful, beloved hair. He could see blood on her scalp where the razor had cut her skin and, at that moment, the cold blanket of vengeance settled over him. Harcourt and his vile daughter would pay for this evil.

As the first man began to read out the charges against them, the crowd gasped in horror when they learnt that 'Mother Lazarus' had raised a man from the dead. Many crossed themselves and murmured prayers. Marie was accused of being an apprentice to Mother Lazarus and of 'bewitching' men with her looks and her hair. Many of the women in the crowd nodded. They could see that Marie was beautiful and they could see how she would use those looks in the service of the Devil.

Catherine Harcourt came on to the platform and Nathan's muscles tensed. If she was there, her father would be close at hand. She began to give false testimony on how she had witnessed the various black arts that the two accused women practised. They had made potions together, she said, and Sister Marie had made eyes at a young man and given him a lock of her hair which had caused him to become infatuated with her.

There was a commotion in the crowd. It was Casado. Unable to bear it any longer, he vaulted up on to the platform and grabbed Catherine Harcourt by the neck.

'You lie!' he shouted in fury, then he turned to the crowd. 'I am that man she speaks of! This woman . . .' he pointed to Marie, 'is innocent. She made no 'eyes' at me; I received no lock of hair from her. This evil girl . . .' he dragged Catherine in front of him and she screamed for mercy, 'is the one who consorts with the Devil! She has made up these lies because she is jealous. She tried to seduce me and I rejected her!'

The crowd looked at the handsome Casado, his eyes ablaze with fury, and they looked at the squirming Catherine – plain Catherine – and they murmured words of belief.

The guards pounced upon Casado and he struggled with them, pushing Catherine to the floor.

'NATHAN!' Pearce's yell dragged Nathan's eyes from the platform. Pearce was advancing through the crowd to the stage, as were de Ferm, Graco and Samson. 'COME, WE HAVE NO CHOICE!' Casado had started something that they now had to finish. Nathan swung from the tree, managing to give a swift kick to the man below him whose speech had incensed him earlier. He ran through the crowd, pushing people aside, until he had a clear space to draw his sword, then he vaulted up on to the platform to join the others. De Ferm and Pearce were already at swords-drawn with four of the guards and Nathan joined Graco against another three. Samson was busy grabbing anyone in his path and hurling them into the crowd.

Panic ensued and the assembled people began to trample over each other in an attempt to scatter. The wooden platform swayed alarmingly with the weight of so many people on it, and those in the front of the crowd were being pushed against the struts that held the platform aloft. Suddenly there was a great cracking of wood and the whole platform buckled forwards and tipped on top of the crowd. Nathan grabbed Marie, whose hands were tied behind her back, and she fell on top of him as he, in turn, fell backwards and slithered towards the crush below. Sister Beatrice fell forwards but landed on top of de Ferm, who slung her over his shoulder like a sack of flour and carried her to safe ground.

Nathan found himself, and Marie, lying next to Casado.

'Take her!' he said, shifting her body across his to Casado's waiting arms. 'Guard her with your life! I must find Harcourt!' He shot a reassuring glance at Marie, who nodded in acceptance, and then he scrabbled over the up-ended platform to the Council Hall behind. He was sure that Harcourt was in there. The only puzzle was why he had not come out to save his daughter.

When he entered the building behind the collapsed

platform he saw why. Samuel Fox, his face contorted with rage, had Harcourt's head in a vice-like grip and a knife held at his throat.

'Nathan!' rasped his father. 'Find this man's daughter and bring her here!'

Nathan swiftly turned on his heel and flung himself back into the chaos. Casado had struggled out of the crush and was carrying Marie back to the waiting horses. Nathan also spotted de Ferm heading the same way with Sister Beatrice. Pearce was still duelling with a guard, Samson was picking innocent bystanders up off the floor and lifting them to safety, while Graco was busy tying up two unconscious guards with some woman's skirt he had ripped up into strips. Then Nathan spotted Catherine Harcourt. She was struggling to her feet and was trying to climb the platform, so Nathan ran round the back to intercept her. As she dropped over the top of the broken wood, he grabbed her and carried her, kicking and screaming, into the Hall.

Samuel Fox bared his teeth in a satisfied grimace.

'Now, my son, you saw what those animals did to your sister . . .' Nathan looked at his father expectantly. 'Do the same to this man's daughter. Cut off her hair.'

Catherine screamed again and Nathan smiled as he took his knife from his belt. Disappointingly, she fell into a dead faint, and Nathan was robbed of the pleasure of showing her every strand of hair as he cut it. Her father was unable to struggle or cry out as Samuel Fox had now placed his very sharp knife between Harcourt's teeth – any sudden movement and he would have a permanent smile from ear to ear. Nathan hacked away as best he could. He had no razor, so the best he could manage was to leave her with short clumps of ragged hair all over her head. Still, it was a good job. He took some of the long straight brown hair and stuffed it into his jerkin as a souvenir for Marie.

'Now,' said his father menacingly to Harcourt, 'I shall settle scores with you.' He took the knife from Harcourt's mouth and placed it to his throat again.

Harcourt spoke at last. 'Kill me and get it over with,' he said, trying to sound noble.

Samuel Fox laughed.

'No, no. A swift death is too good for you. I shall condemn you to something much worse. Nathan,' he commanded, 'get my bag from behind me.'

Nathan obeyed and retrieved the battered black leather bag from the floor at his father's feet.

'Open it and look for a silver bottle.'

Nathan obeyed once more and held the bottle aloft. Except that it was not made of silver. What was *in* it was silver.

'Take out the stopper and come here.'

Nathan advanced.

'Open your mouth, Harcourt.'

The man struggled in vain resistance but Samuel Fox

pressed the knife into Harcourt's throat until it plainly hurt and he opened his mouth.

'Empty the contents of that bottle into his mouth, Nathan.'

Nathan obeyed and the contents slithered out in a great lump on to Harcourt's tongue. It was not a liquid, it was mercury – poisonous mercury.

'Now swallow,' Fox hissed. 'Swallow, man!'

Harcourt obeyed, ingesting the tasteless substance and opening his mouth again to show that he had done so.

'You have just been given a dose of mercury, my friend,' said Samuel Fox, with a small mirthless laugh. 'Just enough to slowly poison you. First your hair will fall out but, unlike my daughter's, it will never grow back. Then your teeth will become loose. Then your joints will ache. Perhaps your skin will erupt in sore pustules. Then you will find that your brain becomes addled and your fingers and toes will become numb. It is not a large enough dose to kill you but you will suffer so badly you will wish that you were dead. And if you ever send anyone after my family again, I will send someone after *yours*. Remember that.'

Then he pushed his stricken enemy on to the floor, picked up his bag and motioned Nathan to follow him.

As they left, Nathan heard Harcourt cry out like an animal, 'I will be avenged, Samuel Fox! Wherever you are, I will find you!'

Then Nathan heard the moaning sound of Catherine Harcourt reviving from her faint and he paused – waiting – until she emitted the bloodcurdling scream that told him she had discovered all her shorn hair on the floor around her. He smiled in satisfaction.

Father and son raced for the place where the horses had been left. No one attempted to stop them. The residents of Oudewater were still busy dealing with the disaster of the day – counting broken limbs and sore heads.

As they ran towards the outskirts of the town, they were met by Pearce running in the opposite direction.

'Thank God I've found you!' he panted. 'Casado ambushed de Ferm and knocked him out. We found the Grande Dame and Sister Beatrice trying to revive him. Casado has taken Marie and gone after the relic. We have no time to lose!'

23

'LIKE FOR LIKE AND MEASURE FOR MEASURE'

*T*hey all stared at the piece of paper in the Grande Dame's hand. It made no sense.

> *'Bring us to our palace, where we'll show*
> *What's yet behind, that's meet you all should know.'*
> The Patriot

'What palace? What does it mean?' Pearce was impatient and angry.

Nathan knew that it was because Casado had played a final move which Pearce had not foreseen. Nathan, too, felt bitter. After all, he had actually trusted the man enough to hand poor Marie over to him during the confusion in front of the Council Hall.

The Grande Dame cleared her throat and seemed embarrassed. Pearce's eyes narrowed. His instinct for spotting deception, which had so failed him with Carlos Casado, was now working perfectly.

'Reverend Mother, tell us exactly what you know,' he said quietly but insistently.

The Grande Dame flushed. She knew that there was no time for games. There was too much at stake.

'The Patriot is the Duke of Amsterdam . . .' she began, looking down at the ground with embarrassment, '. . . and he is my brother.'

For a moment, no one said anything. They were too puzzled by this turn of events.

Then Pearce spoke. 'And where is your brother, the Duke?'

The Grande Dame seemed even more uncomfortable.

'He has been amongst you all the time. Masquerading as the man you know as Friar Lodowick.'

Nathan's head spun. *Yes! It makes sense now. That was why the Grande Dame allowed him to stay in the Béguinage where men were usually forbidden. That was the reason he followed us to the Council Chamber but would not go inside and speak for Isabella. Now I know why he seemed to know the purpose behind the Duke's mysterious disappearance and why he knew so much about Lord Angelo's past. Damn him!*

'Where is he now?' Pearce's voice was even. He was controlling his anger but only just. Nathan knew how much he disliked being toyed with.

'I . . . I don't know. He disappeared completely about five days ago, leaving the message with me. I assume he

307

wants you to go to the Council Chamber – the people of Amsterdam often call it "The Duke's Palace". He must be planning to return.'

'Does Marie know all of this?'

'I didn't tell her everything, only that the reference to the palace probably meant the Council Chamber.'

'My lady,' Pearce's tone was thick with displeasure, 'you and your brother have played a pretty game with all of us. It nearly cost the lives of two women. Let us pray that Marie does not still pay for your folly.'

'What was your brother's purpose in pretending to leave Amsterdam and then disguising himself?' Nathan asked impatiently.

The Grande Dame bowed her head in shame.

'He wanted to unmask Lord Angelo's hypocrisy and he felt that the only way to do that was to leave him in charge. I sincerely beg your forgiveness,' she whispered.

'Many poor people in Amsterdam have paid a heavy price for your brother's cowardly actions,' Pearce said bitterly. 'Let us pray that Marie is not another casualty. Take poor Sister Beatrice back to your Béguinage and give her comfort. We shall ride hell for leather for the Council Chamber.' Pearce was dismissive and angry.

De Ferm was puzzled by the whole business of Casado kidnapping Marie and he asked why the strange message from the Duke was so important.

Pearce sighed. 'As you suffered some injury at the hands of Carlos Casado and we now need your help in rescuing Marie once more, I suppose it is only fair that we tell you of our second mission.' So Pearce told him of the relic and de Ferm's eyes widened – or, rather, one eye did – the other eye had closed.

'Why are the English so interested in some religious relic?' asked the Dutchman with a certain amount of scorn in his voice.

'Why indeed?' answered Pearce grimly. Nathan knew that Pearce had not been in favour of the mission from the start. 'The English want the relic because King Philip wants the relic. It is no more complicated than that. Her Majesty takes the view that any blow we can deal to the Spanish king is worth the effort.'

'Ah.' De Ferm nodded. Skullduggery he understood. Then he mounted his horse with some difficulty. De Ferm, like Nathan, had been on the end of one of Casado's unexpected blows to the temple. Nathan shot him a pitying glance. He knew, all too well, how *that* felt.

So, yet again, Pearce, Nathan, de Ferm, Samuel Fox, Graco and Samson rode off to rescue Marie, and Nathan cursed himself for being the one who had been foolish enough to hand her over to Casado in the midst of the chaos at Oudewater.

They rode hard to the village where they had left their spare horses and collected them. Graco said that they should wait to change mounts until they were nearer to Amsterdam, so they pressed on, running the spare horses in tandem with the ones they were riding.

As they pounded through the countryside, Nathan found himself continually looking at his father. The Samuel Fox in Oudewater – the vengeful father, full of hate – had been a revelation to him. Until then, he had always thought of his father as a gentle man, full of wisdom. Then he remembered his first mission, when Harcourt's paid assassin had been sent to eliminate Nathan, but his father had got there first and one throw of his knife had sent the man to an early grave. *There are many sides to our father*, Nathan decided. *But most of all, first and foremost, he would do anything for us.*

Amsterdam was in a fever of excitement. Word of the Duke's return had spread and those who had had their fill of the reign of Lord Angelo were rejoicing that he would be in charge no more. Time and time again, passers-by would call up to the men on horseback, 'It's a fine day! Have you heard that the Duke has returned?' Although they gave courteous replies, no one in their party, especially Pearce and Nathan, had much respect for the Duke and the joy of his subjects began to grate on their nerves.

Finally they arrived at the council chamber. Samson took the horses to be stabled and the rest of them entered. All visible weapons had to be left at the door but Pearce looked at each of them in turn and received the imperceptible nod of confirmation that they were all carrying concealed weapons. Nathan patted the flat blade which was lying across his stomach under his clothing.

Business was being conducted in the main chamber, judging by the rise and fall of voices, and Nathan showed the others the way to the screened corridor where he had watched over Marie and Isabella in their dealings with Angelo. They stood silently in the dark – Pearce, Nathan, Samuel Fox, de Ferm and Graco – and listened.

The Duke was seated in the large chair of State. It was hard to believe that he had ever been Friar Lodowick, for he now had a five-day growth of beard which altered his appearance dramatically. He was dressed in a knight's outfit, with a full surcoat that bore the black Teutonic cross on the front, and he appeared to be comfortably in command. The thin face of Lord Angelo looked wary and it seemed to Nathan that he was nervous. The unexpected return of the Duke must have unsettled him. Nathan thought some of the other men in the room looked vaguely familiar.

'Where is Marie?' Nathan heard Samuel Fox whisper anxiously to Pearce.

'She is here somewhere, never fear. Casado will have her secreted somewhere in this building,' was the whispered reply.

There was a flurry of activity in the chamber. Two Sisters of the Béguinage had entered and both knelt on the floor before the Duke. Nathan's stomach churned. One of them was Isabella; her usually pale face was flushed. The way she held her head and flashed her eyes told Nathan that she was angry rather than embarrassed.

'My lord Duke!' the vehemence with which she spoke surprised everyone, particularly Nathan. 'I am the sister of one Claudio, who was condemned to death by this man—' she pointed to Angelo, 'for making his girlfriend with child out of wedlock.'

The skin on Angelo's face seemed to tighten in the dim light of the candles and he stepped backwards into the shadows, as if to avoid scrutiny.

'Continue,' said the Duke smoothly. Nathan thought he seemed to be enjoying the fact that Isabella, caught up in her anger, had not recognized him as the Friar who worked alongside her in the Béguinage.

'I came to see Lord Angelo to plead for my brother's life,' she continued. 'I pleaded, prayed and begged him to relent and finally, he agreed to spare my brother if I would become his mistress.'

There was a silence and all the Duke's men looked at Angelo. Nathan gave a small smile of grim satisfaction. *Now, surely, the Duke will punish him!* He was unprepared, however, for what happened next.

'I did this . . . thing . . . he asked of me and the next day he executed my brother anyway,' she said flatly and hung her head so that no one would see the tears she was fighting back.

Nathan felt the blood drain from his face. *She did it?* All his anger was then directed at the Duke who had promised him, as Friar Lodowick, that he would protect Isabella. He felt for his knife and fumbled, because his stomach was covered in a film of cold sweat. Pearce, anticipating Nathan's next move, grabbed his wrist in an iron hold and mouthed, 'Think of Marie!', his eyes glittering a warning. Nathan pulled his hand out of his shirt and nodded resentfully.

'I cannot believe Lord Angelo would ask such a thing!' the Duke cried in horror. Nathan's face twisted in disbelief. *Is he playing yet another game?*

'Arrest her, my lord,' cried one of the men. 'She is obviously a troublemaker and this is a false accusation.'

Angelo said nothing and simply stared at Isabella, his eyes boring into her as though willing her to be silent.

The Duke held up his hand.

'Is there any witness to this accusation?' he asked.

The other Sister spoke up. 'My lord, there is a woman who can testify that this accusation is true.' And, at the Duke's signal, she left to fetch the witness.

Nathan's heart leaped. *Marie! It must be Marie!*

But when the Sister returned, it was with a woman who Nathan had never seen before. A woman who was older than Marie and had once been beautiful but Nathan could see that her face was etched with misery.

When the woman appeared, Angelo seemed agitated and those present turned to look at him again. Nathan held his breath and wondered how this new development would help Isabella.

'My lady, state your name and your testimony,' said the Duke kindly. He was growing in stature as Angelo was diminishing.

'My name is Marianne,' the woman replied. 'I was betrothed in marriage to Lord Angelo some five years ago but he abandoned me when my brother died and I was left penniless and without a marriage dowry.' Now Nathan understood. The Duke, in his disguise as Friar Lodowick, had mentioned this woman. *He means to prove Angelo's evil nature now.*

Marianne's words provoked some murmurs of displeasure from the assembled men and Angelo found his voice at last.

'My lord Duke, this woman lies!' His angular face was gleaming with sweat and it was obvious that he was desperately trying to save himself. 'There was some talk of marriage between our families, five years ago, but it was broken off for many reasons – one of which was this woman's bad reputation. I could not bring myself to marry someone who was thought of so poorly!'

Isabella made a sound of anger and held her hand out for Marianne to hold. Nathan felt outraged. *What a piece of work this man is! He has no thought for anyone but himself.*

The woman Angelo had dishonoured raised her head and summoned up every ounce of her strength to reply.

'My lord Duke, it is this man who lies, not I. Until last week, I was a woman whose virtue was without ques-

314

tion.' She looked at Isabella and smiled, gripping her hand tighter. 'Then I took Isabella's place and gave that virtue to the man who should have been my husband. In the darkness, he did not know that I was not this holy sister that he had *blackmailed*.'

Nathan's mouth dropped open at this point. *So Angelo had been tricked! Marianne went to him in Isabella's place! Was it her idea or the Duke's?*

Angelo was now frantic in his protests. 'My lord, these women have been put up to this by some unknown person! You cannot believe that I, who have done so much to rid this city of sin and vice, would stoop to such actions?'

The Duke smiled, ready to deliver the final blow.

'Oh but I would, Lord Angelo. You see, I know this woman, Marianne. Her brother was my very good friend and, for five years now, I have known the despicable depth of your treatment of her. I was also here, in this city, in disguise, to watch your treatment of the people of Amsterdam. I have seen corruption boil and bubble until it overran the stew. I have seen your interpretation of the law and in one respect, and only one, I agree with you – which is why I now say that for your execution of this girl's brother Claudio, you shall be likewise executed. Like for like – measure for measure. Take him away!'

The guards stepped forward but Marianne cried out and flung herself at the Duke's feet.

'Please, please, my lord, do not deny me my husband a second time!'

'He must die, I am resolved on that.'

Marianne turned to Isabella for help.

'Sweet Isabella,' she begged, 'help me save Angelo's life and I will owe you mine.' She turned back to the Duke. 'I know he is a bad man but they say that if such a man recognizes his faults and learns from them, he will become a good man in time. I pray you, spare him!'

Isabella looked helplessly at the Duke. Nathan watched in admiration as she delivered her next words with slowness and deliberation.

'My lord Duke, there would be no advantage in this man's execution. I mourn my brother but this man's death would not bring him back. I despise Angelo, but if Marianne thinks that her love for him can change him then let her have him.'

Graco nudged Nathan. 'This is better than any play, my friend!' he whispered in astonishment.

The Duke held his hand out to Isabella to raise her from her knees.

'Sister Isabella, for your sake, I will pardon Angelo. The only sentence I impose is that he should take his lady, Marianne, and make of her an honest wife, before the sun sets today.'

The craven Angelo fell to his knees and gibbered his apologies to everyone he had wronged. Nathan curled his lip in disgust, and out of the corner of his eye he saw

Graco do the same. Then he heard the soft-hearted gypsy sniff away an unmanly tear as Marianne led away the unfortunate Angelo.

The Duke turned back to Isabella and said gently to her, 'There is one final thing. Now you may know that your brother is, in fact, alive. I prevented his execution – and you shall be reunited with him very shortly.'

Nathan saw the look of delighted shock on Isabella's face and it seemed as though she wanted to fall to her knees once more in gratitude, but the Duke took her other hand to prevent her from doing so.

Graco was smiling all over his face at this happy ending but the Duke's next words made the smile disappear in an instant.

'Isabella,' the Duke raised his voice so that everyone present could hear clearly, 'I wish you to be my wife . . .'

There was a small gasp of shock from Isabella.

'Mother of God,' muttered Pearce, 'he's old enough to be her grandfather!'

Nathan said nothing. A resignation settled over him. *What choice does she have?* he thought dully. *She is sixteen with only a feckless brother to look out for her. She has no father to step in and protect her. I suppose a loveless marriage to a rich man three times her age is better than spending the rest of her life in the Béguinage – or is it . . .*

No one heard Isabella give an answer and now she was being ushered out by the accompanying Sister. The Duke's men also vacated the chamber.

The Duke then turned, with a strange smile on his face, and walked towards the screening. Looking straight at them, but unable to see them, he simply said,

'I have been expecting you, Englishman. You can show yourself now.'

THE BONES OF THE VIRGIN

*J*o say that the Duke was surprised when five men stepped out from the screened corridor was an understatement. He had been expecting one agent of the Crown of England, not the five who stood before him.

'Why so many – and yet another?' he asked in consternation as they were joined by the giant Samson, who had successfully stabled the horses.

'War makes strange companions,' answered Pearce tersely. 'Where is Marie?'

'Ah, yes, most unfortunate. Such a thing would not have happened had I been there, I assure you.' The Duke seemed genuinely remorseful but Nathan dismissed his assurances.

'Where is my sister?' he asked through gritted teeth.

'She is safe below. Come with me now and you shall see.'

The Duke led the way to a door in the side of a small chapel. Nathan brushed his hand over the knife under his clothes as they made their way in single file down some dark, winding stairs. Not only did he not like the Duke but he did not trust him either.

At the bottom of the stairs there was light, a great deal of light and warmth, and Nathan, who was the last to descend, stepped into a bare crypt that was ablaze with many candles. There, on a raised dais, was an ancient stone box – smaller than a coffin – with strange markings, and before it, on bended knees, was Carlos Casado, deep in prayer. He took no notice of anyone else, so deep were his devotions.

Nathan anxiously scanned the crypt and found, much to his relief, that Marie was lying asleep in a recess of the wall. Suddenly Nathan felt strangely calm. There was a perfume in the air, like the scent of roses, and he wondered whether that was making him feel so relaxed.

He became aware of a movement and realized that his father, Graco and Samson were now kneeling down in front of the dais. Samuel Fox put his hands up to his neck and lifted something over his head and brought it down in front of him. It was a rosary.

My father is a Catholic? Nathan felt bewildered as he saw his father's long fingers move from bead to bead, his mouth moving in silent prayer. *Marie never said that our father was a Catholic.* He should have felt shock, maybe outrage, that such an essential piece of information had been kept from him but he merely felt curiosity.

Marie had never been much of a churchgoer, nor had

she raised Nathan to be anything other than someone who was God-fearing but indifferent to church ritual. *Perhaps she thought that to be a gypsy in England was risky enough, without being a practising Catholic as well.* Ordinarily he would have thought more about the question of his family's religion but his whole body felt so heavy and so tired. He seemed to have shed the ability to produce any strong emotions and he looked at the backs of the three kneeling men with an almost detached interest.

Pearce and de Ferm stood immobile at Nathan's side and he wondered why they had not made any move to capture Casado.

The Duke spoke quietly.

'I can see that you all feel the strength of the Blessed Virgin. She has this effect on everyone who enters her presence.'

Was it that? Or was it the strange perfume in the room? Nathan wondered.

The Duke walked over to Casado and gently touched his shoulder. This seemed to rouse him from his trance and he looked up at the newly arrived band of men.

'Forgive me,' he said in a reverent whisper, as he got up from his knees and faced them. 'I only wished to pray in front of the holy relic – no more. I resolved, once I came into its presence, not to seize it and take it back to Spain. I cannot allow it to become a justification for continuing this war. But you should know that I will do

321

everything in my power to stop the Queen of England using the relic in that way.'

Pearce seemed to find his voice, and he replied quietly, 'Her Majesty has decreed that the relic will not go to England. It has been decided to take it back to the Holy Land and rebury it in a secret place.' Nathan wondered why Pearce had chosen to tell the truth to Casado but it hardly seemed to matter any more.

'Ah! Then I was wise to contact the English!' The Duke seemed very pleased at Pearce's news.

'Does the casket truly contain the bones of the Virgin Mary?' Whatever other emotions had washed away from him, Nathan still possessed a powerful curiosity.

'Yes, I believe it does,' the Duke said with feeling. 'This stone casket is an ossuary – a receptacle in which the ancients placed the bones of the dead once they had lain in a crypt for some time and the flesh had mortified. The markings on the ossuary are in Aramaic and they state that the bones are those of Mary, mother of Jesus of Nazareth and wife of Joseph.'

'And how did it come into your possession, my lord Duke?' asked de Ferm.

'I am a Master of the Teutonic Knights. The Knights were formed to fight in the Third Crusade. The Order discovered the ossuary and brought it back to its headquarters in Prussia. There it remained, until recently . . .' He paused for a moment, searching for the words to explain further. 'Our Order is changing. Many of the

322

branches of the Order are embracing Protestantism and leaving the Catholic faith. Those of us in the Netherlands who have decided to fight against the tyranny of the Spanish Empire have embraced the Protestant religion perhaps sooner than others Nevertheless, such a commitment left us in a quandary about the ossuary. We do not wish it to be a "prize" to be used by the Spanish Empire. If Philip of Spain had it in his possession he would regard it as a sign from God that his cause was just. All of us in the Order, whether Catholic or Protestant, could not allow the Blessed Virgin's bones to be used to justify war.'

'And you trusted the English not to do that?' Pearce was amazed.

'Well, I was right, was I not?' the Duke answered with a smile. 'I judged that Queen Elizabeth, whose own father destroyed so many relics throughout England, would not want to keep it for herself but that, also, she would not anger her own Catholic subjects by destroying it.'

Samuel Fox rose from his knees and his friends followed suit.

'We have been entrusted with taking the relic back to the Holy Land, my lord Duke,' he said simply. 'Rest assured that we shall find a safe place and bury the casket so deep that it will not be found for another thousand years.'

The Duke seemed happy at this and swiftly lifted up

the cloth on which the ossuary stood and wrapped it around the precious stonework.

'It will take great strength to lift it,' he counselled.

Samson stepped forward and it seemed to Nathan that the blond giant had a look on his face that said, 'This is the task I was born to fulfil!' and he lifted the ossuary in his arms as though it were the Virgin Mary herself. Everyone parted to let him through and up the stairs.

'There will be a cart waiting outside, ready for you. Give the man instructions and he will take you any-where.' Obviously the Duke had everything prepared.

Samuel Fox tried to rouse his daughter from her deep sleep but Casado stepped forward.

'I promise you that I will deliver her to the cart safely. Let me carry her these last few steps for you.' He seemed genuinely contrite and scooped her up into his arms where she settled into sleep once more. She was wearing Casado's cloak, Nathan noticed, and her shaven head was, thankfully, covered.

Outside, snow was falling thick and fast and, as Samson reverentially placed the wrapped ossuary in the back of the cart, it was already being hidden from human sight by the gathering snowflakes.

'God is sending his blessing,' said Graco, crossing himself piously.

Casado reluctantly laid Marie beside the ossuary.

'I had hoped that she might wake and I could ask her

forgiveness before I said goodbye,' Casado said quietly to Nathan.

But whatever force had put her in a deep sleep was keeping her there and he had to content himself with giving her a brief kiss on her forehead. Then he looked at Pearce, uncertain about his status as a prisoner, but Pearce merely gave a brief nod, which Casado took as the gift of freedom, so he returned the nod, shot Nathan a rueful smile and left. A lonely figure, without a cloak, he disappeared into the Amsterdam backstreets.

De Ferm took his leave as well, saying that he would meet up with them in Marken tomorrow. Nathan, having been touched by the Spaniard's farewell to Marie, told de Ferm, on a matter of honour, to leave Casado alone. He was afraid that de Ferm would follow him and exact some justice for his injuries at Casado's hands.

'Don't worry, my friend. I have some other business to deal with,' de Ferm said enigmatically and then he disappeared.

As the cart rumbled out of Amsterdam, heading for the Isle of Marken, Nathan turned to his father.

'I did not know that you were a Catholic,' he said matter-of-factly. 'Does that make Marie and me Catholics as well?'

Samuel Fox smiled. 'No, Nathan. A man's religion is his and his alone. You have been brought up in a land where the Protestant religion holds sway. I was brought up in a different land as a Catholic. I am used to it. That is all. We all follow the same road to God, Nathan. Some men think they can see God just ahead of them on the road but the rest of us are merely content to look down and follow his footsteps.'

That was all he would say on the matter and Nathan knew that the discussion would have to continue at another time. He felt a little frustrated, though, by the fact that he had to discover things about his father and their family background bit by bit. Father and son sat in the back of the cart in silence, both with a protective hand laid on the sleeping form of Marie.

Once they were safe on the island of Marken, Nathan thought it was interesting to see the reactions of de Ferm's men to the ossuary. They ranged from devout to suspicious, and the box was kept apart from their living quarters as its effect was somewhat disquieting. Nathan gave it no thought, nor did it seem to make any impression upon Pearce, but Toby and George Silver seemed dumbstruck by the thought that the Blessed Virgin might be watching over them from the next room and became unnaturally subdued.

It was Marie's condition that caused the most consternation amongst all those who had stayed on Marken when she was rescued from Oudewater. Men wept to see her shaved head and some even offered back the locks of hair that they had begged from her when she had tended to their wounds. Though pale and shaken by her ordeal, her father's medicine and everyone's kindness had caused her to find her strength again. Nathan was relieved that she was able to laugh at the thought that a few locks of hair might be plastered on her bald head and make her look better.

A scout was despatched to Amsterdam to watch for the arrival of the two English ships that were to carry both the gold and the relic away from the Netherlands. He returned the next day to say that all Amsterdam was in thrall, as the great Sir Francis Drake had moored his ship that very morning. Pearce looked jaded at the thought of sailing with Drake once more but when Nathan pointed out that he would be able to remind Drake that *they* had captured the gold and not him, Pearce visibly brightened.

De Ferm reappeared that day too, his mysterious business completed. He presented himself to Marie, looking awkward, with a parcel under his arm.

'I have a present for you,' he said with some embarrassment. 'It was a Dutchman who took your hair and your dignity from you and I felt that it was a Dutchman who should give it back,' and he handed her his parcel.

Everyone in the room held his breath as Marie unwrapped the cloth that held the parcel together. At once she was both crying and laughing. De Ferm had got an Amsterdam wigmaker to work through the night to make a wig that closely resembled her natural hair. Marie launched herself at de Ferm and kissed him squarely on the mouth in gratitude. The men roared their approval but Nathan noticed that Pearce bit his lip and looked at the floor.

He also noticed that when they were finally aboard Drake's ship, pulling away from the quayside in Amsterdam, Marie, wearing her new wig and looking much like her old self, stood silently on deck and waved goodbye to not one, but two figures on the quayside. De Ferm was standing where they had left him but, in the shadow of a doorway, watching silently, was Carlos Casado.

Then she turned and grabbing Nathan's hand, they ran to the opposite rail to wave goodbye to Samuel Fox and his gypsies, who were on board the other English ship, heading for the Holy Land with its precious cargo.

'I am lucky, very lucky,' Marie said quietly to Nathan as their father's ship grew smaller on the horizon, 'to be cared for by so many good people.'

'If you give kindness, then you receive kindness,' said Nathan wisely, 'Like for like, measure for measure,' he added, echoing the Duke's words and fingering, inside his jerkin, the itchy clump of Catherine Harcourt's hair, which he would present to his sister later.

Epilogue

*I*t was Christmas at the queen's court, and the Great Hall at the Palace of Greenwich was bedecked with boughs of holly, laurel, ivy, bay and holm oak. The Earl of Essex, the Queen's current favourite, was pronounced 'Lord of Misrule' and to him had fallen the task of making sure that the court was entertained for every available moment of the entire twelve days of Christmas.

Nathan had never been so happy – neither had Marie. From the moment their invitation had arrived, only one week after they had returned from their successful mission in the Netherlands, life had been one long agony of anticipation.

Fortunately, Marie had all the wonderful gowns bestowed upon her by the queen's ladies-in-waiting when she had attended to Her Majesty's teeth and she generously unpicked the seams of three of the plainest gowns and set to work, feverishly remaking the cloth into new clothes for Nathan.

When they arrived at Greenwich on Christmas Eve, along with half the nobility of England, it was just in time for the carrying in of the Yule Log. This was to be something of a reunion, since they had not seen John Pearce for some weeks and, likewise, their great friend Will Shakespeare. Both had been away in the country visiting their families.

Will and the other actors from the Burbage Company were to present several plays for the queen's delight during the twelve days of festivities and Nathan looked on wistfully at their preparations. Despite his new life of great adventure, he sometimes missed the companionship of the theatre in Shoreditch.

On Christmas Day, after the Archbishop had led the service of the morning, Elizabeth indulged in her public presentation of gifts to those she favoured.

Nathan was astonished to hear his name called out and he stepped forward, all eyes upon him, and bowed so low that his head almost touched his knees.

'For service to your queen and to England, Master Fox, we bestow upon you this small gift,' the queen said in a loud and very regal voice. Then she held out her hand and presented him with an exquisitely jewelled dagger, the beauty of which took his breath away.

'Your Majesty does me a great honour,' Nathan said, as loudly as he could, taking the dagger and kissing the queen's hand.

As he backed away, still hunched over in reverence,

he heard Marie's name called. Once straightened up he saw with pride the flushed face of his sister as she sank into a deep curtsey.

'Twice you have done me a great service, Mistress Fox, and so I am doubly grateful. For that reason, I must give you *two* presents!' The queen said this triumphantly and looked expectantly at the assembled Court. Nathan realized she was making a small joke and the courtiers were expected to react. There was a sudden burst of forced laughter and some delicate applause. The queen looked satisfied, and held out both her hands, to show in each palm a large pearl earring nestling.

'Tell your sister *not* to wear them on market day in Shoreditch,' murmured a familiar voice and Nathan spun round delightedly to face a beaming John Pearce.

'Will *you* get a present from the queen?' Nathan whispered excitedly.

Pearce grinned and shook his head.

'No. Thank God! If the queen were to give me a present every time I was of service to my country, I should be knee-deep in the things! No, presents are reserved for those who have given exceptional service, like you and your sister, and . . .'

'. . . the fawning lickspittles who sit around at court all year on their backsides and flatter the queen,' came the rude interruption from Sir Francis Drake, who happened to be passing at that point in the conversation.

Nathan laughed and Drake continued, warming to

his subject, 'God's teeth! I could build and equip three more ships with the money Her Majesty spends each Christmas,' and, having said his piece, he moved off to grumble at someone else.

Pearce pulled a face at Drake's retreating back and then bowed low to Marie, who had come to show her earrings to her brother.

'A word of advice,' Pearce whispered in Marie's ear. 'Put the earrings on now and don't take them off until you leave court. It will please the queen.'

Marie nodded happily. To do so would be no hardship, she said, and she placed them in her ears. Both Pearce and Nathan gave her admiring glances. Today she was radiant and the memory of her experience in Oudewater had almost faded. Only Nathan knew that sometimes she cried out in the night, in her deepest, darkest dreams.

That evening, after a lavish supper consisting of roast bustard, goose, cockerel, peacock and swan, where courtiers were treated to the very rare sight of their Sovereign eating, the Burbage Company staged their whimsical play about mistaken identity and two sets of lovers.

Afterwards, when the players had been thanked by the gracious queen, a blissfully happy but sweating Will Shakespeare threw himself down into a chair next to Nathan.

'It was rubbish, wasn't it?' he said cheerfully, 'but *I*

was good!' Nathan agreed that Shakespeare's portrayal of a doddering old man had been one of the highlights of the play. *The vanity of actors!* he thought cheerily. *It never changes.*

Shakespeare dragged him to a quiet vestibule, far away from the noise of the music that was now being played. Nathan looked back and smiled to see that Marie was dancing a vigorous galliard with Pearce as her partner. She looked a picture of elegance, except for the fact that, occasionally, she would scratch her head, making her wig move a little.

'So,' said Shakespeare, eyeing Nathan seriously. 'I was not there when you returned from your mission and I have fretted, this last month, that you will have forgotten all the details and will not be able to tell me the full story.'

'Never,' answered Nathan firmly. 'It is as fresh in my mind as if it were yesterday.'

'Then come with me to the next room, where I shall find ink and paper and, more importantly, some wine, and you shall tell me everything.'

So Nathan recounted the story – or was it several stories, each interweaving with the other? It was only in the telling that he realized what a complex mission they had undertaken in the Netherlands. He became more and more animated, leaping up to demonstrate the ambush tactics for taking the Spanish gold, flinging himself down to show how Groesbeck had been assassinated.

All the time Shakespeare scribbled furiously, some-times looking at Nathan with the wildness of a man who has stumbled on a hoard of gold. They both became sombre when Nathan related Marie's ordeal at the hands of the witch-hunters and Shakespeare made the sign of the cross when Nathan described the feelings that over-came him when he stood in front of the relic.

Then, much to Nathan's annoyance, when he had parched himself with telling all the adventures, Shake-speare said earnestly, 'Tell me more of the story of Isabella and the Duke. Did she marry him?'

'I don't know,' said Nathan sulkily. 'Probably. What choice did she have? To be honest, in the end, I didn't much care.'

Shakespeare rolled his eyes to heaven. 'Oh, the fickle-ness of youth! One moment you were fighting a duel over her and the next you "didn't much care"! Mark my words, there is poetry in this tale of treachery and nobil-ity. I feel something forming in my head as we speak.'

'It's probably the wine!' retorted Nathan sarcastically and left his friend to his scribbling. *What about the capture of the gold? What about Marie's rescue? Writers!* He felt irri-table with Shakespeare and contemplated never confiding in him again.

He spotted Walsingham seated alone and apart from the merriment. He looked tired, as usual. *Affairs of state always seem to hang heavily on his shoulders*, Nathan thought.

Nathan walked across to him and was rewarded with one of Walsingham's rare smiles.

'You have received just honours today, Master Fox,' he said kindly, 'just honours.'

Nathan offered him the dagger for inspection and Walsingham traced a finger over the precious stones.

'Guard it well, Nathan. Such a gift is beyond value. It is good to see you and your sister at the Christmas court. I take pleasure in seeing new faces – just as I take pleasure in the fact that some old faces are not here this year. Her Majesty was told that Lord Harcourt and his daughter are suffering from a disfiguring fever and are convalescing at his house in France. I shall send him a message advising him to take a long convalescence. It would, I think, be bad for his fragile health were he to return too soon.' Walsingham's eyes sparkled with barely disguised joy at Harcourt's indisposition. Then he looked squarely at Nathan. 'Are you rested from your last mission?'

'Yes, sir. Quite rested.'

Walsingham stood, with some difficulty, and leaned heavily on his stick.

'Come with me, Nathan. We need to talk in private.'

Nathan followed the limping Spymaster down a corridor, wondering what was about to unfold. As they entered a room, he was astonished to see Robey pacing the floor and a grim-faced Pearce standing by the window.

Nathan turned his puzzled face to Walsingham and the old man began to speak.

'My agents abroad tell me that Philip of Spain is building ships all over Europe, to replace the ones that Drake burned. The Armada will be bigger than ever and it will be coming soon. Perhaps sooner than we think. England is now in greater danger than she has ever been. I want all my people to be ready when the invasion comes.'

Nathan felt a cold chill descend on his bones. The merriment of Christmas seemed to melt away in that moment. *England is now in greater danger than she has ever been?*

Robey then spoke. 'Nathan, I am truly sorry to cut short your Christmas festivities but there is no time to lose. Some of the Spanish ships are nearing completion. We have reports of large-scale movements of soldiers and equipment. While we doubt that the Armada will set sail before the spring, there is much to do to prepare for the invasion. This will be the hardest mission that you have ever faced – that we have all faced – and we must start your training immediately. So,' he added firmly, 'pack your belongings and say your goodbyes. We must leave at dawn tomorrow.'

Nathan nodded and left the room. As he was gathering his fine new clothes together and placing them on his bed, Pearce entered and grasped him reassuringly by the shoulder.

'There is no rest for anyone in the coming months,' he

said quietly. 'Particularly for us. This will be the severest test of our skills. When Spain invades it is men like us who will form the human wall to keep Philip of Spain from the English throne. Do you have the courage to do that, Nathan Fox?'

Nathan looked squarely at Pearce and tried to ignore the thudding of his heart inside his chest.

'I do,' he said simply and he smiled. 'This will be our greatest adventure yet, will it not, John?'

The first title in the Nathan Fox series

L. BRITTNEY

Nathan is an actor in the same company as Will Shakespeare. A skilled acrobat with many other talents, he catches the eye of England's Spymaster General. Recruited as an agent – and partnered with fearless spy John Pearce – Nathan is trained at a School of Defence in the arts that will keep him alive.

His first mission takes Nathan Fox to Venice – into the eye of an explosive situation involving the formidable General Othello . . .

THE INFINITY CODE

E. L. YOUNG

Will Knight, 14: Inventive genius.
Creates cutting-edge gadgets (S.T.O.R.M.-sceptic)

Andrew Minkel, 14: Software millionaire
(and fashion disaster). Founder of S.T.O.R.M.

Gaia Carella, 14: Brilliant chemist with a habit of
blowing stuff up (usually schools).

Caspian Baraban, 14: Gifted astrophysicist.
Obsessed with the immense forces of space
(equally immense ego).

Will mocks S.T.O.R.M.'s plan to combat global problems, but then they uncover a plot to create a revolutionary weapon. Will swallows his doubts as they race to Russia to confront the scientific psychopath with a deadly power at his fingertips.

The first book in the S.T.O.R.M. series, *The Infinity Code* is a gadget-packed high-adrenalin adventure.

DRAGON KEEPER

CAROLE WILKINSON

Ping is a slave in a remote royal palace at Huangling Mountain. Her cruel master neglects his duties as Imperial Dragonkeeper, and under his watch the Emperor's dragons have dwindled from a magnificent dozen to a miserable two. Soon only the ancient and wise Long Danzi remains. Ping has always been wary of the strange creatures living in their dark pit – but in a moment of startling bravery she rescues Danzi and the mysterious and beautiful stone that he protects.

Now fugitives, Danzi and Ping race across the kingdom, fighting enemies at every turn. But as they come to the end of their journey Ping must prepare for a heartbreaking loss – and a truly thrilling revelation . . .

An enthralling, magical adventure set in the exciting and colourful world of ancient China

Elizabeth Laird

John was half crazed with panic and grief.
The rocking sea beneath him and the vast bulk of
the ship louring over him seemed to have surged out
of a nightmare. He knew though that they were real.
He knew they had claimed him, in one terrifying snatch,
and that everything familiar, everything he knew,
had been torn away from him.

Falsely accused of murder, twelve-year-old John Barr and
his father run for their lives through the dark and winding
streets of Edinburgh. At the harbour they are forced to join
the navy and posted on different warships.
On board the mighty HMS Fearless, a chance dis-covery
thrusts John into a shadowy world of secrets and spies.
His adventure has only just begun . . .

'Exciting action, alarming plot twists
and breathtaking near escapes' – *Books for Keeps*

A selected list of titles available from
Macmillan Children's Books

The prices shown below are correct at the time of going to press.
However, Macmillan Publishers reserves the right to show new retail
prices on covers, which may differ from those previously advertised.

L. Brittney
Nathan Fox: Dangerous Times   978-0-330-44116-2   £5.99

E. L. Young
S.T.O.R.M. – The Infinity Code   978-0-330-44640-2   £5.99

Carole Wilkinson
Dragonkeeper   978-0-330-44109-4   £5.99

Elizabeth Laird
Secrets of the Fearless   978-0-330-43466-9   £5.99

The Garbage King   978-0-330-41502-6   £5.99

A Little Piece of Ground   978-0-330-43743-1   £5.99

All Pan Macmillan titles can be ordered from our website,
www.panmacmillan.com, or from your local bookshop and
are also available by post from:

Bookpost, PO Box 29, Douglas, Isle of Man IM99 1BQ
Credit cards accepted. For details:
Telephone: 01624 677237
Fax: 01624 670923
Email: bookshop@enterprise.net
www.bookpost.co.uk

Free postage and packing in the United Kingdom